ONCE UPON
A
TIMEZONE...

Neelesh Misra was born in 1973 in Lucknow, India. He worked with the India Abroad News Service and the Associated Press before joining the *Hindustan Times* in New Delhi as Senior Roving Editor.

In a career spanning seventeen years, he has covered some of the biggest news stories in South Asia including the Kargil conflict, Orissa's super cyclone, the Gujarat earthquake, the massacre of the royal family in Nepal and its transition to democracy, the Asian Tsunami, and the Kashmir earthquake. When he's not chasing the news he also writes songs and scripts for Bollywood films.

ALSO BY THE AUTHOR

173 Hours in Captivity: The Hijacking of IC-814 (2000)

End of the Line: The Story of the Killing of the Royals in Nepal
(2001)

ONCE UPON
A
TIMEZONE...

Neelesh Misra

HarperCollins *Publishers* India
a joint venture with

New Delhi

First published in India in 2006 by
HarperCollins *Publishers* India
a joint venture with
The India Today Group

Copyright © Neelesh Misra 2006

ISBN 10: 81-7223-664-6
ISBN 13: 9788172236649

Neelesh Misra asserts the moral
right to be identified as the author of this work.

First published in 2006
Second impression 2006

HarperCollins *Publishers*
1A Hamilton House, Connaught Place, New Delhi 110001, India
77-85 Fulham Palace Road, London W6 8JB, United Kingdom
Hazelton Lanes, 55 Avenue Road, Suite 2900, Toronto, Ontario M5R 3L2
and 1995 Markham Road, Scarborough, Ontario M1B 5M8, Canada
25 Ryde Road, Pymble, Sydney, NSW 2073, Australia
31 View Road, Glenfield, Auckland 10, New Zealand
10 East 53rd Street, New York NY 10022, USA

Typeset in 11.5/15 GoudyOldStyle
Nikita Overseas Pvt. Ltd.

Printed and bound at
Thomson Press (India) Ltd.

For my wife,
Nidhi Razdan,
and her two significant others:
Calvin the Labrador
and
Hobbes the Golden Retriever
(both of whom I don't get along with)

SOME RAMBLING FIRST...

Maybe I'll begin with the rules.

I am just a storyteller and a storyteller is an imperfect god. So don't blame me if things go wrong. And most importantly, don't you ever tell Neel that I told you any of this. He will die of embarrassment.

Somebody once asked me: How do love stories begin? That's like asking: Why does a river flow? Or, how is a poem born? Or, how do birds learn to fly? I said: Because that is their destiny. They were born, or they flew, or they flowed, because they were destined to.

Some say that's rubbish. Some say that's the first rule of everything. The first law of life. Do you believe in destiny? Well, I do, and I do it all the more because Neel's love story is before me. It followed its destiny like a calf follows its mother home from the fields after sundown in a dusty village.

It was a journey in search of a dream — and whenever you undertake that uncertain voyage, often the journey itself becomes the destiny, and the path itself becomes the destination.

Which brings me to the second rule I strongly believe in — that whatever happens, happens for the good. It is something that the all-knowing Krishna told the nervous and wavering Arjun when they stood to battle Duryodhan's army. The wise Krishna said something you might consider ridiculous: That what has happened, what is happening, and what will happen, are all for the greater good.

Do you believe in that law? Maybe you don't. It's kind of old-fashioned.

But I do.

It helps me keep my blood pressure down.

AN AMERICAN DREAM

New York City was in a hurry to get home.

It was a late August evening, and a slight drizzle was coming down on Manhattan. The roads, awash in a thin film of rainwater, slowly got lonelier. Long, lazy caravans of yellow cabs headed home. Those lucky ones without cars had started the drowsy ferry ride home across the Hudson. Beaming theatre-lovers, their jackets sprinkled with water, stepped out after a Broadway show and unsuccessfully hailed cab after snooty cab. Newsstands shut down. Two bikers pedalling with the accuracy of synchronized swimmers cut through an imaginary maze on the wet, empty pavement. Someone swore at someone else from a window above. Someone swore back. A lonely bearded man muttered incoherently into a pay phone as he caressed the coin slot mischievously with his fingers, his alcohol-heavy breath fuzzing up one panel of the cubicle. The bald Yemenese deli owner and his wife mopped their floor, brought inside the sign offering sandwiches for three dollars and smiled cheerfully at the day's last customer. The only buzz was in a corner of Manhattan, in Greenwich Village, the city's narrow-laned bohemian hub where the art and culture types, the lovers of Italian cuisine, forlorn men trying outdated pick-up lines at strange bars, and other such eternal wanderers, came flocking after dark. The air was bogged down with laughter, heavy perfume and small talk. Two men argued about the *Da Vinci Code* over Irish coffee, pretzels and honey-roasted cashews. A Hispanic woman hummed an ancient song of longing to an awestruck friend from the Middle East. Back on the street, a man and woman kissed deeply under a lamppost, their lips clinging like lost lovers, with sheets of falling raindrops lighting up a thousands pearls around them...

❦

Thousands of miles away across the globe, in the heart of bustling middle-class India, one man could hear all of these sounds and see all of these sights. Neel Pandey refused to wake up and lay curled in bed, his eyes closed, his arms hugging his pillow, his mind transported, as it was every night, to the land to which he believed he belonged, but had never visited — America.

Outside his window, morning had long arrived in New Delhi. Trains pulled into packed and messy stations. Capricious jaywalkers, shoeshine boys, bribe-seeking policemen, pickpockets, stoic hermits, and cargo carts pulled by dusty, sinewy men who had long started to look like the silent, oppressed horses that once plied these colonial-era thoroughfares, got about their business. Expensive sedans and Mercs jostled for space on the roads with three-wheeled cycle rickshaws and reckless public buses. Villagers, who had escaped the crushing poverty of their faraway homes, rapped their knuckles on the cool car windows, some ingenious ones with their hands swathed in ketchup-laced bandages, begging for alms in the name of real and imagined droughts and devastations. A row of cars at the traffic intersection honked mercilessly because the light had turned green. But the car in the front could not move because a little girl who was asking for money in the morning heat had placed her sunburnt cheek against the cool air-conditioned windowpane and momentarily closed her eyes...

The alarm rang. It was a hideously sharp alarm by Neel's bedside that ripped his eardrums each morning, but it was his insurance from oversleeping and landing into trouble with his overbearing father. The Manhattan dream was hastily yanked off his mind's screen. He could hear his father, Ravi Pandey, growling angrily at his wife in the next room. 'Jesus ... good morning to you too, Dad,' he mumbled to himself as he lumbered towards the bathroom. Thank goodness, his staunchly Hindu father had not heard him instinctively invoking the son of the Christian god.

The Pandeys' apartment wasn't big but it was large enough for the husband-wife and their only son. Neel's parents had saved for many years before being able to buy it. Those were the days when the so-called economic boom had not happened and there were no private banks hungry to give loans and fleece people. So his mother had sold part of her jewellery and Neel's father had bribed the manager of the government bank to be able to get a house loan. The early years had been tough. They were barely able to pay the interest, let alone repay the principal. Many cheques were delayed. Many jargon-filled reminders came in each day with the postman. But in the end, it had all worked out fine. The mortgage had been all but paid off, the house was nearly theirs, and the bank manager had become their neighbour (diligently scraping together his bribe money to buy the apartment on the floor above theirs).

At Neel's birth, Ravi's grandfather had made his own investment. He had put one lakh rupees (his entire savings until then) into a post office scheme under which the money doubled every five years. By the time Neel turned twenty, the money had grown to sixteen lakhs. Ravi planned to spend the money on his son's higher education. Or to buy him a two-bedroom apartment in a middle-class neighbourhood when he got married.

Ravi's only other possession of some significance was an obstinate Lambretta scooter that he had got twenty-six years ago as dowry from his school-professor father-in-law. This machine had a mind of its own, refusing to budge when it had to, and not stopping when it should have, which often meant earning the daily glower of a familiar, benevolent enemy – the traffic cop at the intersection near his house.

Ravi Pandey was a senior clerk in the Prime Minister's Office. That didn't make him any better than his counterparts in, say, the Ministry of Agriculture, or the Ministry of Coal and Mines, but it gave him a social standing among his peers, and evoked an unstated jealousy when the other clerks sat around at lunch; he worked in the PMO, after all.

Ravi Pandey regaled his friends with stories of how the Prime Minister sometimes cracked jokes with his staff, or inquired about the health of his chef's little daughter, or, once, stumbled on the lawns when trying to kick his grandson's football. Of course, he never told them that these stories were all hand-me-downs; that he had never really seen the Prime Minister in person. But the stories made him something of a Prime Minister himself, in his circle.

Oh, and believe me, he was Prime Minister at home as well.

So, exercising this self-invested authority and breaking the serenity of the autumn morning, Ravi growled angrily to his wife about that which he had growled angrily several times in the last two hours: 'Where *is* he?'

'He is still sleeping,' Narmada spoke to her husband with the nervousness of their first night, twenty-six years ago.

'Do you know the time? It's nine o'clock. How can he still be sleeping?' Ravi thundered.

'Please let him sleep for a bit today. He was studying until two,' Narmada replied, her eyes fixed on the blue refrigerator in the corner of the room. (She looked at the cool fridge whenever she had to escape the heated gaze of her husband.) Of course, she was lying about her son studying until two. Honestly, Indian mothers have to lie so much for their sons, it's not funny.

'Studying? I know what he was "studying" ... I heard the TV when I woke up to go to the bathroom. He must have been watching those dirty films ... that's all these young men do these days. I want to have that conversation with him today. Otherwise, you will tell me I never speak to him,' he shouted taking a few threatening steps towards his son's room.

She held his arm. 'No, not today. Today is a Friday. Not a good day for such things,' she said.

Who could defy superstition in the Pandey household? 'Well... tomorrow then ... we'll *definitely* talk about it tomorrow,' Ravi blustered uncertainly and stomped out.

C

The person at the centre of this scathing scrutiny was hiding behind a newspaper in his room, his eyes pretending to read but his ears twitching and straining as if they had an in-built radar, picking up every bit of the conversation.

Twenty-five-year-old Neel knew this clockwork of sounds well. This was the time when his father's black leather shoes marched towards the door, his office keys jangling, his mother's flip-flops flip-flopping behind him. Then the creaking door would open, his mother would dutifully say 'come home early', his father would mumble something incoherent, walk down the stairs, and putter away on his self-willed scooter past the enemy traffic cop. That daily drill over, Narmada would walk quietly into Neel's room, close the door behind her, lean against it, pat her face dry with the edge of her sari, and in a near-whisper announce: 'He's gone.'

'You are telling me like I am *scared* of him and hiding here or something,' Neel said looking up indignantly from his paper.

'Yes, of course you are hiding, Neel,' his mother giggled and a large dimple formed on her left cheek. It was one of those things that used to make the guys swoon over her in college. With her beautiful face, glowing skin and gentle streaks of grey, Neel's mother was still more Mrs India than Mother India.

The August sunlight lazily filtered into the apartment. Shafts of sun rays peeped through the glass, wherever they could, warming up long rectangles of space on the concrete floor of Neel's room. A large wooden rack in one corner stood next to an ornate teak box full of love letters from Neel's past girlfriends (all, alas, happily married now). It was crammed with thick books on computer software that Neel had studied for two years after completing his Masters, trying to get that fancied job in a software company. He couldn't. So he studied hotel management for a year until he was posted to the Food and Beverages department, where his delicate upper-caste Brahmin stomach turned at the sight of the blood-laced cleaver. So now the jobless son spent his days listening to 'I told-you-so' tirades from his father.

On the study table, beside a list of immigration counselling services in New Delhi promising a U.S. visa, and a miniature U.S. flag, were books on the GRE test and a thick list of American universities. The walls of his tiny room were plastered with pictures of the Statue of Liberty, the Niagara Falls, Hollywood celebrities and rock-stars. In one corner of the room, God Bless America played on a CD player. It was programmed to play at this time each day.

'So what are you reading?' Narmada said.

'The news. What else will I read in a newspaper, Mom?' Neel rolled his eyes.

'But these are the matrimonial pages, Mr Pandey, the green-card girls looking for good Indian boys,' she said, chuckling.

'Oh, shoot! They have printed the marriage ads where the international page used to be,' Neel said and looked at his mother sheepishly. Mother and son understood each other well. They had shared years of hopes and aspirations, grudges, laments, and unfulfilled dreams.

Narmada looked across the room, at a large poster of the Statue of Liberty. Then she smiled and asked her son his favourite question: 'So, what's happening in America today?'

'Basketball. There's an NBA match. And George Bush's dog has choked on a pretzel,' he said, looking at the switched-off TV.

Neel was completely sold on the United States of America. That's all he thought about from the moment he woke in the morning — looking at the stars-and-stripes poster across the room that said 'Born in the USA' — to the time he went to sleep at night, looking at the same poster. Neel loved everything about America: its style, its accent, its women, its sports, its technical superiority and material wealth. He wanted to migrate there. He wanted to marry an American girl and make a stackload of dollars.

Neel was also a deep admirer of American values. Every little thing he saw, and every little thing he read about America made him compare it to his bustling country of a billion. It made him wonder why his nation, that had given the world a sixth of its people, was able to produce only a tiny fraction of its wealth; why the nation that had some of the world's best software professionals or doctors or engineers was competing for development indices with tiny faraway blobs on the map run by tin-pot armies and crackpot despots. It made him dislike his nation — an attitude that his parents could never understand or accept.

In his dreams, Neel had stood, oh so many times, on Ellis Island, the chilly wind biting his face, numbing his cheeks and lips, his hair blowing about as his eyes drank in the stunning vista before him — the breathtaking skyline of New York.

Even in his dreams, Neel felt a spectacular sense of awe and admiration as he imagined the waves that had carried shiploads of weary travellers to the American shores where they had built a nation from scratch. More than anything, he told himself, it was its pride in nation-building that had made the United States so great, like post-war Japan or Germany, and it was pride that had been missing, for such a long time, from India.

Neel would do anything to be in New York — a city that realized the worth of hard work — where, in many ways, there was no distinctive culture except work. New York was a factory of the mind; a city teeming with ideas and drenched in small and big ambitions. There were thousands of these ambitions walking down Manhattan's avenues and streets draped in jackets and suits — some worth the next million, some worth the next meal. And it was here — to the capital of the Big Ideas — that Neel wanted to go. He had to get to New York. He was destined to, he had told himself so many times.

Naturally, it didn't help that Neel's father hated America.

Neel had only to mention McDonalds, Pepsi, George Bush, or Microsoft to get a rise out of his dad. Ravi Pandey would have quite a mouthful to say to George Bush or Bill Gates if he ever came face to face with them, but, since that was a slim possibility, he made do with his son. Lunches and dinners often extended to an hour-and-a-half. No one could leave the table until the father did, and the father couldn't get up until he had abused America to his heart's content. Neel would stagger back from the dinner table each night, his brain bursting with suppressed retorts, sink onto his bed and hold his head in frustration.

C

Like her son, Narmada — who had nurtured her family as devoted daughter-in-law, wife and mother for years — had her own dream. She had successfully performed the duties expected of her in a middle-class Indian family, from searching for a dry nappy for her shrieking son to rummaging for a clean handkerchief for her restless husband. Now, she didn't want to be just a housewife. She wanted to open a beauty salon and make people look beautiful. And she knew she would be pretty good at what she did. After all, she had kept herself quite well, hadn't she? At forty-six she hardly wore any make-up and could still make the teenage brats in the neighbourhood swivel and stare when she walked past them, a string of jasmine flowers adorning her long braid.

Unfortunately, Narmada was held back. The big dam in Narmada's way? Her husband, Ravi — from the conservative Hindu heartland of Allahabad.

Narmada looked out of the window at two of her young female neighbours, carrying fancy leather handbags and wearing layers of make-up, stepping out to hail a taxi to work. She took a deep breath. 'There is something I want to tell you, Neel,' Narmada said. Like a good dutiful wife, she had been entrusted with doing her husband's dirty work.

'So do I, Ma,' Neel said.

Narmada paid him no attention. 'Look, we all have dreams. You know I have one. I know you have one. They are very special to us ... they are what keep us going...'

Neel looked up. 'But?' he prompted.

'I know that you desperately want to go to America. That's your dream. But your father ... doesn't agree,' her voice faltered.

'I know. So what does he want me to do? Open a scooter repair shop?' Neel said scornfully.

'Um ... no ... he wants you ... to get married to a nice Brahmin girl from a family like ours and to get a job ... or else he will send you to the mushroom farm in Allahabad to look after cultivation. He says there is a lot of money in mushrooms.'

Neel had a sudden vision of himself wearing a dhoti and kurta, munching on freshly plucked mushrooms and chasing his young shy bride through the green fields of a sprawling farm, as his favourite cow silently chewed his Statue of Liberty poster. It was a difficult dream. He took a deep breath and returned to the moment before him — which wasn't much better either. Neel the reluctant groom or Neel the reluctant farmer? Neel was stuck — squashed, in fact — between a rock and a hard place, with a javelin between them sticking into his posterior!

'I know how you feel, beta ... though I must admit even I would love to have you walk in through the door with a beautiful bride in a red Banarasi sari and a lot of bangles and henna ... But I won't ever pressure you, beta ... um ... your father is adamant, though. He has already started looking...' Narmada said.

'Well, Ma, I have some news for you too. I have got a letter from an American university — I wanted some information about a management course — and I have applied for a U.S. visa, the interview for which is in a few hours from now. So, I am going to grab a clean shirt, shave my face ... and go.' Neel paused. 'And I hope my old man will let me use the sixteen lakhs my grandfather gave me to pay part of the admission fee, if it is correct, as he says, that the money is for me.'

Narmada heard her son out in silence, watching him fetch his towel and pick up his clothes. She was terrified of what she and Neel would have to hear from her tough and stubborn husband when he came to know of his plans. Of the volcano that would be unleashed inside him. But she also knew, deep in her heart, that she was relieved. She was grateful for the spark of rebellion. She wanted her son to fly free and pursue his life.

To live his dream.

To do all that which had so emphatically been denied to her.

AN AMERICAN NIGHTMARE

The burly, clean-shaven guard at Gate No. 4 of the U.S. Embassy straightened his back, puffed up his chest and looked with smug satisfaction far into the leafy New Delhi avenue. Shyam Lal Banarsi came from a small dusty village in Uttar Pradesh, but you couldn't really blame him for thinking sometimes that he was the U.S. ambassador himself – or St. Peter at Heaven's Gate! The six-foot-something man was Chief Guard at the hallowed entrance everyone had to pass through for a visa interview. It was the portal to more prosperous lives or better jobs or reunions with faraway loved ones — and all could enter only after he had ushered them in. It was a position of great seniority and great responsibility. That's what Shyam Lal Banarsi had told folks back in his village, anyway.

There were people scattered as far as he could see. They had all come in expensive chauffeur-driven cars and brought along packed lunches from flashy restaurants. They squatted on the grass. They sat on the pavement. They stood on the road. They sprawled in their cars. They paced up and down. They fretted. They waited patiently, wherever they got to wait, for their watches to strike 11:30 a.m. when the interviews would begin. The line for the U.S. visa was the great leveller. All people, no matter how rich or well connected, had to wait their turn. All of them had to go through Shyam Lal Banarsi. There was a strange kind of socialism at the doorway to the kingdom of capitalism.

When his turn finally came, Neel Pandey, wearing a blue check shirt and khaki trousers and clutching a thick file of documents, swaggered in. After he was frisked, a clerk gave him a number and asked him to sit in a large hall where other nervous, solemn-faced men, women and children waited. It was a seat in the front row. Behind him, the murmur of rows and rows of whispering people swelled to a giant wave of last-minute checks combined with the anxious rustling of photocopied and original documents.

High on a wall in front of where Neel sat, a TV-set was tuned to an old Hindi film in which the bad guy, with an oily-looking wig, was ordering a woman to dance. Clearly, the woman had a lot of free time on her hands that day, as she was obeying willingly, twirling and circling and letting her long skirt swirl and rise to her waist. Now don't get any ideas — nothing Marilyn Monroesque happened, she was wearing the mandatory, modesty-ensuring, tight white churidar pajamas underneath. Neel couldn't bear to watch. In fact, he wondered how such a crass old movie was being shown in a place like the U.S. Embassy at all.

One after the other, the names of people were announced. Neel began a small game, trying to guess who was who, whether they were going as tourists or visitors or as potential immigrants. Then he tried to eavesdrop on the visa interviews, straining to catch the answers the applicants gave to the questions put to them by the officers seated behind the glass windows.

Mostly he got it wrong. The Tamil woman he thought was a housewife, going to join her husband, turned out to be a Citibank executive going for a conference. The forty-something Sikh gentleman in white, whom he had put down as a farmer visiting his son, was actually a Punjabi author going to receive a community award; and Neel could have sworn that he heard one of the white visa officers behind the windows speak in Bengali to a man who was asked to prove that the woman accompanying him was his wife.

As the interviews droned on, Neel switched off his mind and the sounds seemed to fade away. He stretched his legs and slipped back a bit in his chair, feeling his tight muscles loosening up. After all, he was in the American Embassy.

He was already beginning to feel at home.

C

Narmada Pandey had just showered and shampooed her hair, and was running her long sensuous fingers deep into its furrows, imagining they were her husband's caressing fingers and not her own. She watched herself in the large mirror in the bathroom, looking straight into the eyes of her reflection, studying the glint and sheen of her long wet hair as it dripped onto her bare shoulders. Narmada smiled languidly to herself, feeling like the young woman she had been years ago, when she was just about discovering the magic of her body and the effervescence of her soul. She closed her eyes and let her mind float back to a time when she was becoming aware of her body; when she was realizing that she had bloomed from a giggly teenage girl to a full grown woman, stepping out after her bath in a wet, white, translucent cotton dhoti and watching herself in the mirror with the hungry eyes of a lover, letting her hair fall over her sensuous breasts and then lifting it off slowly, feeling a surge of passion inside her that she never had felt before...

She had grown up by the Ganga, in a village near Varanasi, where millions flocked each year, seeking riches and salvation, to the Kumbh Mela. The childless wanting children, the failed businessmen wanting money, the newly married wanting joy, the sick wanting good health, and the dying wanting a place in heaven. Some wanting nothing, just the presence of their bodies and souls at a place where the divine was believed to merge with the earthly in a magical, disorderly union.

Narmada had watched them make this arduous journey in the face of insurmountable odds. They had left behind their homes, put their elders and children in others' safekeeping, sold their cattle and come packed like cattle themselves in the Kashi Vishwanath Express to the Mughalsarai railway platform, just to be at the river of their dreams, to take a dip and seek the salvation that would one day rid them of their wretched lives. They had come hundreds of miles from their families and shops and mustard fields and risked being lost in the millions or being trampled upon in a stampede, just because they were chasing their dreams.

Narmada understood their need. She knew that what they were seeking was not just money and fame and children and jobs and the resolution of old enmities. They were giving up control of their chaotic, directionless lives to a power they believed was stronger than themselves and would control them.

Like those millions, Narmada, too, had grown up chasing her dreams.

There was no husband back then, no children, no responsibilities — just herself and her small charmed circle of beauties who went from their village to bathe in the Ganga and were drenched everyday in the scorching gaze of male attention. She didn't quite know it but Narmada had been one of the most beautiful women in her neighbourhood. She had large, expressive, kohl-laced eyes, long flowing hair, the figure of a well-groomed city model, and fragile silver payals on her feet, whose teasing susurration as she walked by, aroused desire in the most stone-hearted of men.

Then Narmada had grown up and come to New Delhi to study at the university, joined the student union, contested an election and was the joint secretary of the Delhi University for a year. She wowed audiences at debates, fought with hostel authorities for the rights of docile junior students, and dreamt of making it big one day in politics. One day, her father died abruptly and she had to get married to the only man who would marry her without a dowry — Ravi, three years her senior at the university, and known to her through their small-town bonds in the big city.

Ravi was a decent man. But still...

She looked up into the skies, her eyes filled with a potion of hope and despair and, as if on cue, the skies joined her. It began to rain, an unintended and unexplained shower long after the rainy season, that once again took Narmada back in time...

Deep inside the unknown alleys of a dense apple orchard, a woman of nineteen moaned loudly, making wild love to her unstoppable lover on a stack of hay. He pinned her down, holding her hands as she willingly submitted to his raging desire, long thin strands of hay scattered across their bodies. She bit his ear in a rush of pleasure, her hair open, her kohl smeared, her necklace beads strewn, her hairpins lost. That woman, tasting the forbidden fruit and muffling her screams of agony and ecstasy, was the young Narmada.

Narmada smiled with a secret satisfaction as she remembered that day. It was only one of the two days in her life when Narmada had rebelled — the second was when she had thrown her wedding ring at her dominating husband, screamed and fought with him like a wounded tigress, threatening to walk out of the house with their tiny son. But I will tell you more about that a little later.

She took a deep breath and turned back into the room. The phone. The phone was ringing outside. Narmada clicked her tongue in irritation but, fearful that it might be her husband, quickly put on her clothes. It was Ravi. He just wanted to know where Neel was. Narmada hesitated for a second, then quickly made up a story about how he had gone to a job placement agency to hand in his CV. The mini crisis blew over.

Narmada sighed deeply as she hung up. Her son had put her in the awkward position of a conspirator, an accessory to the crime, as it were. But she felt calm. She had to be like the mother sparrow, helping her little one learn how to use his wings rather than pulling him back into the nest. So Narmada draped herself in her favourite red sari, and made her way to the secret mission that she had planned since morning. Neel had a dream and he was pursuing it. She wanted to make sure her son would be happy in whatever path he chose for himself.

Narmada closed the door of the prayer room behind her and sat cross-legged on the carpeted floor. She lit a cotton wick dipped in mustard oil and jangled the small copper bell, as she hummed a Sanskrit sloka. Then she looked Ganesh straight in the eye. The speech opened with a flat lie, routinely spoken before their gods by millions of Indians, all of whom had learnt it from Bollywood. 'I have never asked you for anything,' she said with a deadpan face. 'But I am asking you today ... '

Ganesh listened intently. The other gods watched in silence from behind their photo frames. They had to get their facts right before granting any wish. Even gods have some accountability, after all. The oil wick flickered, then started burning with greater intensity. Good sign. Narmada strengthened her attack: 'I promise you, he will stop eating meat and fish if he gets the visa. And he will also wear the yagyopaveet thread that he deliberately forgot in the bathroom after the ceremony last year.' And then, the final swoop: 'I promise I will fast an extra day every week. I will make the pilgrimage to Vaishno Devi, I will walk barefoot up the mountain and offer five gold coins at your feet.'

Narmada took a deep breath and got up, satisfied with her morning's work.

☾

'Neel Pandey, Counter 45 please!' a voice boomed across the Embassy waiting hall. Neel had dozed off, and he woke up with a start. His lips were dry. His heart was racing. He wanted to go to the loo. A sudden attack of nervousness made him wobbly. His hands trembled as he gathered all his papers and walked up to a charming young Indian woman behind the glass. He felt reassured and smiled at her. She felt upset and didn't smile back. Apparently, Neel was at counter 54, not 45. He picked up his papers again, trudged back eight windows, and came to counter 45. It was the same grouchy Bengali-speaking white American. He looked listlessly at Neel. Perhaps visa officers were trained to never smile at anyone, like the Secret Service was trained to be gruff and pushy and never nice. Clearly, if there was a God of Visa Interviews, he (or she) was not on Neel's side today. 'Your papers, please,' the officer said disinterestedly. He had an intense, pockmarked face, gold-rimmed glasses, curly black hair and a disconcerting way of tapping his pencil on the table. Nonstop. The tapping made Neel even more nervous.

He slipped his sheaf of papers through an opening below the window. Minutes passed by. The visa officer seemed to be going over every goddamn paragraph and every goddamn sentence and every goddamn word and every goddamn letter. After what seemed like three years he turned one page. He made some marks with a pencil. He took a sip from a coffee mug with an American flag printed on it. Then he read further. Each line, Neel told himself. Each syllable.

'Passport, please, Mr Pandey,' the clerk finally said.

Neel slid his passport across and then wiped his sweaty palms on his backside. Behind him, a girl in the front row of the waiting area giggled. Neel hated her. He suddenly realized the importance of the moment: the moment in time that could mark his first step into the future. A single sticker and stamp on a small blue booklet that could change his life. He was closer to that one spot of ink he had dreamt of for years, than ever before. If the man across the window wanted, Neel would get to see the real Ellis Island, the real Statue of Liberty, the real Rockefeller Center ... and, perhaps, even meet the American woman of his dreams.

God takes so many forms. Is this visa officer the benevolent Vishnu, sprawled on the mighty multi-headed Sheshnaga, with his wife fanning him? Or is he the angry Shiva, serpents slithering all over his body, his neck blue from the poison of the ocean that he drank to save the universe, firmly clutching the long and lethal trishul, with the havoc-causing third eye half open? To Neel, one flick of the pen would decide the fate of his future. Would it be Vishnu, then, or Shiva?

'Your photograph is taken against a blue background. It should be white,' the visa officer observed.

Possibly Vishnu, but most probably Shiva, or even a male version of Kali, tongue sticking out and all, Neel thought. Luckily he had a photograph with a white backdrop and he slipped it to the grouchy man behind the thick glass.

'This letter from the university does not state whether they are offering a scholarship. It's just a general letter with information about the courses. Well, OK, you can collect your passport after 4 p.m. from the window outside the visa entrance, Mr Pandey.'

'Make that a ten-year multiple-entry visa, please,' Neel said grandly to the visa officer, before sauntering out of the U.S. Embassy, hailing a taxi, and speeding away. He had decided to go spend a few hours at a friend's place before coming back to pick up his visa, and then, maybe, he thought, a few beers later to celebrate.

Five hours later, Neel walked back into the house. His shirt grimy, his hair tousled, his eyes defeated. He rang the bell, and Narmada came running. 'Where were you all day, Neel? I was about to die with worry. How was your interview?'

Neel looked away. 'I'm not going, Ma.'

'What? *Why?*'

'Because the God of Visa Interviews was not on my side, Ma,' he said as he walked away to his room.

The God of Visa Interviews was not Shiva or Vishnu or Ganesh.

It was Yamaraj, the God of Death.

AMERICAN SWEETHEART

Thousands of miles away, a crispy morning had just popped up from god's great sandwich maker, in a county outside New York, in the America of Neel's dreams.

A young woman sat sprawled on her bed, her coffee mug by her side, as she picked low-cal snacks every once in a while from a coloured glass bowl balanced on her pillow. Her apartment complex overlooked a sprawling park by the Hudson River, where many residents of Upper Plymouth jogged and walked. Upper Plymouth was a wealthy county outside New York, a thirty-nine minute train ride from Grand Central Station in Manhattan, close enough from the city but yet far removed, as the realtors would say. Inside her room there was a beautiful silence. The pictures on the wall were large and evocative, some dreamy, some sensuous, of faces, sunsets and waves. They were pictures of faraway lands that she had never gone to and people she would never meet.

Through the large French window, Angela Cruz watched the morning sunlight shimmer on the massive glassy walls of an office building in the distance, and the young men and women laying out chairs at roadside breakfast joints that would soon be abuzz with lazy, yawning chatter.

Angela liked to think she was a determined young woman who knew what she wanted in life and, sometimes, even knew how to get there. But, in truth, she was a dreamer, making long, untiring journeys in her mind and never reaching a destination. For instance, she read an account of an unknown Italian schoolteacher dedicating his life to blind schoolchildren and the next moment she was actually searching the Internet to learn Braille online. She heard of a prostitute in Chile who sold her body to bring up the daughter an unknown man had impregnated her with, and Angela immediately pictured herself consenting to strangers each night, thinking only of the needs of her tender daughter, as they bit her breasts and egged her on with foul whiffs of bad breath. Once, she'd actually begged on a Manhattan kerb after reading about an undercover journalist who broke a huge story about a millionaire's mistress by staking out in front of her house disguised as a tramp!

But in the real world few things could please Angela — this was as true of her sushi as of her men. She liked the idea of falling in love, but more often than not she would always end up sitting on her balcony shaking her head at her last date and wondering how she could have gone out with a dull guy like that. She hated the idea of a regular romance. She wanted adventure. Like falling in love with a pastoral nomad in the Prairies. Or lusting for a wandering mendicant in Egypt. Or kissing a poet in Kashmir as they glided on the Dal Lake in a dainty shikara boat…

Angela had recently started working as a reporter with the *Upper Plymouth Journal*, the popular county newspaper. As she dreamily sipped her coffee, Angela suddenly remembered she was late for her morning appointment with the children from the school across the Village. It was a story that her best friend and news editor Hema Easlay had told her about. Shoot.

On the other side of the Hudson, in the less posh side of town, was the Plymouth County School, where Angela should have been headed by now. It had shabby, discoloured walls, a small playground, and the dubious sight of sullen children skulking about. If you walked down the chemistry lab and trod soft-footed past the library, you might even find innocent-looking children surreptitiously passing around tiny amounts of suspicious white powder. Which, let me hasten to clarify, the school bosses were working on, so don't let this grainy image mar the overall humdrum nature of this all-American school — with no more than its normal share of school-related problems.

But for once this school had been in the news for a very proud reason. To tell you about which, I will have to take you to the grassy expanse to my south, near the tennis courts of the school, where the lazy sun seemed just about stretching itself and waking up. Gentle sunlight lit up an untended tennis court otherwise lost in the shadows of the lofty trees surrounding it. Birds flew overhead, spreading their wings as far as they could to hug the sky as they headed for some unknown destination. Who knows, they thought, whether they would ever be able to come back again to embrace and be part of this piece of sky?

On the ground, twenty-four children ranging from ages six to sixteen sat on the grass or paced the rows of the spectator seats of the tennis court. They were unusually silent, talking in hushed tones, huddled in a corner. These kids were members of the exceptionally talented band of the Plymouth County School. Most of the kids were from different parts of the world. Hispanics, Indians, Africans, Chinese, Arabs. A lot of them were backbenchers in their classes — silent, reserved, barely talking to the teachers or to each other. Most of them had grown up feeling ignored by their classmates. Because they did not fit in with the rest, they felt unwanted, or unloved, or plain unlucky. They had become used to hearing sniggers and smart-ass comments hurled at them behind their backs.

One year ago, they had recognized that to be heard in America, they had to have their own voice. And they found it — in a rambunctious fusion of the uplifting sounds of calypso, bhangra-pop, and rap. And, as they swung to their new beat, they'd realized that if there was one thing that gave them more joy than a chocolate cake with icing; more pleasure than watching Harry Potter or playing computer games; more excitement than having a bittersweet crush on the school heart-throb, one thing that uplifted their spirits so much that they did not feel deprived, or poor, or awkward, or unloved or dumb — it was music.

This year, their music was sounding sweeter than ever before; it rang, after all, with true happiness. They were the only marching band from the entire northeast chosen to perform during the half-time extravaganza at the Orange Bowl in January! It was a rare and very prestigious honour for the students of the Plymouth County School. The achievement was especially inspiring since most of the band members had no formal training in classical music. For them and their parents, it was akin to winning the Nobel Prize in Chemistry. The children would play before tens of thousands of frenzied spectators and millions of prime-time TV viewers cross America. Not to mention thousands of awestruck viewers in Upper Plymouth! It was a passion that was inspiring, and rare. These were valiant warriors riding a dream.

But, as with every dream, there was a little hitch.

The school only provided them with a place to rehearse — not the money needed for instruments and outfits, and for the band members to fly down with their truckload of equipment to Miami and stay there for at least four nights. So they had to raise the money themselves. Over the past year, the school and the band had done everything they could think of to try and raise the amount. They had sold raffle tickets, made colourful posters seeking donations, painted T-shirts, made exciting Halloween gifts that the local stores agreed to sell, and gave public performances. Money came, but it was way too little to take them to the sunny beaches of Florida.

That afternoon, as she covered their practice session, Angela stood spellbound. As she heard the children play – their eyes closed, their faces awash in a steely determination – she was enthralled by the sheer brilliance of their performance. And among them all, was one that spoke to her most eloquently with her silent eyes and shy smile. A six-year-old Mexican girl, Juanita. A sad small thing with thin arms, who did not dare look anyone in the eye, but when she opened her mouth to sing it was as if an angel had revealed the goodness of her soul. Angela did not understand the nuances of the music, but she knew very well the patterns of emotion woven by every note in that little heart.

Can you recall a moment that changed your life? Years and years from now, Angela Cruz would remember this moment as the one that changed hers. The moment when Angela Cruz, the mental gypsy, had finally found a cause. The drifter had got her anchor. The vagabond had found a place to rest. After years, the young woman who always wanted to live someone else's life, to be someone else, had found a dream to pursue.

The kids milled around her as she took notes, telling her how they had overcome great odds to set up their show, and how they now needed a crucial contribution from the community to be able to go and perform at the Orange Bowl. She knew that the kids needed at least fifty thousand dollars and that it was going to be a herculean task – but Angela was confident that her writing would move the community into shelling it out. Because, suddenly, bringing a smile to the faces of Juanita and her band had become the single-most important thing in her drifting cloud of a life.

Angela had written several stories for the college paper, so when she had first reached the office of the *Upper Plymouth Journal* for her interview with a stack of clippings, she had no doubt that she would get the job. She did. But she took some time catching on. For months now she had been dumped with covering ladies' garden parties and other social events. Now, she decided, she would take up the cause of these brave kids and write the individual stories of each of these twenty-four immigrant children — their lives, theirs fears, their dreams. She would move people all over Plymouth into opening their hearts — and their wallets.

C

That afternoon had been the kind of break that Angela had always craved for in her work day. Far away from home, Angela's first job gave her freedom and excitement and a good fresher's salary, but also some mixed feelings. She sometimes missed her small-town life, her friends, her mother and even her father — famous for throwing things when riding the wave of high temper and fixed ideas. Every year, when she went home for Christmas, she imagined that he would have changed, but in truth little did, Christmas over Christmas.

In his heart, Gavin always measured a person by the colour of his skin. He thought little of Angela's work; he would freak out when he got to hear that she was trying to do something for a bunch of immigrant kids.

She felt sorry for her father. She had tried to understand his point of view over the years, tried to imagine what might have made him so racist, but Angela could never justify the depth of his hatred for non-whites. That, in a way, balanced out her aching desire to leave New York and go back home, hundreds of miles to the south, to Jackson, Mississippi.

C

The man who caused Angela so much heartache was sitting far away in Jackson City, watching the 9 p.m. news on TV. Gavin

Cruz groaned and threw up his hands, one holding a cigarette, the other a newspaper. Then he took a deep breath and looked around to make sure his wife was listening as she worked the dishwasher after dinner.

'What's wrong, honey? Do they want more tax?' she said loudly, thrusting a wooden ladle hard to scrape the obstinate remains of meat from a pan.

'No. Just come here and take a look at this, Martha. There's been a murder right here on our street,' Gavin said. 'Lord knows next time they might come and drive that chain-saw through me.'

The story on TV was about the killing of a black youth the previous night on Maine Street in Jackson, the largest city in Mississippi state. The address — number 53, a large house with white picket fences — was just a few hundred metres down from where the Cruz family lived. Martha shuddered as the TV cameras lingered on the partly shrouded face of an eighteen-year-old boy with close-cropped hair, his closed eyelids hugely swollen and his face apparently bludgeoned with a blunt object.

There were many things that the blacks and whites of Jackson had to ask forgiveness for. This city of some 180,000 had once been the hub of racial hatred in Mississippi, where the blood of many an African American had spilled at night-time, on the same streets on which hundreds of Klan members paraded during the day. Those days were gone, Jackson residents often said, but they were kidding themselves. Race was still a very powerful issue for the residents of Jackson City. Most killings were labelled racial attacks, even though they were often linked to the gang wars that every now and then erupted on Jackson's streets. Black kids were stereotyped as thugs, trigger-happy freaks and drug peddlers. The whites were seen as more educated and affluent, and hence, the blacks said, got preference in jobs. All social tension was linked to race. If a white businessman tried to buy up a prime piece of property or laid off a few workers who happened to be black, it was quite natural at black family dinners to use that as a tool to trace it all the way back to the Klan – to evoke the fear of the dreaded days of the white supremacists who bombed their homes and killed their kids. And if the black mayor spoke of the rights of coloured people, or of the need for more affirmative action, the 'N' word was sure to come up in hushed tones in white men's conversation over a few rounds of beer in the local bar. The whites said that now it was racism in reverse – blacks discriminating against *them*. The shadows of suspicion still loomed large; racism was quite in fashion in Jackson.

Gavin's grandfather had come to America from Puerto Rico many decades ago and found work in a bar. His father, scraping together every penny he had, eventually ended up owning the place. When Gavin's father died – and expressly against his last wishes – Gavin promptly sold the bar, bought a car, filled it up and drove all over the United States. Somewhere along the way he met Martha, who said she had been mugged and assaulted by three drunken men. He gave her a ride to wherever he was headed. On the way they had sex. Six months later they were married and came to Jackson.

Over the years, they had three beautiful daughters and moved from a small apartment at the edge of town to a slightly bigger house closer to the school where Martha taught and their three lovely girls studied. The neighbourhood seemed so perfect, away from the uncertainty of the rest of the city.

But before Gavin and Martha could realize it, their city – which had survived the social catastrophe of the racism era – began to crumble about them. Martha heard of too many brawls at her school that were traced to problems between whites and blacks – often over issues as trivial as a striker's seemingly harmless joke at a baseball game, or a student of one race asking the other not to sneeze in everyone's face and circulate the blessed virus. Then, within some years, the white students themselves began vanishing. Worse, the white teachers began vanishing as well. Gavin and Martha's home was robbed twice, and Gavin was quick to tell the officer that he suspected the black kids he saw loitering around his property the previous day.

Gradually, the Cruz couple bound itself in, withdrawing to their own small home and social circle, as thousands of other whites and blacks had done across the city. Without their realizing it, the crime, fear and aggressive racial overtones in the city slowly but certainly changed Gavin. And though his own grandfather was Puerto Rican, Gavin convinced himself he was white.

Gavin developed a fearful obsession for controlling the lives of his daughters. He slowly began dictating what his daughters could do, whom they could meet, where they could go. No black boyfriends. No hanging out at the Pizza Hut in the black district to the east. No coming home after eight. No listening to rap music because it was blacks singing most of it, anyway. And no posters of black male artistes with bare chests, because Gavin was prone to ripping them off the wall and tearing them to shreds.

Martha realized the injustice, but could do little. Also, she saw that Gavin had gone through a lot that the daughters had not, although he was not always the best man when it came to explaining his point of view or communicating things. If he decided on what he thought was right for the family, that was pretty much it. Even the Pope could not change that.

His eldest daughter, Elaine, was now married with two sons. When she'd wanted to marry her boyfriend, Gavin had thrown a fit because he attended a church group that sang in choirs in black areas for racial reconciliation. She ran away from home and didn't come back for two years. Then there was twenty-four-year-old Jane. She'd graduated from the University of North Carolina and majored in American History (because Gavin had asked her to). She now worked at a school in Indiana.

The youngest — Gavin's favourite — was Angela. He often used to brag that Angela was the most beautiful girl in Mississippi. That might well have been true. At twenty-two, she was a 5-foot-7-inch stunner, with black hair inherited from her father, large hazel brown eyes, and a mind-blowing figure. Of course Angela had a tough streak and an occasionally sizzling temper — but she was also intelligent and funny and the one who got the most laughs at the Thanksgiving dinner. She had gone to NYU for a degree in journalism and then stayed on in New York. This meant that Angela only had to hear her father's sermons once a week, when she called home on weekends. Invariably, he would grab the phone and launch into his favourite diatribe about not mixing with blacks and Asians.

Asians. Yes, another sore point in Gavin's life. A serious one. After all, they had taken his job away from him.

You see, in his first ten years in Jackson, Gavin tried out many ways to make money. Nothing worked. Finally, on Martha's advice, he joined a nice little office near the city council. He worked for what he pompously called a 'software company' though it was basically a call centre and involved lengthy phone conversations with irate customers. The office was on the first floor of a building which also housed the offices of two insurance companies.

Gavin had had no clue about computer software. This was the Eighties, after all, when people were just about getting used to letting machines take over their lives. So, on Martha's egging, he had gone and enlisted himself in a local college. Few offices had computers. People wanted thousands and thousands of pages of data fed into computers to be saved for posterity (the computer virus that wipes out entire hard disks had not been invented yet). There were death records from the insurance companies, birth records from the hospitals, police department files from the chief's office, schools, colleges, authors and poets, everyone who had ever scribbled anything on any damn piece of paper wanted it punched into a computer and printed out on a screeching dot-matrix.

People wanted to buy computers but no one knew how to use them.

Gavin found himself a job in a call centre, answering their queries. Soon, he was in a steady job, with easy hours and enough comfort. He became a manager, and was on his way to becoming an associate vice-president. Gavin bought a house on Maine Street. He bought his wife a car. Life was easy. Gavin had never had it so good.

Then, one day, in the late Nineties — I think it was 1998 — Gavin's boss invited all his employees for a fabulous dinner to meet his new partners, Ramanujam Krishnapalli Ramaswami and Madanjeet Singh, both engineering graduates from IIT, India. In his after-dinner speech, Gavin's boss announced that he was expanding his business overseas beginning with the opening of a call centre in Bangalore, India. Then, almost as an afterthought, just as his employees were savouring the mouth-watering dessert, he added that none of those present at the party need report to work the next day. Or, indeed, ever again.

They were being laid off. As the world would learn to say later, Gavin Cruz had been Bangalored.

Six months and two weeks later, Gavin had to sell Martha's car and put his house on mortgage. He had made an addition to his list of Most Hated People as he struggled to pay his bills every month. Until now, it had only been the blacks. Now it was Ramanujam Krishnapalli Ramaswami, Madanjeet Singh — and all Asians ever born on this earth.

PROPOSALS AND DISPOSALS

On several evenings when he sat with Narmada having ginger tea, exasperated by his son's joblessness, Ravi Pandey wondered what life would have been like if he had never come to the big city.

Good old Allahabad had simple rules by which it had run, unquestioned, for centuries. Allahabad. Where thick-skinned, fat-tummied, bald Hindu pandas fleeced the illiterate like a benevolent Mafia gang, offering an array of ceremonies for all occasions. They had a ritual and a mantra for just about everything: whether you had just been born, or were about to; whether you had just died, or were about to; or whether you were just plodding along life, like a stoic sage on the banks of the Ganga, kicking up the silt, and wondering how far further you had to go on the dreary, desert path to salvation.

Like the millions of others who had lived and assembled in his city, dripping with faith and the waters of the holy Ganga, Ravi Pandey had for decades carried the plough of religion unquestioningly. The ancient people had laid down rituals, so they had to be followed. Past generations had laid down unwritten rules, so they had to be adhered to. Religion had little to do with these practices. It was the pandits who had started them, and arrogated to themselves the right to be revered and followed.

Now don't get me wrong. This old world had a million good things worth sticking to, but it also had a few million bad, and somehow good old Ravi Pandey, like many other conservative Indian parents, unfailingly picked all the wrong ones. This meant that a low-caste person would sit on the floor while the high-caste sprawled above him on a bed. This meant that Ravi's mother could not be at the forefront of any religious ceremony because, being a widow, she was deemed inauspicious. This meant that his wife could not step into the temple when she was having her period. And Ravi Pandey had clung on to memories of his boyhood — of a world where women covered their heads in long veils and stepped out of their homes only to attend birthdays and wedding parties. A world where men worked diligently all day and had the right to force themselves on their women at night. Where women rarely went to college, and never took up jobs, and where the menfolk were required to get the security of government jobs after they graduated, so that they could be married off (with a big dowry, of course).

Of course, to be fair to Ravi, being a bigot and a male chauvinist was only one part of his personality. Ravi Pandey was otherwise a nice guy, a concerned father who stayed awake all night when his son had a slight fever, and a caring husband who could be romantic in silly ways. Ravi was a poet once and sneaked off to the post office to send his poems to literary magazines when his brothers were not at home. Well, a few actually did get published, but he never knew this. The miserly publishers never sent him a copy or a cheque, and he did not have the money to buy every issue and keep track. One day, in the monsoon season, he threw away all his poems, scattering them with a dramatic flourish from the third floor of his building. The poems floated and drifted away — unsigned, fluttering, directionless — like his own dreams. There was more than the usual fleet of paper boats the next day in the neighbourhood's roadside puddles.

Some of the adolescent fire survived through his youth, through his stormy college days when he got swept into student politics and was elected to minor union positions that earned him enough respect to bum a free paan off the roadside cigarette shop each day. Then he got married and found himself a clerical job in the PMO.

Somewhere along the way, he stopped dreaming. He began to dislike overt expressions of joy, or passion, or any emotion, really, except anger. The creative, sensitive Ravi, transformed into the archetypal office clerk, pushing files, trading office gossip and waiting for lunch hour. Working for so many years as a lower functionary, always taking orders and sticking to the mindless procedure of government red tape, he now carried the same rigid adherence to small unnecessary matters into his home. And rules were rules.

Ravi had mandated that his son would marry whom *he* decided, get a job that *he* thought was good for him, and that his wife would not work for a living as long as he was alive to earn the bread for the family.

Unknown to him, these were precisely the rules that his wife and son wanted to defy. If they were successful, it would be the biggest-ever social revolution in generations of Pandeys since the time, during the days of Ravi Pandey's childhood, in his large joint family, when the daughters of the house had finally been permitted to wear salwar-kameezes instead of saris and ride cycles to school.

C

So that evening, Ravi Pandey walked into his house with a wedding invitation in his hands and some strong feelings on his face. His son was falling behind in the Great Indian Wedding Race. A colleague in Accounts was marrying off his son — about the same age as Neel. The invitations had been sent around today. It was the final provocation. Ravi came in with the determination of a bullfighter.

'This room is so dirty! What do you people do here all day?' It was unusual for Ravi to start cribbing the moment he walked into the house; normally he waited for his tea before doing that. But he was clearly a bit worked up and Narmada soon discovered why. 'Mr Sharma and his wife are coming,' he told Narmada, directing his gaze at the cushions rather than at her. This was because he knew how she would respond.

'What? But you didn't tell me anything in the morning. How can I cook for them at such short notice?'

'Mrs Pandey, will you ever let me finish? They won't have dinner. Just tea. That's all. He said so himself. The three of them were, anyway, coming to the neighbourhood, so they said they would drop by,' Ravi said.

'Three? You don't mean...?'

'Yes. Meenal is coming too.'

'You know this is not fair to our son. You call your friend, you call his wife, I understand. But you also call their young daughter, of marriageable age, for whom I know they are looking for a boy? I know what will be on *your* mind and *their* mind when they are here,' Narmada said lashing out uncharacteristically. 'I still remember what Sharmaji said when Neel was a baby and they came for his first birthday. He said, "One day this little master will be my son-in-law."'

Ravi's cover was blown; he quickly went on the defensive: 'What does this have to do with Neel? They are my friends, they are coming to see me. And his wife is your friend.'

'No, she is not my friend. She makes it a point to mention that she is working in a bank, that she's a "working woman". She will never admit that all she does is lick stamps and count notes all day!' Narmada snapped.

'I know ... that is something I never understood. When Hari Sharma gets a good salary, when he has his own house, what's the need to ask his wife to work? What kind of a man is he? Does he have no self-respect?' Ravi Pandey was momentarily diverted by the perplexing motivation of working women.

Of course, despite what she had said to her husband, Narmada was secretly quite thrilled. If this was what she thought it was, then it would be the first real marriage proposal for her son; an occasion that sends hopes and dreams soaring in most Indian mothers. A beautiful daughter-in-law, all dolled up and bejewelled, is great to show off to the jealous women of the neighbourhood. If she comes with a dowry, it is an added bonus. The refrigerator, the double bed, the television set, sometimes even the car, all still packed, are proudly displayed in the hall where the neighbourhood women are invited to sit, gawk at the goods, and sip tea. That way, they can soak it all in, get really jealous, go home and tell their husbands and make them envious too — before leaving to tell the *other* neighbours who haven't been invited. It has such a great social ripple effect! It can change a brand-new mother-in-law's standing at community parties and religious congregations, indeed in society at large — where everyone wants to give or get loads of dowry. It's all very good for the economy. And all the treatment for hypertension gets the doctors good money.

Even beyond the dowry, there are so many other spin-offs for the mother-in-law. The daughter-in-law shares the housework which the mother-in-law has slogged over, unaided, for years. She tells her other people's gossip that she's promised not to tell anybody. And then, one day, she shyly tells her mother-in-law she is going to be a mother herself. This is a day of great jubilation. But the jubilation continues only if the child brought out of the labour room is a boy.

If it is a boy, his uncle climbs to the topmost floor of the house or the water tank and performs a traditional ritual also guaranteed to invoke the fierce jealousy of the neighbours. He bangs a large steel or copper plate with a wooden ladle to declare that a boy has been born in the family. If twins are born, two plates and two ladles. Double the pleasure! It just sends blood pressures soaring and foreheads sweating and envious mothers-in-law grumbling across the neighbourhood. Perfect.

But if it is a girl ...

If it is a girl, they say, 'I told you the daughter-in-law is unlucky, my right eye was twitching on the day of the wedding,' or, 'Did you drink the water with honey and lemon and cardamom I gave you on your first night? I *told* you to do that if you wanted a son!' or, 'Oh, well, keep trying.'

But Narmada was made of saner stuff. She wanted a daughter-in-law not because she was tired of doing the chores around the house, but because she could see that, between them, she and her husband had made their son a lonely, lonely young man. And though Neel had wanted to escape to America – to seek freedom, to come into his own, and to do what his heart told him, that possibility seemed more remote than ever now, with the failed visa interview and the Sharmas walking in through the door.

They were Brahmins like Ravi Pandey's family, and belonged to one of the highest levels called the Shandilya Gotra of Brahmins. Hari Sharma was an officer in the Accounts department of the Prime Minister's Office. Everything fit like a glove, thought Ravi gleefully as his guests sat down. Engagement in two months...wedding in four... a grandson in thirteen...Great. Fantastic. Just perfect.

Tea was served, fragrant with expensive cardamom and a few cloves — Narmada's innocent way of showing the guests that they were special. Narmada had used her most expensive crockery and served the salted snacks that she normally saved for VIP guests. This family could be their future in-laws so why be miserly? Why give them an opportunity to gossip later about their shoddy hospitality?

From the kitchen, she peeked out at the guests. Meenal sat on the sofa, wearing a traditional, embroidered salwar-suit in cream with a red dupatta. She was beautiful, her face like that of goddess Lakshmi's on the large calendar in Narmada's prayer room. She wore a red bindi on her forehead and her shoulder-length hair was smooth and shampooed. Her long eyelashes embellished the beauty of her large eyes as they darted across the room, partly shy and partly curious. Her nervous fingers did a sort of tap dance on her thighs. Poor thing, Narmada thought. She looked like Narmada herself had when Ravi's family first visited her house.

Meenal's mother coughed and looked hard at her daughter's twiddling fingers. The twiddling stopped immediately. Narmada saw this exchange and smiled, remembering the subtle but tough ways her own mother used to employ to keep her 'disciplined'. A warm motherly feeling for Meenal surged through her, as she remembered the time when she and her cousins were all being 'considered' for marriage. Later, when they huddled about in a giggly bunch sharing their experiences, it turned out that all of them had felt pretty much the same — like nervous young goats put up for scrutiny before prospective buyers in an animal market. The only source of excitement — the shy anticipation of their first lovemaking. They had all been saving themselves for their husbands, naturally.

It was always the same for the girls: the groom's parents would ask her questions, look for obvious flaws like a club foot or a speech defect, ask her what she could cook, and decide whether she came across as too flighty or of 'bad character'. Only then would they cross-check horoscopes and discuss the dowry, the would-be mother-in-law quite forgetting that she had once been put through this humiliation herself. On many occasions, after all the examination and close questioning, the groom's family would reject the girl. So the poor girl would lock herself up in her room, cry for some days, then doll herself up again for another potential suitor and another round of interviews and scrutiny. It was like a job hunt. Just much worse on the self-esteem.

☾

'So, where is Neel?' Hari Sharma looked around the house and cleared his throat.

Meenal's fingers began to twiddle furiously.

'In his room. I'll just call him,' Narmada said, thinking she had already broken her promise not to disturb him, but then she had little choice.

Inside his room, Neel had overheard all. He didn't want to risk a scolding from his father. So he was ready, his hair combed down, wearing a clean shirt and trousers and waiting for his mother to walk in.

'This is about marriage, right, Ma?'

'No, no, Neel, they are just family friends who have dropped by ... though I must say, the daughter is very beautiful,' Narmada said with a smile and a wink.

'I can't think of any woman suggested by my father without imagining her in a mushroom farm.'

'Oh, come on, just say hello to them, sit for a while, make some excuse and come back, OK?'

'Do I have a choice??'

'So, Neel, I hear you are studying computer software,' Hari Sharma said as soon as Neel sat down.

'I was, Uncle, but I have given it up for now. There is a big slump in the software industry. There are no new jobs, in fact, a lot of people are being sacked,' Neel said.

'So what are your long-term plans when you go back to the software industry?' Hari wanted to know as Neel's father looked on with anxious pride, smiling as if he had been allowed to sit in during his son's job interview.

'Well, I want to go to America' — Neel caught his father's disapproving look from the corner of his eye — 'or even stay in India. There are so many companies here,' he bleated meekly.

'I am sure these jobs pay a lot of money,' Hari Sharma said.

'Sort of, Uncle.'

'So how much do you hope to earn, Neel?' Hari asked shamelessly.

'I don't know, Uncle. Depends on the job.'

'Will they give you an apartment?'

'I am not sure, Uncle.'

'Provident fund?'

Neel looked at his mother helplessly.

'Medical allowance?'

No answer.

'Bonus?'

Tight smile.

'LTA?'

Straight face. Slight frown.

'Transport allowance?'

Clenched jaw. Hands clutching sofa cushion.

At this point Ravi Pandey butted in, eager to change the direction of the conversation. Ravi's ego was a bit hurt because his guest was not playing by the rules — he was interrogating his son rather than having his daughter interrogated by him. After all, the onus of being an able spouse was entirely on the girl, wasn't it? Over the next fifteen minutes, Ravi asked Meenal seventeen questions, beginning with a harmless 'how is everything at college?' arriving in three minutes at 'so you must love cooking

... all women cook' and progressing at breakneck speed to 'you must wear the purdah at all times before the family elders when you get married'.

Narmada cleared her throat. 'More tea, anyone?'

Neel pounced on the slight break in the conversation, excused himself and walked away to his room as his mother got up to make more tea. But Ravi Pandey was one up. He was the father of his son, after all, not the other way round. Despite all that you or I or Neel or Narmada might have thought about him, Ravi fancied himself a progressive, in-step-with-the-times sort of father. Before putting his stamp of approval on the girl, he wanted to get his son's views too. He wanted Neel and Meenal to spend some time alone so that they could understand each other better and make up their minds. Of course that meant, in essence, that the two had just about fifteen minutes together to decide whether they wanted to extend it to a lifetime. 'Meenal, beti, didn't you want to see Neel's CD collection?' Ravi Pandey said.

The Sharma couple cleared their throats in unison.

Poor Meenal. A minute later, she was softly knocking at Neel's door.

'Hi,' Neel said, looking up from the bed, on which he sat cross-legged. He was twiddling his fingers as well, quite furiously, as a matter of fact.

Meenal saw this and smiled. It helped that someone else was in the same state she was. She pulled the door shut after her. 'Um ... I am sorry to come in like this ... but they asked me to,' she said.

'I know. I know what this is about. You know what this is about, right?'

'Yes.'

'They want us to get married.'

'Yes.'

There was a long pause. Neel realized Meenal was still standing. 'Please sit down, sorry about the mess.'

Meenal smiled as she looked around and sat down on the only clean spot on the bed. 'Everything here is about America! You like America a lot,' she smiled. 'Your mother told me so many years ago.'

'Yes, I do. I hope I can go to America some day. That's my dream. I almost got to go, you know, but the visa office nixed it...'

'I can understand how terrible you feel, Neel. I did my Honours in Psychology. I should understand things a bit, I guess.'

Neel paused. Was he making a mistake by not even considering marrying this beautiful, understanding, sensitive girl? 'Hey, do you remember when we were neighbours? You had those tiny ponytails and cried when I didn't let you play with my stuff?'

'Come on, yaar. I have seen childhood pictures of you bathing naked in a tub! We might not have met for many years, but I remember everything ...' Neel and Meenal laughed with the warmth of an old friendship. 'We were best friends ... then you moved out of the neighbourhood and met me only at birthdays and weddings. After that you didn't meet me at all,' Meenal said.

'I know ... we used to have fun ... and since we are friends again, can I say something honestly to you?'

'Of course,' she said.

'I am not sure how to say this, Meenal. I really like you and you are a great person. I would have been very lucky to marry someone like you...'

She looked up at him and raised her eyebrows.

'But the truth is that I do not want to get married right now. Maybe I am making a mistake, because you are so ...

perfect ... You are intelligent, and beautiful, and witty, any guy will be lucky to have you as his wife ... But you know about my dream ... maybe I can never make it true, but like you said, I will keep working on it ... I want to go to the States and get a good job and settle down there...'

'I know,' Meenal smiled. 'I also remember you wanting to marry an American girl.'

Neel flushed. 'Oh god, you've heard about that ... I'm sorry, it is not a reflection on you or anyone else...'

Meenal smiled understandingly. 'So sweet. And so stupid.'

'But you know how my father is ... he is hell bent on marrying me off to the girl of his choice, which I think is you. And if I refuse, I don't know what will happen. They are expecting that we will walk out of this room hand in hand, ready to get married,' he said.

'I understand what you are saying. So how do you want to deal with this?' said Meenal.

'First, you tell me what you think about all this, Meenal. This cannot be one-sided. If you feel strongly about it, maybe there's some wisdom in it.'

'You mean, if I want to marry you, you will agree to the marriage?'

Trick question.

'Um, maybe not right away ... but I will certainly respect your opinion and give the issue serious thought because I know that you are a very mature person...'

'So, technically, the destiny of your life is in my hands right now, right?' she said with a wink.

Neel smiled and shrugged his shoulders. 'Come to think of it, you are right. Hope you are on my side ...'

'Well, you do seem likeable enough for me to say yes ...'

'You are teasing me, right?' Neel quivered.

'Actually, I am. I don't want to marry you, either.'

'What? Oh wow, that helps. Great, it is all sorted out then and...wait a minute' — his male ego suddenly asserted itself — 'wait ... why don't you want to get married to me? Am I not worth getting married to?' he asked incredulously.

'Gosh, you men are all the same! No, no ... you are a nice guy ... good husband material, I guess ... but I have other reasons,' she said.

'OK, I understand. Who is he? You know you can tell me, Meenal.'

'Actually there is no "he". It would have been so much simpler if there was.'

'Then what's the problem?'

Meenal paused. 'Can you keep a secret? It's the biggest secret of my life,' she said.

'Of course, you don't even have to ask.' Neel was happy at the trust that Meenal had placed in him.

'There's no man in my life ... because I don't like men,' Meenal said.

'I know. Men are all such assholes ... but you used to talk about marrying a prince and all that when you were young?'

'So much has happened since ... I discovered some changes in myself. How do I say this? It's so difficult ... I don't like men because I like women now.'

'Huh?'

'I like women. Is that so hard to understand? I want a woman as a partner, not a man. Why are you making me embarrassed?'

There was suddenly total silence in the room. 'You are a lesbian?' Neel asked finally, recovering from the shock.

'I guess.'

'Wow!'

'What's there to go wow about?'

'I have never met a lesbian ...'

'That sounds like "I've never met an alien" — don't make me sound like a freak, Neel. I can't tell my parents, they will kill me. They will disown me. This sort of thing is just not done in India, especially in "decent" families like yours and mine, you know that.'

Suddenly, Neel felt liberated. A wave of fresh, jasmine-scented air swept through his mind clearing the cobwebs of despair. 'What's the problem? We'll tell them you are a lesbian and I am gay ... It's a total mismatch! They have their priorities all wrong — they should seek a guy for me and a girl for you!' he laughed out loud.

(Outside the room, Ravi Pandey walked furtively out of the guest bathroom near Neel's room and reported back to the waiting audience that everything was going well; the boy and girl were laughing and sharing jokes.)

❦

'*What?* What do you mean you don't want to marry her? What's wrong with her?'

'There's nothing wrong, I just don't like her, that's it,' Neel mumbled like a scared duckling, crouching near the kitchen door. His puzzled mother listened silently and nervously as she put the dishes away.

'Look! Good Brahmin families and girls like this don't pop up everyday! You listen to me ... she is a great girl and she is just right for you ... I know this...I *know* what's good for you and what is not ... I am your father, not your enemy! As your father, I didn't even have to ask you whom you wanted to marry, but I did, because I am not like those other didactic dads ...' Ravi thundered.

Neel just heard him out in silence. Then offered another feeble defence. 'She does not like me either. She doesn't want to marry me.'

'Yes, she does! Yes, she does! She wants to marry you ... Her father *told* me she does!'

'But, Papa, she told me she doesn't like me.'

'What does *she* know? Does she know more than her father about her likes and dislikes? Look, it is like this ... I can give you a month. You think about this whole thing and also find a job. If I find a better match for you, I will take another chance. Otherwise, Meenal is the one for you. And if you don't find a job in a month, I am packing you off to the mushroom farm!'

THE GOD OF VISA INTERVIEWS

Neel woke up late the next morning, after he was absolutely sure his father had left for work. After his Dad's outburst the previous evening he had been unable to sleep. So he'd watched a rerun of *The Sopranos* late into the night, too depressed to watch *Everybody Loves Raymond*. Soon, he told himself morosely as he finally turned the TV off, he would be watching the farmers' channel, to catch the latest breakthrough in fertilizer development for mushroom cultivation. As he lumbered out of bed, slouched down to the dining table and reached for the newspaper, he saw Narmada, the edge of her sari tucked into her waist (interpretation: she meant business), briskly walking past the kitchen, stopping short, and on an afterthought, summoning the housemaid.

Bittu Bai, the fifty-three-year-old housemaid, was Neel's one-time confidante. After Neel began senior school he used to come home bursting with tales of beautiful girls with long hair and shy dimples, all high school heart-throbs, whom he claimed liked him (and only him!) in the entire class. When he wanted to brag, Bittu Bai was his usual victim. On days when Neel's father was not around, Neel would throw down his schoolbag, yank off his tie and shirt, and inflict his stories of adolescent infatuation on the maid. She would nod and hum in the kitchen, peeling potatos, hearing each minute detail but pretending not to, as Neel recounted wildly-embellished tales of how a certain woman walked up to him or brushed past him or sat (almost) touching his elbow in the noisy class. But he always, always, stopped at the most tantalizing moment, just before the kisses, and Bittu Bai, whose own man had abandoned her before she could kiss him enough, secretly yearned to listen to it all. Those were days of carelessly peeled potatos and overcooked gossip.

Now Bittu Bai was waiting for Neel to get a new job. Narmada had promised her a sari the day her one-and-only got his appointment letter. And so the two of them were determined to aid him in his efforts. It was the fight back of the Sari Squadron!

The two women marched into a cramped storeroom piled to the ceiling with old newspapers. Narmada knew what she was looking for; Bittu Bai's was not to reason why. The two women picked up newspapers from the dusty shelves like diamonds from a coal mine. They sneezed, they frowned, then covered their faces with the ends of their saris. Sometimes, the maid stopped, distracted by pictures of the movie stars in the weekend colour supplements. This earned her an angry glare from Narmada who once again reminded the illiterate Bittu Bai what to look for. After two hours of work, they had produced the finest collection of job advertisement pullouts ever put together in New Delhi.

Neel looked at each of them, weary-eyed and a bit traumatized as he sipped his tea. The two women stood at the entrance of the room, like gladiators expecting the emperor to look up and honour them with a bowl of gold coins.

'Ma ...' Neel began.

'You're welcome, my son,' Narmada said with satisfaction.

'No, I was just saying that the dates for most of these ads are over, and in any case I am not qualified for them,' he pointed out.

'Oh ... uh ... ahem ... Bittu! Didn't I tell you?' Narmada said, turning as always in her moments of frustration, upon the poor maid.

Luckily for Bittu, the phone rang just then.

C

'Hello, is this the residence of Mr Neel Pandey, please?' said a deeply resonant baritone.

For one wild moment Neel thought it was the Big B himself playing telephone operator for the Phone-a-Friend helpline on the latest show of KBC. 'This is him,' Neel said in a suitably awed voice.

'Nice to be talking to you, Mr Him. Can I speak with Neel-ji please?'

'This is Neel,' Neel said unable to mask his disappointment as he realized this was definitely not a superstar response.

'But, I thought you are saying you are Mr Him? Anyway. Sorry for the misunderstanding. Well, can I meet you personally, in person? It is very important,' The Voice said enigmatically.

'No. Look, are you from a bank or credit card company? Don't bother me, OK?' Neel said, about to hang up.

'I am helping people go to foreign countries, f-r-i-e-n-d.' The 'f-r-i-e-n-d' was stretched out, like a password to a hypnotic trance that took you to Visa Land, where ten-year multiple entry visas and green cards dangled effortlessly from dollar-draped trees and visa officers in leopard skin loincloths pressed your feet and stuck visa stamps on their chests to seduce you.

'Huh?' Neel almost fell off the bed into the dustbin.

'I have heard through reliable sources that you are wishing to be going to the United States and your visa request has been rejected. I can help you,' The Voice offered. Visa Land and a Welcome Drink. Neel was gulping them down fast and quick to save himself from a Happy Heart Attack.

'What? How? And how do you know all this?'

'My sources, f-r-i-e-n-d, my sources,' The Voice said.

Neel curbed his shameless fit of happiness, composed himself, and rewound the events of the previous day. Oh yes, he had narrated his woeful tale to the neighbour's gossipy son the previous evening. 'You met Adarsh from my neighbourhood, did you? Whew ... anyway, how can you help me if my visa has been rejected? There's no way!'

'As you are knowing, f-r-i-e-n-d, there is a way for everything in India.'

Why did he have to say f-r-i-e-n-d in that seductive drawl, in slow motion, like a Mallika Sherawat kiss watched before the family? 'What do you plan to do?' Neel said, beginning to lose patience.

'We are having many many schemes, f-r-i-e-n-d. We are having foolproof methods to fool destiny. For a fee, of course,' The Voice clarified. 'Can I meet you in person? I am being liaison officer.'

'You mean you are a tout,' Neel snapped, feeling as if the goblins and fairies in Visa Land had suddenly been carpet-bombed by a Musharraf of Misfortune. The dream had gone *phussss* like a football that landed on an evil thirst-less cactus plant.

Was the caller's mesmerizing magic wearing off? Nah. The Voice injected extra sexiness in his next 'f-r-i-e-n-d'. 'Tout is a bad word, f-r-i-e-n-d. I am being a liaison officer.' The Voice was pained.

'I am sorry, I cannot meet a stranger just like that. You have to tell me more about how you will do it. I hope it is not illegal,' Neel said. He was sitting up now.

'You have to meet me first for me to explain, ' The Voice said.

'Tell me a little more. At least tell me how much you charge?'

'I can't tell you everything on the phone. We will have to meet in person. These days they are tapping phones left and right. Tapping them in the centre also. One of my friends was arrested for terrorism.'

'What? And you expect me to meet you even after hearing this?'

'No no, f-r-i-e-n-d, it was nothing of that type. He is not a terrorist,' assured The Voice.

'Then why was he arrested?' Neel wanted to know.

'His phone was tapped after his girlfriend called saying that she was wanting to see his big gun.'

'Oh?' Neel said. 'Just for saying that?'

'No, actually my friend replied that he wanted to be testing her grenades first.'

☉

Unbelievably, Neel was sitting at a coffee shop two days later, waiting for The Voice. The Voice wanted to meet here, in a restaurant near Mandi House, New Delhi's watering-hole for wannabe theatre actors, about which they made up sad struggle stories after they had become famous. Not really Neel's kind of place. But then, big dreams often had small beginnings, and Neel had come here with a bit of hope and a bit of what-the-heck recklessness.

The man who approached Neel was a skinny runt, a shifty kind of guy with a face like an enthusiastic musk rat. The Voice, it turned out, was only a rat hollering down a water-pipe.

The Voice had first come to New Delhi from Gadahila village in a crammed train squashed with sweaty passengers. He had wanted to be an actor. Back in his village, he had played several parts in the local Ram Lila each year. Through the ten days when the epic was performed, The Voice got to enact different parts. When he had to join Hanuman's army and play a monkey he puffed out his cheeks like a rhesus, stuffed one end of a tightly coiled three-metre cloth in his underpants, and jumped around the stage pulling it out tantalizingly, bit by bit. When he played Sita's female companion, he pinned a braid behind his sideburns, caked his face with make-up, and stuffed two rubber balls up his shirt. When Ram's army attacked Ravan to rescue Sita, he became a skinny demon in a deadly mask, held a heavy cardboard sword in one hand and hitched up his dhoti, that threatened to come undone and reveal the holes in his underwear, with the other.

With such a rich theatre history behind him, it was natural that The Voice was not cut out for farming and milking the cow. So when the first opportunity presented itself, he ran a line of kohl under his eyes for good luck, snatched the money stashed under the paper that lined his father's pooja cupboard, and caught the first bus to the city.

However, things did not go quite as planned for The Voice. To become an actor, one had to get into drama school. To get into drama school, one had to write an exam. To write an exam, one had to have brains. And therein lay the catch. So he tried essaying different roles at the traffic roundabout near Mandi House, as shoeshine boy, crippled beggar, tea-shop assistant, tyre-shop trainee, and pickpocket. The last profession promptly got him a rupee-less wallet, a sound thrashing and a trip to jail, where he met his boss, the King of the Overseas Travel business. His life was transformed. The Voice was looking for a Guru; the Guru was looking for a nitwit of a disciple. They did well together.

'Mister Pandey?' said The Voice, as he shook hands, offered himself a chair and took a long gulp of water. He was wearing a red shirt with the most hideous print Neel had ever seen.

'Yes,' Neel said. He didn't want to pin too many hopes on this shady-looking character. Maybe later, like Lord Krishna, this skinny piece of slime would manifest his real form and grant Neel three boons. But for now, he just seemed a pathetic might-have-been in the dark dungeons of crime.

'I could recognize you from your way of looking,' The Voice said.

'What's wrong with my way of looking?' Neel asked, confused by what he meant but crossing his arms belligerently, in case.

'Nothing, nothing, f-r-i-e-n-d, just a psychological observation. You are having a deep hunger in your eyes. A kind of lust that refuses to go away. You know how to enjoy the orgy of life. I am reading that desire in your eyes. I can give you what you want. I am having what it takes.'

'Excuse me?' Neel said.

'I am sorry, f-r-i-e-n-d. Mean to say, that we are having all the facilities, and we can do all that is needed to help you go to the U.S.'

'First, who's "we"? And second, how?'

'"We" is my boss, his R&D team, and I. As for "how" — that Boss-ji will tell you.'

'R&D? You mean research and development? What R&D does he do? And what's that got to do with this?' Neel asked, amused.

'Boss-ji will tell you the rest. He is being very knowledgeable. He is knowing all about passports and visas and visa rules. His visa applications have been rejected by so many countries. Twenty, I am thinking.'

'What? And he claims to be able to send others abroad?'

'That was being only his trial and error. To study the system from inside. He stayed back only to help the youth of India like your good self.'

'I think you guys are just con artists, and stupid ones at that! This has just been a total waste of time,' Neel said as he began to get up in frustration.

'No, no, Pandey Sahib, one should not be kicking destiny like this. Someday destiny might be kicking you,' The Voice said philosophically, holding Neel's hand and gently coaxing him back into his seat.

'It already has,' Neel said. But by making that lousy statement on destiny, The Voice had touched a raw nerve. Neel dithered.

That was the clinching moment as far as he was concerned. The Voice knew that the client was his. 'Then what are I and my boss sitting here for, f-r-i-e-n-d? We will turn the lines of destiny on your palm. We have various options. That Boss will explain with all technicality. Right now we need to go, he is waiting for us. He hates to wait. There is only one place in the world where Boss-ji doesn't mind waiting.'

'Where?' Neel asked, despite himself.

'The police station.'

C

Boss-ji was a tall man, a robust Sikh with a promising paunch trapped in a yellow designer shirt, a matching yellow turban with sequins down the primary fold, innumerable gold rings on his pudgy fingers, and expensive-looking but ugly suede shoes. He had two mobile phones with identical ring tones – of shrieking bagpipes. 'Welcome, Mister Pandey. I am Rocky,' he beamed, 'and this is my humble office.'

Rocky Randhawa's humble office was a three-storeyed building in an out-of-the way neighbourhood in east Delhi. Next to the heavily carved, gold-edged, plushly-upholstered sofa in his room, was an old AC that leaked water in a steady dribble into a broken plastic mug. Rocky's shining Sanmica topped table had a miniature flag of India, bunches of plastic flowers in dazzling crystal vases and many, many files. But to Neel the most reassuring sight was the large number of certificates on the freshly painted bright orange walls, presented in appreciation for services rendered, by the heads of the consular sections of several embassies and high commissions.

Hmmm. Impressive. Neel's attention went, naturally, to the one from the United States Embassy. It was a certificate 'in appreciation of the services and advice rendered by Mr Rocky Randhawa to the consular division of the United States Embassy in New Delhi, and to the American people'. Next to it was a close-up of Rocky with Ambassador Robert Black himself – the ambassador, in a smart black suit beamed happily with Rocky's arm, ensleeved in a shiny fabric with red and yellow stripes, draped around his shoulder in a warm hug.

Quite pally. Maybe these guys aren't con artists but angels in disguise sent by the God of Visa Interviews, Neel thought.

'Would you like something to drink, Pandey-ji, some thanda-shanda?' Rocky said, banging the table and yelling for the skinny office boy without waiting for Neel's reply.

'Sure, Mister Randhawa. A soft drink will be good.' The 'mister' was an involuntary add-on.

As Rocky instructed Babban, the skinny boy in ragged undershorts, to bring a cold drink from Dabbu's shop on the double ('Tell him to put it down in the register'), Neel walked over to another corner of the room, where pictures of Rocky on foreign trips filled the wall – in a ferry in New York by the Statue of Liberty; in Paris, on a fishing trip with the French Ambassador (oddly dressed in a suit ... whew, these Frenchmen); in London, birdwatching on vacation with the British High Commissioner.

'Quite impressive, I must say,' Neel said.

'Ojee, it's nothing, but thanks,' Rocky said, his chubby cheeks flushing red with embarrassment.

'So how can you help me?'

'Well, we offer many services. We can help you get all the information you want about the job and study opportunities available in different countries. We can help you get visa forms. We can help you get acquainted with immigration procedures. We can guide you through everything you need ...'

Neel was disappointed. 'Is that all? Didn't this guy tell you that I have already applied for a visa and it has been rejected? So clearly I don't need your counselling and all that. I have already screwed that up. All I want to know is this: Can you still get me a visa?'

Rocky took a deep breath and looked daggers at The Voice. The rat. 'Why didn't you tell me it's a special case?' Rocky snarled, momentarily dropping his sweet voice. Then he turned back to Neel. 'So sorry about the confusion, Brother-ji. But no tension. We have a multilayered operation. We can use Plan B or Plan C,' he said.

'What are those?'

'Or we'll do a U.P. trick.'

'A U.P. trick? What the hell is that?' Neel asked

U.P., or Uttar Pradesh, the home state of Neel's father, is known for many things – like, it is the largest state in terms of population in the country with some 180 million people; or that it is India's political heartland and has given the country most of its Prime Ministers; also that it is a great centre of learning, music blah blah blah. But most of all, U.P. is known for trouble. Poverty, caste rivalries, crime, fraud, criminals who became lawmakers, lawmakers who are criminals ... U.P. is a free-for-all. In this fertile atmosphere, citizens and politicians all need a little nefarious help to get by. They need the U.P. trick.

'Dekhoji, every state has its speciality, its USP. Just like Punjab is known for its agriculture, Maharashtra for its stock market and onions; Karnataka for its high-tech and software; in the same way, U.P. is known for its U.P. trick. It's all about using the brain. When nothing else works, you got to use a U.P. trick. It always works,' Rocky explained.

'Hmmm,' Neel said. Rough ways but maybe they were effective, he thought. After all, the French Ambassador wouldn't go fishing with any Tom, Dick and Harry.

'So we can do many things for you under Plan B. But it might cost a bit more. You are our first customer today, so I will give you a discount. Just give us fifty thousand rupees now ... rest when the job is done.'

'What job? What Plan? I don't know even now what you do.'

Rocky turned to The Voice and said in an icy tone — (a premonition of more heated things to come later when the guest was gone) — 'Haven't you *told* him, you donkey?' He fixed his assistant with a lethal look before turning to Neel and saying in his sweetest salesman voice, 'Sir, we make fake visas. Fake passports. Fake IDs. Fake credit cards. Fake bank cheques. Fake certificates. Fake photographs with celebrities. Anything.'

Neel looked around the room. The images swirled before him: Rocky's certificates; Rocky's pictures with the diplomats; Rocky in his synthetic shirt with red and yellow stripes arm in arm with U.S. Ambassador Robert Black; Rocky vacationing in New York and Paris, on a fishing trip with the French Ambassador in a suit; Rocky with the British High Commissioner.

Neel reached out for the glass of cola before him. 'You mean ...?' he said weakly.

'All fake, Pandey,' Rocky beamed proudly. 'They are all fake. Cent per cent fake. Same to same, no?'

'I-I d-d-on't believe this. How can you do this? They look so real. I mean ... what if you are caught?'

'We are offering these services only for educational and entertainment purposes, Pandey-ji. If they are used to commit illegal acts, that is not our responsibility,' Rocky said. 'As for getting caught, we have some checks and balances in place in the police department. And if one of our customers complains about us, we have ways of finding out and dealing with it. This is a very professional set-up, Pandey-ji.'

Neel was scared. And fascinated. The devil in his mind wanted him to get a fake visa. He wasn't a terrorist sneaking into a country to commit a crime, after all. He just wanted to make his career and life out there.

'So you can get me a U.S. visa?' Neel asked.

'Yes, we can get you a ditto-same duplicate of a U.S. visa. However, let me caution you that those guys have become very careful since this terrorism-sherrorism started.'

'Oh. So?'

'That is when I use the U.P. trick.'

'You have a U.P. trick for this one too?'

'We have a U.P. trick for *every* problem on this earth. From non-proliferation to – what do they call it? – greenhouse gases to population control. It's just that no one asks for our opinion. Their loss ...' Rocky shrugged, taking a deep breath. 'Anyway, returning to the matter at hand, since the U.S. is not the U.S. it used to be, and since they look with suspicion upon South Asians, we will give you a passport of another country, to show that you are a national of another country visiting India, and you also have a U.S. visa.'

'Huh?'

'Like we will give you a passport for Zanzibar,' Rocky said.

'Zanzibar? Where the hell is Zanzibar?'

'Nowhere! There was once a country called Zanzibar. But it's now called Tanzania. So by giving you a passport for Zanzibar, we have broken no law, because there is no Zanzibar law, and that's because there is no Zanzibar!'

'But what about the visa?'

'We have U.S. visa designs, with the embossing and the sticker and everything. We'll put one on your Zanzibar passport.'

'But that is illegal.'

Rocky smirked. 'I say again ... I am not asking you to do anything illegal. I am just selling stationery. How you use the stationery is your problem,' Rocky said with a wink. 'This is a creative company. We sell ideas.'

'And suppose I was to take this ... um, stationery ... to the United States, how will I get through their immigration guys?'

'The level of education differs from country to country, Mr Pandey. Fortunately, it is not very high in the United States. Geography is not one of the strong points of the American people. So the immigration guys haven't the foggiest idea that there is no such country as Zanzibar now.'

'Hmmm. So what are the other countries whose...er... stationery you sell?'

'British Honduras.'

'Where is that?' Neel asked.

'Nowhere. It is now Belize.'

'I should have known.'

'Netherlands East Indies.'

'That's somewhere in Europe, right?'

'Wrong. In Asia. It's Indonesia.'

'Dutch Guiana. It's now Suriname.'

Neel leaned back in his chair, took out his handkerchief and wiped the beads of sweat off his forehead. 'Mindboggling,' he said.

'You are a bit young to look like a First Secretary, otherwise I could have made you a diplomatic passport. That would give you diplomatic immunity, *and* you could have taken in anything you wanted without being checked.'

The Voice had been sitting in silence all this while, absorbing each word of his boss with blind admiration. Finally, he spoke. 'Boss-ji, he is a friend. Can we give him a tour of our office before we tell him about the different schemes we have to offer?'

'A tour ... hmm. Of course. Come, Pandey. I will show you the other three storeys in this house. I have built it all with my sweat and blood. Come, Pandey. I will climb slowly as I don't like people staring at my butt when I climb, so you go ahead.'

C

Neel climbed three flights of stairs, waiting for Rocky to tell him to stop. But the signal never came until they reached the top floor, because Rocky was busy taking his revenge on the world and staring at Neel's butt.

On the top floor, an exciting sight awaited them. A sprawling hall had been divided into many large wooden cabins. On a faded blue carpet in one of the sections were strewn a range of musical instruments — two sitars, many dholaks and tabla sets, a discoloured harmonium of warped wood, some cymbals and other side instruments. A thin guy in a shiny kurta tested a dholak, played it out of tune, and rubbed its skin furiously with talcum powder. Like the Hindi proverb goes: When you don't know how to dance, you blame the tilt of the floor.

They then walked through a narrow corridor into a cabin with a large blackboard near a glass-panelled wall in front of six rows of wooden benches. On the blackboard were large letters that explained the purpose of that particular section: ENGLIS CLASS. A pile of thin notebooks, covered once in brown paper and then again in thin plastic sheets, were stacked on a large stool. The walls of the cabin had several large charts — with the letters of the English alphabet and their Hindi translations, the meaning of simple words and simple instructions informing students when to say 'I am happy to hear that' and when not to say 'Same to you'.

The adjoining room was bare. There was a big green mat, and little else. The only clue about what happened in that room hung from a nail in the wall: a judoka's dress.

Neel uttered the same words of dumbfounded bewilderment he used every time he had sat for a maths exam and seen his maths examination paper. 'What the hell is this?' he asked Rocky.

'This is Plan C.'

'Plan C?'

'Yes. When you can't get a visa like you are supposed to, you sing and dance your way to it.'

'What do you mean?'

'We train people to apply for visas as part of music troupes going abroad for concerts, or as teachers in Punjabi schools abroad, or even as part of sports contingents.'

'Yeah, but that must be for short trips,' Neel said.

'Who says they have to come back? Once they are in, they are in. Some call it human trafficking, we call it the international traffic of humans,' Rocky said. 'So they go with music troupes. But the problem is, you see, that my average customer is a good old farmer from good old Punjab who just wants to go to Canada or Britain or the U.S. He cannot tell a Sa-Re-Ga-Ma or Do-Re-Mi-Fa from the clanging of a bucket. So what do we do? We help him. We train him. We nurture his hidden talent. We teach him to play a few tunes.'

'You mean they can actually be asked to play an instrument as proof?' Neel asked.

'Yes, of course. There have been instances when people were asked to play their dholaks or sitars at immigration. But we make sure it doesn't come to that. We supply our clients with abundant proof that they are upcoming performers who are the best in the region and that's why they have been invited abroad for concerts.'

'Really?' Neel said. 'You make them that good?'

'No, yaar. We have friends among local journalists who print news about these men in newspapers, claiming that they are the next big thing after Madonna. When we have four or five clippings with pictures, our file is ready. Of course we also have to do something to keep the journalists happy ... you know, get them and their relatives a visa or two. It is a perfect understanding, you see. Just a good example of a healthy working relationship with the media.'

'Right,' Neel said.

'But then, music sometimes does not work, because many of the visa applicants are blockheads who would rather work a spade than a flute. So we teach them sports, especially those related to what they often do in real life. Like fighting. That's why we have judo classes. You see, yaar, there are so many sports tournaments overseas, no one even keeps track. So we send people pretending to be participants at these events. The last batch of our men had gone for the World Rural Olympics.'

'Really? Never heard of that. Where were those held?' Neel asked.

'Nowhere. But our men reached Canada! Sports bring people together, you see. Sports also take people places.'

'Fascinating ... but tell me, how come you haven't gone abroad yourself? Your man here tells me your visa application has been rejected by many embassies.'

Rocky turned to The Voice and suddenly blazed, '*Why do you keep telling everyone that?*' and then smoothly re-entered his serene self to reply to Neel, 'Actually that was only trial and error, to understand the system from within.'

'Yes, so I was told by His Master's Voice.'

Rocky took a deep breath. It was a tender moment. 'But I do have a dream, Mr Neel. I want to go to America some day. Because someone there awaits me. My woman is seven seas away. I have her address. God willing, I will be able to go there one day ... You might be wondering why I am telling you all this. I am telling you because you are my first educated customer. I feel a sense of pride in exchanging my thoughts with a fellow intellectual ... So which Plan would you like to opt for, Mr Neel? B or C? I will give you a big discount. We can discuss the money after you have made up your mind whether you want to go as a karate black belt or a sufi singer,' he said.

'Let me think about it. I've had something of an information overkill this afternoon. Besides, it might be unsafe ...'

'If you want, we also have a Plan D,' Rocky said, as he gave Neel his business card. *Rocky Randhawa, Chief Liaison Officer, Money's Worth Immigration Services* it said.

'Plan D?'

'Yes. We can arrange a mob to burn down your house, attack you and beat you up, so we can claim that you are facing religious persecution in India. Then you can get into the U.S. as a refugee.'

'Wow. No, I think I'll skip that. I'll get back to you.'

'Of course, of course. I will wait for your call. However, I want to strongly advise you not to tell anyone about this place and our operations. You see, I have had to deal with many friends who tried to give away my secret and became my e-n-e-m-i-e-s.' A glint of a threat came into Rocky's eyes and Neel shivered with the chill that suddenly descended in the room. But then Rocky smiled his warm, fake smile and pumped Neel's hand with gusto.

'It will be a pleasure to do business with you.'

C

Six days later, Neel's father was relaxing in the sun in the balcony when he began reading out a newspaper report to his wife. The words filtered into Neel's room as he struggled to open his eyes.

'Narmada, did you see this? They make fake currency notes, they put pesticides in cold drinks, they put worms in chocolates, now they are making fake visas too!'

'Uff,' Narmada said, without listening as she poured the tea.

"'Police raided a neighbourhood in East Delhi on Saturday and arrested three men associated with an immigration racket involving fake visas that had defrauded both customers and immigration officials,'" Ravi Pandey read aloud. "'Police are now searching for the kingpin, a man identified as Rocky Randhawa —'"

In his room, Neel sat up in his bed with a sudden jerk.

Ravi continued: "'— Randhawa used to fool immigration officials by training his clients as musicians, sportsmen and priests so that they could get visas. Randhawa and his assistant were arrested and his building raided and sealed. Police Commissioner P.C. Poojary said Randhawa also has close links with the mafia and all his accomplices would soon be apprehended. A high-level source told *The Delhi Today* that police had been tipped off by a decoy customer who went to Randhawa's office pretending to be seeking a U.S. visa." Can you believe this, Narmada? Teaching people to dance so that they can jiggle their way to foreign countries?'

'Uff,' Narmada said, still not listening.

But Neel was. O my god o my god o my god, he thought. Rocky will read this in jail and think it's I who told the police. I am screwed. I am dead. I am dead, he muttered to himself.

Ravi read further. "'Police recovered about 100 passports. 35 forged stamps of different embassies and 150 visa stickers of the United States, Britain, Canada and countries in the Middle East were also seized." What has happened to this country, Narmada, hain, what?' Ravi demanded.

I don't think he expected an answer. But he got one.

'Uff,' said Narmada.

How May I Help You?

The half-ready, greenish yellow cane billowed gently in the wind. Dusty cows with small bells jangling around their necks, sauntered along the narrow mud path that bordered the fields. A lonely farmer squatted purposelessly by a mud path in the distance, chatting with his goat and doodling on the ground with a small bamboo stick. A young girl in chunky silver jewellery plucked and chewed a bright yellow mustard flower from a blossoming field.

All of a sudden the cows grew fidgety. They sensed danger. From within their cosy burrows, angry snakes slithered out, followed by farm rats, marching like obedient armies vacating their positions before the enemy attacked. Birds struck up a noisy, out-of-tune chorus from the safety of their nests on the banyans and the peepuls, then flew out in swarms that covered the skies, fleeing the coming catastrophe.

Then, with the intensity of a nuclear explosion, the earth split open in the middle of the huge farm field with a deafening roar. A massive crevice opened up with brute, supernatural force, shearing through rows of densely cropped sugarcane and throwing up a mountain of fertile alluvial soil. The terrified village people watched frozen in horror as an ocean of dust was whipped up in the centre of the vast farm field.

Then a moment of silence.

And suddenly, as if by magic, a massive apparition rose from beneath the ground, wearing a cowboy-style hat, with muscles as strong as three-and-a-half Schwarzeneggers and the anger of a crazed demon on his face. 'I will get you, you destroyed my life ... I will get you,' Rocky said in a Punjabi Robocop voice...

c

'Neel!? Neel? Neel? I have been calling you for so long, son! Are you dreaming?' It was Narmada, standing at the edge of Neel's bed, with a cup of tea.

He shook his head from side to side, as if shaking off a ghost. Morning nightmares have an especially vicious sense of humour. 'What can I do, Ma? He won't let me do anything. He won't let me live in peace, he's threatening me in my dreams now ...' Neel mumbled still in his sleep finally managing to squint at his mother through one eye. He didn't understand why his mother would want to smile in the middle of his trauma.

Narmada ignored his antics. She had a big, victorious smile on her face and a newspaper in her hands. She cleared her throat. 'I have found you a job, beta,' Narmada said, holding up the newspaper's job supplement and gesturing with her eyebrows at a huge quarter-page ad on the front page. 'America Beckons You,' the ad announced in huge letters.

Neel jumped off his bed and snatched the newspaper from his mother. '"Walk-in interviews for call centres",' he read. It offered dozens of job openings for 'agents' in call centres. But what did that have to do with America? What was a call centre? What was the job? Neel was clueless. He had finally spotted a job opportunity in which America was beckoning him but what was it? What did one have to do, and what did one have to be, to get there?

Neel looked up at his mother. She shrugged in a don't-ask-me-dude-I've-found-the-paper-so-say-thanks-and-lemme-go way. Neel rushed to the phone to call the only person he could think of, who might be able to help. 'Meenal?'

'Hey, Neel. What's up?'

'Hey, how are you? You don't sound yourself ... Just needed to ask a stupid question and know you are the only person who won't mind my asking,' Neel said.

'Sure, Neel. In any case I was about to call you myself.'

'Really? Anyway, what's a call centre all about? And what does it have to do with America?' Neel asked, even as he thought, *God, please let a call centre be someplace where I can work and not a rocket science sort of place.*

'A call centre? A friend of mine works for one. It's like when you buy a TV or a computer in America, or have to fill out your tax returns, you can ring a call centre to help you over the phone. These centres were earlier in America itself, but now they are moving them to India because it's so cheap, like, it costs one-fifth of what it costs companies there. When a customer in the U.S. calls the service people, he doesn't know that the phone is actually ringing in Bangalore or Hyderabad or Gurgaon ... 'cos the call centre works and responds exactly as if it was in the U.S ...'

Neel was confused. 'How's that?'

'You pretend to be American.'

'*Pretend?*'

'Yes. You speak with an American accent, learn the American way of life, and go to office at night when it is daytime in the U.S. You talk to American customers all night pretending you are an American staffer in a call centre there. Are you getting a job with one? It might be good for you, because for a person like you who's crazy about America, I would say this is a good second-best. Maybe someday the company will even send you to America ... Of course, the job completely screws up your sleep and digestive cycle ...'

Neel thought aloud: 'Sleeping and waking with America ... and talking to Americans all day ... Hmmm. I am going there today.' Then he looked with longing at the Statue of Liberty poster, as if gazing at a long-time crush whom he was finally going to be able to get familiar with. Perhaps he would actually see it some day. Oops. He suddenly remembered that Meenal was still on the line, waiting for several minutes now. 'Oh, I am so sorry. What was it you wanted to talk to me about? I was so impatient earlier, I am all ears now.'

'Is there an extension on this phone, Neel?'

'No, no... why? You can speak. It's totally safe,' Neel said. He sensed that Meenal wanted to talk about something serious and felt a little embarrassed about badgering her like a kid about the call centre.

'I needed to talk to you ... there is no one else I can talk to. And if I don't share this, my head will explode,' Meenal said. Her voice had grown softer. Actually she sounded like she was choking back her tears.

Neel imagined her face, tears welling in her large, beautiful kohl-laced eyes. 'Hey, hey, easy, Meenal, what's the problem?'

'I am in trouble. Major trouble.'

'O god, what happened?'

'My parents know.'

'What? How? Did you tell them? You should have waited, Meenal. You should have prepared them for this,' Neel said.

'My mother walked in.' Meenal's voice was trembling.

'Walked in when?'

There was a pause. 'Walked in when I was kissing my girlfriend in my room.'

⟨⟩

It does not happen too frequently in India (or such is the conventional wisdom) that a mother walks into a room and finds her young, beautiful, ready-to-get-married daughter kissing a woman, who has been routinely coming to the house for a year now, posing as her daughter's friend, and has spent several hours with her alone. It was the worst possible betrayal as far as Mrs Sharma was concerned. She had stood stunned as she saw the two in each other's arms, kissing each other on the mouth with a passion that Mr Sharma, her husband of many years, had never displayed for her. She thought she would have a heart attack on the spot. She had, however, somehow lived through it to tell her husband about the calamitous kiss in the evening.

As expected, both her parents had not spoken a word to Meenal ever since; it had now been over eighteen hours. At the age of twenty-four, Meenal thought she was up against *the* worst crisis of her life. It was hard enough being a woman in her conservative Indian family; it was so much harder being a woman in love with another. Meenal had locked herself in her room, too afraid to step out, feeling like a criminal under house arrest. A maid acted as scared courier and messenger, bringing her food and informing her when her parents left the house and when they were expected home. It was a set-up of course: the husband and wife were hiding in the storeroom, keeping watch through the small storeroom window with a view to the gate, waiting to see if their wayward daughter would go the corrupt woman's way again. Before this black day, the worst social slur that Mrs Sharma could have possibly imagined was her daughter having sex before marriage and getting pregnant. That was equal to blasphemy as far as she was concerned. But this, this was much, much worse than that. Pregnancy was something she could hide; she could force an abortion, marry her off, send her to another town. But this, Hai Durga Ma, she couldn't even begin to comprehend this...

C

Meenal's love affair had started a year ago at a bus-stop, provoked by a young man who was itching to prove his manhood.

The roadside Romeo had been watching the road for about ten minutes, looking at his cheap plastic watch repeatedly, clearing his throat and pushing back greasy tufts of long hair from his forehead every thirty-five seconds. Romeo had taken a fancy for a young woman who used to get off at this stop each day at the same time, wearing the same stoic look on her face and carrying the same red bag. She was lean, slightly taller than Meenal, and with much shorter hair. She had never noticed Romeo, and, believe me, never would have were it not for the incident about to take place. She was on the same route again, and when she got off, Meenal did as well. Both girls began crossing the street after looking to the left and right, as sensible Delhi girls are cautioned to do, to ensure the absence of a rich brat in a BMW or a lurching DTC bus run amok looking for people to mow down.

Anyway, that was the moment when Romeo released the cycle brakes, giving it a little forward push with his left foot, and began slowly pedalling towards the women, who were walking a few feet behind each other. Cars raced by. Some scooter drivers honked and swore at him. A bus passenger threw an orange peel that almost landed on his head. But Romeo pedalled on, mesmerized. He was so hormonally charged that he thought he would explode. As he reached the woman, he stretched out his arm and lunged for her left breast and then began cycling wildly ahead, speeding as fast as he could, scared and yet overcome with a feeling of grand, manly achievement.

Did your blood boil? Mine did.

The woman stopped dead in the middle of the road, feeling utterly humiliated and helpless. A man had just groped her in the middle of the road, and all she could do was cover her chest with her arms and burst into tears. She wanted to shriek, to curse the man, to call him the worst possible things, but she knew it would only make her a spectacle on the busy Olof Palme Marg. She felt giddy and was about to fall when she felt the reassuring warmth of Meenal's arms around her. She had seen what had happened and had raced forward, trying to catch the man but realizing she would not be able to.

Meenal held the other woman, and as she looked at her scared, stunned eyes, Meenal seemed to be reassuring her that what she had witnessed would remain their secret, that she understood the pain and the helplessness. In that moment of humiliation, the two young women had each found a friend.

Her name was Sonia Shah. She was a trainee teacher in the college where Meenal studied. They realized that they were also neighbours. That made it convenient for Sonia, who lived alone, to come over to the Sharmas' house almost each day. Mrs Sharma was happy that her shy, introvert daughter had found a friend. The two women found they had much in common — from their taste in fiction to music to their favourite shade of lipstick. They began calling each other several times a day, exchanging books and recipes, visiting each other's homes and watching movies together. They cooked ghastly and heavenly dishes, they danced to the latest Hindi songs, they sneaked out of their homes to have ice-cream from the vendor at the corner of the road. In an excited, discordant chorus, they hailed the man selling the locally-made and popular 'chuski' — crushed ice layered with tasty syrups — or sat in the neighbourhood park, chatting late into the evening. Sometimes Sonia rented DVDs and Meenal went over to watch movies late into the night. Sonia had a one-bedroom, top-floor studio apartment. In New Delhi, it was, for some reason, called a 'barsati,' a raincoat. Anyway. It was private, the room was cosy and very welcoming, done up in a minimal way with wrought iron furniture, candlestands, a couple of ornate teak stools, beautiful blue curtains, matching lampshades, and a double mattress on the floor facing the TV. On a few occasions, she stayed over. They were best friends. They filled a void in each other's lives that was hard to describe. They had become too special for each other.

Months passed. One night, Sonia dragged Meenal away to her house as she often did, all excited about a new movie she had rented.

It was a winter evening. But it would sizzle soon.

Sonia's barsati had a large balcony overlooking the park. The two women stood there for a long time, the cool breeze gently blowing into their faces, sending gentle shivers down their spines. Meenal wore a cotton T-shirt and a long black skirt. Sonia was in a loose pullover and pajamas. Sonia turned around and walked into the room and returned with the only shawl in the house. She draped it over both of them, and as Meenal huddled closer, their arms touched. The warmth was soothing.

'Have you ever realized that we never talk about guys? Any guys?' Sonia said softly.

'I know,' Meenal said, looking at a building across the park where two women stood staring at a couple of muscled hunks as they got off their bikes.

Abruptly, Sonia undraped the shawl, went inside and sat down on the mattress. Meenal shut the door and sank down beside her, fumbling awkwardly for the TV remote and finding it after a few minutes. Strangely, the two talkative friends were not talking and a high tension cast itself about them for several vacuum-like moments.

Then Sonia reached out, pulled her friend close and placed her mouth on Meenal's. The remote dropped from Meenal's hands accidentally pressing a button and raising the volume.

Riz Khan was anchoring Q&A about another roadblock in the Middle East peace process. The voiceovers added to the haze of the moment, the sudden rush of hormonal pleasure, and the tantalizing unexpectedness of their kiss. Meenal took a few seconds to recover from the shock and then surrendered to the sudden rush of excitement coursing through her. She didn't think twice about what she was doing as she looked Sonia straight in the eye, cupped her face with her palms and kissed her back, nervously nibbling her lips, feeling them shyly with her mouth and staying there much longer than she had expected to.

When both recovered from the dazzle of that moment, they wanted to sit back and laugh and shrug it off as a stupid experiment that they would tell their future husbands about. But they realized that they both wanted more. Sonia smiled, looked naughtily at Meenal and gently pushed her onto the mattress. Both women had decided to flow with the moment. They wanted to see how far this would go. It seemed fun. It seemed so, so sexy.

It went far. The long evening melted into a sensuous night, and the night dissolved into a dreamy morning. All inhibitions slipped away. The skirt and the T-shirt lay on the floor, as the two women took each other in a hungry embrace. They discovered each other all night, their lips making the sensual journey of desire across each other's bare bodies, their fingers running through each other's hair, their hands caressing the welcoming warmth of each other's bodies. By morning, there were no secrets left to hide. They had discovered each other.

Soon, Meenal's parents had discovered them as well.

☯

The phone rang just as Angela was about to jump into the shower. It was her mother.

'Hi Mom, how are you? I'm sorry I couldn't call last weekend. I was busy,' Angela said.

'We're good, honey. Just missing you. Your dad just becomes more cranky every day …'

Angela burst out laughing. 'I don't envy you living in that house! But you are clearly the only one who can handle him! Where is he?'

'He's taking a shower. Should be out soon. Ah, here he is now. Here, talk to him … Gavin! Can you please put on something? You still live in a civilized world!' she shouted. 'Sorry, honey, your father …'

'Why am I getting to hear all this? I …'

Gavin took the phone mid-sentence. 'What do you mean, why are you getting to hear all this? You might have gone to New York and become the smart woman from the big city and all, but you are still a Jackson girl, Angela,' he said.

'Hey, Dad … missed you too,' Angela snapped.

'Don't you snap at me like that, young lady … I won't be around for long, and then you will regret not treating me better.'

'All right, I am sorry. I didn't call to fight yet again. You are a nice guy, Dad, but there are many things about you that I disagree with. That doesn't make me love you any less, but I still disagree. All right, does that make you feel better?'

'Yeah, whatever. Anyway, we hope you are doing fine…I just don't want to get morality lessons from my own daughter …'

'I can see that you are at your cheerful best, Dad.'

'I'm just waiting for some black hoodlum to stab me and end my misery. You ran into any there?'

'D-a-d-d-y!'

'What did I say now? I am just telling you the truth! Your mother and I have seen the world much closer and much longer than you. We want you to find a good guy, our own type, soon, and get married. Joseph Mitchell keeps coming over. He's a nice guy ... And I hope you aren't dating any of those ghetto guys and those ... P-a-k-i-s-t-a-n-i-s. I don't want you come home one day with a grey baby.'

Angela was so furious that she couldn't say anything. 'Bye, Dad. I don't know why I called at all,' she whispered, and hung up. Tears welled up in her eyes. Not just because she was outraged by what her father had said, but out of sadness that her father had not changed a bit, in the time since she had left home.

❦

If it wasn't for the flirtatious lady at the reception, Neel would have promptly made a coward's escape from the impressive glass and sandstone building. The office of Axis BPO was much more huge and imposing than he had imagined it would be. There were uniformed guards at the entrance with fancy truncheons, like British Bobbies, and employees had to swipe a card and set off some high-tech infra-red device before they were permitted to cross the threshold. The reception was a large hall where the sound of leather shoes clacking importantly on the black granite floors mingled with the swish and squeak of the sneakers that many casually dressed employees wore to work. The walls were lined with paintings — most of them abstract modern art that seemed to Neel like the work of spiders dipped in colour, crawling across the canvas. Soft music resonated from hidden speakers. In one corner stood vending machines for tea, coffee and soft drinks. Neel quickly understood the main purpose of having these huge imposing offices. It was to make job seekers feel small.

It certainly worked that way with Neel. He felt nervous. The file crammed with certificates that he had brought for the walk-in interview was almost slipping from his sweaty hands. He cleared his throat several time. The large hall seemed to be closing in on him and he began to play with the idea of escaping the building and cooking up a brave-faced story about how he got caught in a traffic jam and was late for the interview for his mother. He began telling himself that he wasn't good enough for this job; the memory of the U.S. visa interview was not entirely behind him yet.

Business was booming at Axis BPO since every small and big company in the west had decided to shift their back-office work to India. Thousands of new jobs were being created. That meant that there were so many jobs open right now that any twelfth grade student who could speak decent English could hope for at least some sort of job, at a starting salary they could never have hoped to get otherwise.

Outsourcing had given jobs to tens of thousands of people all over India. Of course, it was creating a lot of upset in the United States and Britain, where many workers had been laid off. It was, in a way, a cruel form of see-saw justice from the gods that ran the cut-throat world of business. The young American men and women who were furious at being laid off had perhaps never heard of the hundred-thousands of Indian workers in Bombay who had lost their jobs a few decades ago when huge American corporations began doing business in India, shutting down large numbers of Indian factories. The times were changing. The dinosaur of globalization had decided to turn his face the other way.

But none of this was on Neel's mind as he was ushered into a room where he was interviewed for thirty minutes by three very corporate looking men. They asked him about his educational background, his family, and whether he would be able to keep long working hours. They said they were impressed with the way he spoke, his pronunciation, and his confidence. After five hours of tests, they asked him how soon he could join work.

Neel Pandey had just taken one step closer to America.

NEW DELHI YANKEES

P lease spare me your pathetic American accents! I can't stand it any more,' said the accent training instructor, Ms Lily, in a pained voice. She was a lean, mean sort of woman with dramatically enhanced kohl-lined eyes who had once studied theatre in the United States.

Neel was at work, sitting in his first training class, part of a three-week program after which he would be ready to face the world with a headphone. Many of the guys in the class, including Neel, had been trying to show off by talking in their version of an American accent when asked to introduce themselves. But, for all their nasal twanging and Archie-comic-book phrases, their accents were so strongly desi that the instructor winced every time they opened their mouths.

Ms Lily's first words were not very encouraging: 'Look, this is a tough job. This is not an easy job. You will have to stay awake all night, and try to sleep all day, but you won't be able to, because the rest of your immediate world works the opposite way... doorbells will ring, cars will honk outside, the bai will come in and turn off the fan to dust your room, you will toss and turn, you will get hungry at the wrong times. Your mind will want you to sleep when you are at work and *not* supposed to sleep. You will not be able to meet your girlfriends and boyfriends for days... perhaps weeks. Your families will have to adjust to your weird working hours. *Then* you will wonder why you took a call centre job. I repeat, this is not an easy job — those of you with sleep disorders or high stress levels should opt out *now*.

'But' — Ms Lily paused with a dramatic flourish — 'for those of you who *still* choose to stay, despite my discouragement, let me tell you that we will make this a fun job. This job is not just about taking calls from foreign customers and talking to them in their own accent. It is about connecting with cultures and people and timezones that you would otherwise never have been able to. This job will open up to you a world that comes alive only when you sleep; a world that you have snoozed through until now. This job will open up that window to you, a window to the world!' (Ms Lily emphasized her point by widening her eyes and flinging out her arms to shape a huge geoid.)

'To excel at this job, you have to adapt to many new things and have to give up some things. Apart from your sleep, the most precious acquisitions that you will have to sacrifice at the workplace' — Ms Lily placed her hand on her heart — 'will be your *identity* and your *name*.'

©

So Neel Pandey became Neil Patterson — a white guy working in New York, ostensibly to save money for an interior designing course the next year. Customers in America would never dream that the pleasant man with the American accent taking their call was, in fact, the only son of Ravi and Narmada Pandey, an upper-caste, middle-class, low-income Brahmin boy, resident of New Delhi, a dreamer who had joined a call centre to be able to talk to Americans and go to America, operating from India.

At BPO Axis Neel quickly realized that his mind too would have to work as if his office was actually in the United States; observing American traditions, speaking American slang, eating

American food and generally being an all-round American. Swell! Giving up his Indian identity was not difficult for his subconscious. I mean, don't all of us sometimes live out another identity? Don't we all want to be Cinderella?

Of course, as he was learning, the job was not the cakewalk many of the new guys thought it would be. Speaking the English language was a fine art. Though all the new recruits knew how to speak the language, they still had to be taught that it was spoken differently from, say, Sanskrit or Malayali.

Neel's batch, the other new hires, were a motley bunch from different parts of India. The battle was not to speak English well, but to speak it in the tongue-rolled, accented, deeply-drawled way Americans spoke it.

'Roll your R's! Wat-urr, Daugh-turr, Laugh-turr, Thea-turr! Roll your R's!' Ms Lily implored. 'Give me the right pitch! Don't speak like a mouse! Americans like to pronounce their words hard! Gimme the right intonation! Stress on the right syllable! No, no, *no*. Control your breath! You are not having sex!'

Before Ms Lily was a nervous assortment of young stars-and-stripes-eyed aspirants trained only to mumble in agreement with their eyes downcast in front of their elders and bosses. They had very little confidence and were not terribly excited about rolling their R's or controlling their breath. A shuffling, awkward bunch of stutterers and stammerers who had to be crafted into a gang of smooth talking pretenders. At first glance, it seemed like a very daunting task. To make matters worse, they all spoke English in uniquely different ways: India's colossal cultural diversity was displayed here, in this classroom, in all its dialectical and linguistic finery.

There were young recruits from the rough-and-tumble of Uttar Pradesh and Bihar — states in which many kids struggled to clear the competitive exams for government jobs with tens of thousands of others from across India, while, as many others, chose the easier Plan B (the U.P. trick) and scurried up a different and swifter career graph. They became hooligans, university brats, molesters, rapists, bandits and, later, politicians, and they went on to become the bosses of these fine bureaucrats. The remainder were jobless, landless, lawless and generally clueless. The English language had not made much foray into their sprawling lands and minds. So, as far as the U.P. and Bihar blokes went, 'nervous' was to be pronounced 'narbhas' and 'voter' was 'bhoter' and 'lawyer', of course, was 'liar'.

Then there were the hardy men and beautiful women from Uttaranchal and Himachal, where 's' was pronounced 'sh'. So 'sit down' became 'shit down'; 'suits me fine' became 'shoots me fine' and 'sagging' became I can't-even-say-what.

There were fine youngsters from the great Punjab, the granary of India, but also known, as you know, for its dazzling dances by majestically muscled and moustachioed men (and often equally muscled and moustachioed women). Several among them had come from families that had sprawling farmlands back home, and had grown up gorging on tandoori chicken and the sight of good-looking Punjabi dancers doing the bhangra, which they had quickly made India's unofficial national dance with their irrepressible enthusiasm. But pronunciation was obviously not the forté of the Punjabi. They would say 'I'm sorry your dog is dead' and it would sound like 'I'm sure your dog is Dad'. They would say: 'I was just thinking of you' and it would sound like 'I was just stinking of you' and 'Be my guest' would become 'Be my gas'.

There were some young women from Assam who would pronounce 'there' as 'dare' and 'the answer' as 'dancer'; from Kashmir, where 'stop' would be pronounced 'sa-top', 'strong' as 'sa-trong', 'sixth' as 'seeksth' and 'strength' as 'sa-trenth'. There were many enthusiastic recruits from Tamil Nadu where

'H' was pronounced 'Hech' and 'What are you doing?' would be rendered: 'Vaat aar yoo doingggg?'

As you can see, the first job at hand was to undo the different ways of speaking English that they had learned in different parts of India, and to give them what Ms Lily called a 'neutral accent'. Soon, the instructor unveiled her sophisticated weaponry.

The members of the class were asked to record their voices on machines that then replayed different versions of the same sentence using voice software, showing them how they should have said what they said.

'Major Montgomery married the marshal's missus.'

'The rain in Spain stays mainly in the plain.'

'The bandmaster played the band with a magic wand in the sand.'

'Tell me your thoughts through and through.'

'There was a lot of laughter by the valiant Walter after the slaughter.'

Sometimes, they were played tapes of two Americans conversing, and the students had to hastily scribble details of the conversations — because, as you know, one of the worst sins for a call centre agent is asking a customer to repeat a piece of information. Most of the time was spent laughing at the others — or scowling when the others laughed back. But, as the days went by, the classes became a lot of fun; the youngsters were asked to shout whatever they wanted and belt out pop songs with thick American accents. They decorated the office with pumpkins for Halloween, and read accent books aloud, swooping down on each other whenever the accent slipped.

The young men and women in the call centres were foot soldiers for the massive American corporations. The battle was to create a surreal, seamless call centre world where there would be no continent, no country, just a huge network of transcontinental phone links, where thousands of sleepy men and women would chat nonstop with tormented, impatient, angry, rude and sometimes just plain dumb customers.

After three weeks of extensive training, Neel's class finally got its sentences right, and most of them were ready to take up their positions by the phone. The few who did not make it, went back to selling mosquito repellent, whizzing aimlessly around town on their motorcycles, or bunking their anthropology class.

©

Neel's probation had ended. He was now secure in his job — at least as long as the outsourcing boom lasted. You can hardly imagine the happiness this brought to Neel's mother. It meant an end to much of the agony that her son had to go through, and hence she herself had to endure, almost on a daily basis, at the hands of her husband. It meant that her son would be financially independent, more confident; and even if he didn't like Meenal maybe he would find a girl at work who would be nice, who knows?

As for Ravi Sharma, though he never said it in so many words, he too was secretly extremely happy for his son. Although he remained the gruff dad, he was proud that Neel had taken up the challenge and landed a job at such a short notice. It sort of rounded off the edges of the father-son relationship; and to further add to Neel's relief, the son and father barely got to see each other now.

Neel became a totally nocturnal animal. His shift began in the late evening, so he would leave for work before his father came home. And he would come back from work past 9 a.m., critically timing himself to appear just minutes after his father had left for the day. It was all perfect as far as Neel was concerned. No more dinner-time admonishments; no more daily exhibition of photographs of girls of marriageable age; no more prodding about Meenal and other prospective candidates.

There was just one downside. Narmada was much more lonely. Her son would come home from work and sleep much of the day; she would wait to tell him her little titbits of gossip, her funny jokes, her tiny jealousies, but he would always be in a rush to leave. And, she couldn't possibly share all this with her husband. So she started feeling more and more left out, immersing herself in newspapers and religious books and television or just standing by the door and watching the other women go off to their places of work. Sometimes she walked several hundred metres inside her house each day, like a restless ghost flitting from place to place.

Narmada would sit by the window and pass silent afternoons. She would write little poems on newspaper pages and throw them away, lest anyone would see them and laugh. She would eavesdrop on children laughing and playing in the neighbourhood. She would stand on the balcony and wait for the rains. But now, even the raindrops of her dreams were playing hard to get. She wanted to meet her friends but they were all so busy – they had all suddenly got jobs, or were taking tuitions at home, or were knitting socks and caps for their grandchildren.

One day, Narmada was all alone at home, as always deep in thought, when she picked up the newspaper. Her eyes ran over it for a few minutes, and then, suddenly, she sat up. She leaned across the sofa for a pen and circled something with it. After clearing her throat several times, Narmada nervously picked up the phone and dialled. 'Hello ... Evergreen Beauty Parlour? I am calling to find out about the fees and enrolment details for the beauticians' course,' she said.

C

Back in Upper Plymouth, a trail of kids trotted into Angela Cruz's cosy apartment. She lead from the front, carrying two large bags, software and stationery in one and groceries in the other; followed by six breathless and excited kids. Behind them, two men from the Buzz Electronics Superstore brought in one huge carton and two other smaller boxes. Angela had been finally able to save enough to buy a new computer and printer.

After the delivery-men left, Angela closed the door and turned around to find the kids perched about on bits of furniture, settled into whatever place they could find. These were members of the school band I told you about, and they had bumped into Angela when they were cycling back after practice. They were excited that Angela had bought a new computer, because she had promised them that the first thing she would do on it was to write another story on the band.

She unpacked the computer, set the printer by its side, put in all the wires where she thought they should go, and turned it on. The kids cheered.

'Orange juice, everybody? Mark, shoes off the table, please,' she said and Mark, keen to win back the points he had just lost over his dirty shoes, trooped over to the kitchen to fetch some glasses.

'You'll interview *us*?' said Juanita shyly.

'Yes I will, sweetie, because the story is about you! You guys really rock!' Angela said.

'You make me feel so good... and... like... so important like... ' said eleven-year-old Chang Lee, the shy violin player with thick glasses. 'Y'know all the other kids used to make fun of my glasses, and called me four-eyes and I just wanted to like, run home, but now they think I'm cool and they want me to teach them how to play. They don't call me a geek any more since my picture appeared in the *Journal*.'

'You are not a geek, man. You are so talented. You know more about music than most people I know,' Angela protested. Then she looked around the room a trifle embarrassed. The kids were looking at her with such awe and admiration that she suddenly realized how much they were counting on her to help them get to the concert. She realized that she could help shape their love for music, and make people around them realize they were not kids who could be dismissed because their skins were not the right colour. They were exceptionally gifted children — with their own music and their own voice. 'You make me proud, kids,' she said, trying to mask the emotion in her voice, 'but, hello, we still have some work to do!'

'We are thirty-five thousand dollars short. That's all the counting I do these days. Angela, will we be able to fly to Miami?' asked Nyasa Okri whose parents had migrated to America from Nigeria ten years ago.

'Yes, sweetie, of course, but we have to work hard and get there. I have convinced my editor that we should do a series of stories on each of you. The photographer will come by tomorrow to take your picture when you are playing. And we need to think of some new money-making ideas for you kids!'

'We could rob a bank!' said Mark.

'Naah, too much work ... let's stick to this,' laughed Angela, tousling his hair and switching on her computer as the children scampered around her excitedly to answer her questions. The computer screen lit up, and Angela moved the mouse and clicked on the MS Word icon. Nothing happened. She clicked again. Nothing. For the next half hour she battled with the computer trying to make it come alive.

'Jeez, and this is a new computer! Sorry kids, we will just have to do this tomorrow ... let me try and call these guys and see what's wrong,' Angela said.

Angela dialled a toll-free number. Then there was an endless wait on the phone, after an irritatingly sweet recorded voice assured her it was very sorry to keep her holding, that her call was very important, that all the operators were very busy and that someone would attend to her call, very shortly.

☾

Neel Pandey — oops, I mean Neil Patterson — had just walked into his work bay. It was around 10 p.m. He pulled up a chair, logged on to the computer, punched his code on the phone, picked up the headset and took a deep breath. Today was only his second day taking calls. Colleagues walked by. An overworked agent was dozing off in the adjacent workstation. This guy is inviting trouble, Neel told himself.

Within minutes a tiny light on the phone flashed with a 'bing' sound, indicating that a customer was calling.

'Good morning, my name is Neil Patterson. How may I help you?'

Neel was going to have a tough day. He had just run into Angela Cruz.

'Hi, I have been holding for like ten minutes? First you give me bad software and then you treat customers like this. I want to write a friggin' official complaint,' she said.

'I'm sorry you had to keep holding, Ma'am, how may I assist you?'

'I want to talk to your manager! I was put on hold for eternity, for Chrissakes, and all you have to give me is your honey-coated "sorry to keep you waiting" shit,' she said, mimicking Neel. 'Why don't you guys get some more phones so that people don't grow old hearing an inane machine say stupid things, and waiting for one of you to take mercy and pick up? How hard can it be to buy more phones?'

'I'm really sorry, Ma'am. May I have your name please? How may I assist you?' Neel said.

'No, you may not have my name ... And I'm not sure you can assist me ... but I bought this new computer and I am clicking on where it says "MS Word" on the screen and it won't open,' Angela said.

'What do you see on the screen, Ma'am?' Neel asked.

'Stars and stripes ... of course I see nothing, Mister, that's why I am calling you,' she snarled.

'Could you try clicking on an icon other than MS Word?'

'What's an icon? The only icon I know is Abraham Lincoln. Can you please talk in non-geek?'

'Um ... an icon will be one of those logo-like signs on your screen? Please close all other windows,' Neel said.

'Excuse me?'

'Please close any other windows.'

'It's not happening...Oh, you mean on the computer... god, you must think I'm so without it, right?'

'No, no, not at all, it can get really confusing, sometimes I think they need to put a new command in the computer, something like "Smash forehead on keyboard to continue". I mean, I think could write a book on "How to be a Geek and Not Know it",' Neel said.

Angela laughed — grateful for his bad jokes. 'Look, I'm sorry for yelling at you like that but I was in the middle of something real important and you know how it feels when your computer doesn't work and then it reprimands you: "Bad command or file name!" and you feel like you should go stand in the corner?'

'Don't worry, Ma'am. In fact your call was a great relief,' Neel laughed

'Really, why?'

'Because the customer before you was asking me whether her computer can get a virus because she has the flu!'

'Oh my god! You're kidding me! Well, I guess I didn't come off so badly after all ... anyway, about my computer ... where are you guys located? Can someone come and take a look at my machine?'

'Um ... New York. Oh, of course someone can come in, if you want, but I think I can help you sort it out right now ...'

'Great.'

'Let's try to begin again and solve our problem. You want to get some coffee for yourself? This could take a while,' Neel said.

'Good idea. Before I go, what did you say your name was?'

'It's Neil Patterson, Ma'am. While we're on the subject may I just take a few seconds to fill up a customer profile form for you? Of course it's totally confidential and only for our in-house research on who our customers actually are...'

'Um. OK, but make it quick.'

'May I have your name please?'

'Angela Cruz.'

She told him her name and age, truthfully I may add, but when he asked her what her profession was, she couldn't help herself. 'I am a model,' she said, just trying the words out on her tongue.

'Oh, wow, that's terrific! I will need your name and email address to send you a feedback form.'

'Sure... my email ID is thinking_aloud@yahoo.com ...'

They both laughed. Neel suddenly began to enjoy his job. He got himself a mug of coffee, and started over.

They spoke for forty-five minutes.

☾

Neel was humming an old Kishore Kumar song when he reached home the next morning. It was unusual for him to sing a Hindi song. He hated Hindi music. But the song – *Haal Kaisa Hai Janaab Ka* – had leaked gently into his ears from an MP3 being played at extra high volume, and he had been singing it to himself all the way in the taxi.

The song stopped and the cheer on his face disappeared the moment he stepped into the house. His father was still home.

He was dressed in a kurta-pajama and was reading the newspaper; so he wasn't going to work either. Had he been sacked? Had he taken long leave to supervise the marriage and mushroom farm? Neel felt like running out of the house, but he knew he would be caught. Plus, he was too sleepy. Before he could think of a way to sneak into his room, Bittu Bai the maid announced his entry: 'Ah! Neel bhaiyya has also come!'

Bittu the Blah. Yapping at all the wrong times!

The father looked up and, uncharacteristically for him, smiled. This was a first in the Pandey household. He set his newspaper aside and asked Bittu Bai to get tea for Neel as well. 'Come, sit, Neel,' he said. 'So how are you doing, son?'

Son? The father was calling his son 'son'? Wow! It felt nice to hear Ravi talk like that. Neel smiled meekly and began narrating his work day — or rather, work night — to him. He was surprised to see that Ravi was not flipping through the pages of the newspaper and nodding absent-mindedly but listening with interest. Narmada also joined them with tea. After a long, long time, the three of them sat together, like a family, relaxing and chatting.

'So what do you get to eat?'

'We have a very big cafetaria, Papa. It is open 24 hours, and we get cheap, good food. We also have a recreation facility with table tennis, badminton, even tennis ... it is a lot of fun.'

'What? Sports? You can play in your office? That's fantastic! I wish the Prime Minister's Office had something like that! Ha! ... and does your boss like your work?'

Narmada could not restrain herself. 'His boss *loves* his work and he might get a promotion much sooner than the others,' she said, bursting with maternal pride.

'By the way, Neel, your friend Rocky called several times during the day. Your mother told him that you were sleeping,' Ravi remembered suddenly.

'Rocky who?' Neel pretended not to know whom his father was talking about but of course he knew. Exactly. Rocky Randhawa the con king. Rocky, who believed Neel had a prominent part to play in busting his cover. Rocky whose sequinned turban plagued Neel in his nightmares. Rocky, who was baying for Neel's blood.

'Rocky ... what's his name ... Rocky Randhawa, I think ... He is some sort of liaison officer or something ... I couldn't catch the name of his company ... He said he wanted to return you a favour.'

'Did he say he might come here?'

'Yes, but I said you are not home during the day. So he said he will call again. He said you had helped him with something and he and his friends wanted to pay you back.'

DIAL-A-DARLING

'Neel, there's a customer here who wants to talk to you ... I tried telling her I can help her but she wants to talk to no one else. Don't know what you are up to, buddy. I think I should tell the supervisor ... unless you want to buy me dinner tonight!' smirked the cheeky chap two chairs away from Neel.

'Good morning, my name is Neil Patterson ... how may I help you?' Neel said in a smooth, near-perfect American accent, as he smiled at his colleague and made a rude finger gesture at him.

'Yes, hi, I was referred to you by a friend of mine whose problem you had solved a few days ago ... I am having software problems and because of that I have run up a huge phone bill...' the customer said huskily.

Neel imagined a voluptuous blonde in her late thirties. 'May I have your name please and the nature of your problem, Ma'am?'

'My name is Kathy Sylvester and I am calling from Jersey City.'

'I will try my best to assist you, Ma'am. What is the nature of your problem?'

'Honey, I have been getting these huge phone bills, listed as some entertainment calls, month after month,' Kathy drawled.

'Does it say adult entertainment calls, Ma'am?' Neel asked.

'Yeah, yeah, something like that. See, when I go to the Internet, these pop-up screens come up all the time ... and I clicked on them a few times by mistake. That's all. And now I get hammered by these bills. Must be a software problem.'

'I'm afraid it's not a software problem, Ma'am ...you inadvertently clicked on an adult entertainment site and there are some, based in places like the Comoros Islands and Solomon Islands and Guinea Bissau, which automatically start charging you international call rates the moment you log on, without your knowing it,' Neel explained.

'Adult entertainment ... you mean *porn* sites?' The husky voice was scandalized.

'Yes, Ma'am, I mean porn sites,' Neel said, taking care not to let her know he was dying to laugh.

'Honey, do I sound to you like a woman who *needs* to go to porn sites?'

'I am just stating a common problem with these sites, Ma'am,' Neel said. He knew that the agents' calls were monitored by seniors and he had to be at his polite best even with the most difficult customers.

'Look, if I need sex I can have it anytime, OK?'

'Yes, Ma'am,' Neel said.

'I am not a horny single woman looking for sex, OK?'

'Yes, Ma'am,' Neel said.

'Don't forget that this is the United States of America, kid. I can have sex anytime I want. I have five boyfriends, you know that? I can do it with any of them any time I want. Why do I need to log on to the fucking Net to have sex? If I want sex I have it in my bedroom ...'

'Yes, Ma'am ... is there any other software-related problem I can assist you with?' Neel asked solicitously.

'Where are you right now, Neil?'

'We are accessible anywhere Ma'am, to solve your problems,' Neel said in his best call centre voice.

'I asked you where *you* are, Neil,' she said.

'Um ... in New York, Ma'am,' Neel finally said, hoping that she would hang up.

'Would you like to have sex with me?'

'E-e-xcuse me?' Neel stammered.

'I like your voice. Would you like to have sex with me?'

'No, thank you, Madam... uh...is there anything else I can assist you with?'

'I can drive down to wherever you are and pick you up, Neil ... just tell me your address,' she said, sounding really turned on.

'I am sorry, Ma'am,' Neel said, wiping the sweat from his forehead and looking to see if his colleagues were laughing at his discomfort.

'I'll get you for this, you stupid little dick!' the woman screamed suddenly as she slammed down the phone.

Neel sighed with relief, took a deep breath, and reached out for the bottle of water near the phone.

The woman at the other end hung up, started laughing hysterically and dug her face into her pillow. Angela Cruz, now rolling on her bed amid squeals of laughter, had gotten her daily fix. It had been one of her most successful phone operations ever. And by refusing an invitation for casual sex from a strange woman, Neil Patterson had done something that men are genetically programmed *not* to do — and passed Angela's friendship test.

℮

Narmada waved to her husband as he sputtered away on his polluting scooter, following the belches of smoke as far as she could down the busy street. She gave it a few minutes more — in case he came back to pick up something he might have forgotten — then she rushed back inside and walked briskly to a secret hiding place behind the bedroom window. She pulled out the newspaper advertisement she had read earlier, grabbed a rolled-up roti stuffed with vegetables and gulped it down with a glass of water. This is the way working women eat when they are late for work, she thought, as she stepped quickly out of the house – like a thief stealing away from his own home — boarded a bus and headed to her secret destination.

The woman at the reception of the Evergreen Beauty Parlour was very courteous and smiled excessively. There were many women sitting about, some young and apparently just out of college, others rich with time to spare, waiting for their pedicures and manicures and waxing and facials. Narmada felt at ease. This was the temple of fashion. This was where middle-aged women brought their creased skin and sagging tummies and tree-trunk-like thighs and were chiselled back into a semblance of beauty. This was the place where lipstick and rouge and mascara were given the respect they deserved.

The receptionist, a young poker-faced woman, sat surrounded by posters, course brochures, and a pile of cheques. Narmada looked at her for a second and thought: 'Didn't anyone tell you that you need to work on your eyebrows?'

Some ten minutes later, she had signed up for the course. She had opted for the slot just before noon — when her husband was busy at office and rarely called home. It would cost 2,000 rupees a month. Narmada made a quick calculation. She had a secret stash of money, amassed over the years from the little she had saved buying vegetables on discount and selling off old newspapers and empty bottles as raddi. She would dip into some of that kitty for the course and, if necessary, she would borrow from her son. He was a working man now, after all.

The receptionist with the shaggy brows directed her to the business development manager — a restless woman with short cropped hair in a business suit, who seemed to be programmed to constantly move about and click her tongue every seven minutes. Narmada watched, perplexed, as she set the files on her table in order, then picked up three and put them on a stool and pasted 'urgent' stickers on them. Then she ordered tea and offered some to Narmada. Before she could have a sip, and before Narmada could even hold her cup, she zipped to the phone, asking her secretary for confirmation for an appointment at the health secretary's office. She came back and raised the cup to her lips, but felt the room was dark, so she got up abruptly and opened the windows. Then she bent over and replaced the three 'urgent' files on the table with the rest of the bunch, and impatiently changed the page on the spiral calendar in front of her. Narmada was about to finish her tea, when the restless woman took her first sip. It was cold. She picked up the phone. 'Irene, how many times have I told you not to give me cold tea? Why is my tea always cold?'

At last she looked at Narmada. 'I am so sorry, Mrs Pandey. I like my own slow pace of work. But these guys just drive me nuts. So, you want to open a franchise of the Evergreen Beauty Parlour, eh?' she asked.

'Yes, but I want to first do the course myself.'

'Well, our rules are quite simple. We have a special scheme for housewives who want to become financially independent working women. You need a minimum of 200 square feet of rented or owned space, and an investment of at least five lakhs. We will train your people, we will help you in every way, and in return we will take 15 per cent of your earnings.'

Narmada's heart sank. 'Five lakhs? That's a lot ...'

'Not to worry. We will also help you get loans from the government's small entrepreneurs' programme at heavily subsidized interest rates for five years. The small industries boss is also our client,' she chuckled. 'But you need to list something as collateral. Can you do that? A house? A plot of land? A shop?'

'Umm...'

'That's just a formality ... I suggest you consult your husband and then come with him for signing the papers, etc.'

'So his signature is necessary?'

'Ya. If the property is in his name ... so we'll be in touch ...' She took the three files marked urgent and started tearing off the stickers — 'And now, if you will excuse me, I have work to finish ...'

Narmada walked out of the Evergreen Beauty Parlour; her determination to pursue the course still as strong, but her steps much slower than when she had walked in.

☾

It was night, and Angela lay on her bed curled up under the blanket. She looked out of the window at the dark, emotionless sky and thought about herself. She cursed herself for the cock-and-bull story she had fed the computer-assistance guy. What was the need to pretend to be someone else? She pulled out the childhood diary that she once faithfully wrote in every night. It was the secret window to her mind.

Growing up in Mississippi had been very different from growing up in say, New York. The shadow lines of race were deeply etched across this city of Southerners. Those invisible lines were drawn at each weekend party, each teen hangout, each pizza joint. Then, when she went home, the shadows persisted there too. There was rarely a day when race, or blacks, or the insecurity of all non-blacks, was not brought up by her father and mother. Sharp racial clusters had sprung up in this pocket of multiracial, rainbow America. Gavin Cruz, who once proudly canvassed his Puerto Rican descent had started listing himself as white when he filled up the census forms.

Gavin's excessive control over his daughters' lives meant that Angela had never really had a chance to explore her emotions on her own. She had liked a couple of boys but could not talk to them as they were not in the social slot her father considered appropriate. The guys that were OK with her dominating father — the well-to-do white guys — sickened her because they brought the same words of prejudice to every conversation, every joke that she heard each day at her dinner table. So she had arrived a virgin in New York — something her friends in both Jackson and New York would never fail to rib her about. She had experimented with her sexuality here, piling up a small list of ex-lovers, but, really, just muddling through relationships. She had even spent a few weeks wondering whether, maybe, she was attracted to women.

Angela Cruz in New York City was just an innocent wanderer, with a tough exterior that men like her father got to see. She would have liked to fall in love, but most lovers seemed to play out a kind of predetermined script, act after act, waiting to live happily ever after or bringing down the curtain and beginning a sequel.

When in her own private space, Angela would find solace in books and music. She would look out at the sunset and watch it transfixed; she would gaze at the evening sky and search for a falling star. She would run the tip of a feather down her arm and feel aroused. She would close her eyes and imagine herself in the eyes of her own imaginary lover. Angela was a dreamer who wanted to fall in love, but on her own terms. And when she did, she wanted to belong, she wanted to give herself completely to her man. There was a place that Angela had kept in her heart for years, for that one special guy — just an ordinary, funny, decent, regular fella — who's uniqueness would be his unconditional love for her.

For some reason she began to think of Neil Patterson – the stranger with the great voice whom she had just spoken with twice, over the phone. Was she stupid? So what if he had a sexy voice and sounded like a sweet guy. Aren't they all *paid* to sound good on the phone? What if he was a drug addict or stalker or some such thing? What if he was a murderer? Angela tried to imagine the worst. What if he was married with three kids? I mean, if he was such a nice guy, why would he be single?

Angela opened the pages of her diary and began writing, her daily contribution to world literature. She wrote fast and steady:

He knelt by her on the grass, and looked at her straight in the eyes. He was lean, his muscles taut and his body glistening with the perfumes and sacred oils that his tribesmen had rubbed on his body. There was a thin muslin shawl draped over his bare chest; he took it off. Then he reached out, bent over her and began to run his warm fingers through her hair. He ran his fingers deep into the furrows, down to her neck and along her shoulders. She closed her eyes and felt the warmth of his fingers on her skin. The expectation and the anxiety of the moment sent shivers down her body. She gasped. Her body was responding to his magical touch in a thousand ways.

He gently touched her face, feeling the warmth of her burning skin, and kissed her forehead. He ran his fingers over her closed eyelids, then mischievously over her nose, felt the slight depression in her dimpled cheek, and then caressed her lips – her sensuous, full lips. He ran his fingers from one end to the other, feeling them softly, parting them naughtily. Then he slipped his thumb inside her mouth as she took a deep breath and played along with the sensuous surprise, sucking on it and feeling it with her tongue. She slid her fingers inside the wraparound on his waist.

He took off the white loincloth and threw it away, letting it drift for some distance in the evening air. Then he helped her slip out of her sarong. The wetness of the dewdrops on her bare skin made her shiver.

Her bare body felt a wave of a tingling sensation, across every inch.

There was a strange hunger welling up in her body.

(

The cookie jar was filling up, but slowly. One by one, the dollars bills were stuffed inside. A riverside performance was underway, and the spectators were less stingy this afternoon.

Members of the Plymouth County band were performing 'Rawhide', one of the scores they had shortlisted before finalizing what to play at the Orange Bowl — if they ever got there. Today's event was one of the weekend performances they had started at different locations in the Village to raise funds from those people too lazy to put it in the mail, or unsure whether the band deserved it. They had been invited to perform by a reader who had been sufficiently moved by Angela's piece to want to help the kids make some money.

Nyasa Okri, trumpet player and unofficial band accountant, kept looking at the cookie jar from the corner of her eye. If it filled up, she would have to gesture to the person closest to the table to set out another one. She had brought along seven jars.

It never hurts to be optimistic, Angela had told her.

(

'Hi, I am having trouble installing the printer to my computer.'

'Sure, Ma'am. You sound familiar. You were the one having a problem with MS Word ...?'

'Yeah, how do you...?'

'This is Neil Patterson.'

'Oh, yes. Oh, yes. It's you again. Hi! You remembered my voice?' she said, smiling secretly as she remembered the prank she had played on him. Did he know that it was her? She hoped he didn't, because she had called today half hoping she would get him on the line.

'How could I not remember? This voice was outraged the other day, and it gave me the time of my life!'

'Ha ha ... oh, that ... I'm sorry about that outburst ...'

Oh no, not at all, what a heart-warming outburst it was, and how lovely it is to hear your voice again, and why don't you have many more such outbursts with me please, Neel thought. He had had a long day. He needed to talk to someone who sounded like a real person, someone with at least the lowest common denominator of intelligence.

Several people had called during his shift asking, without reading a single word in the manual, how to switch on their computer (that was even before they had opened the box). An elderly gentleman had called asking him to ask the phone company to promptly shut off his Internet connection. 'I am calling to inform you that I can die anytime, and I don't want them to keep billing me even after I am dead,' he had said in all seriousness. One woman wanted to know whether she should wrap up her computer in her dog's spare muffler because the weather channel said the mercury would drop.

So after a night of innocent, rude, restless, stupid and purely brain-dead customers, Neel felt as if a surge of fresh air had swept into the room when Angela came on the line.

'Did you have to hold for a long time today as well?' Neel asked.

'Eleven minutes, as a matter of fact, one whole minute more than the other day ... but did I complain? See, some customers have more patience on some days than other days. I did some deep breathing, counselled myself and then kept reminding myself that my call is important to you, that someone will be with me in a moment, and that I should stay on line!' she said, wickedly mimicking the customer service recording.

Neel laughed out loud. The other agents turned to him in the middle of their conversations. He quickly controlled himself.

From a flashing red light in his supervisor's nearby cabin, Neel and the other agents could tell if their calls were being monitored. It was a trick he had learned from the old hands. After a few seconds, once he was sure he was not being monitored, he spoke more freely. 'Of course, patience is a weapon we have to be armed with all the time. It always comes in handy,' he said. 'So what can I help you with today?'

'I'm having problems installing my printer,' Angela said.

'No sweat. Switch on your comp, connect the printer cord, and tell me what it says.'

'OK ... it's taking time ... So what was the stupidest thing you heard today? Worse than mine or better?'

'I wouldn't say "stupid".'

'Aw c'mon, I am not going to tell your boss!'

'Well, OK, certain "challenging" situations do come up each day ... like there was a gentleman this morning who was having printer problems like you. His computer kept telling him it could not "find the printer".'

'And?'

'So he tried troubleshooting himself. He turned the computer's monitor to the right so that it faced the printer directly. But it did not work, he said. The computer said it still could not "find the printer"!'

Angela burst out laughing. 'I am feeling so much better! Don't worry, I had no such problem and I did not try any such solution,' she said.

'I'll bet... of course the trophy for this week went to the woman who called me from New Jersey and wanted to have sex with me ... what does the screen say?'

'It's asking me to enter the printer CD ... She did? Ha! How weird is that! So did you take her up on her offer?'

'Oh, god forbid, no! Please put in the disk. It's the yellow one ... Yeah, it was bizarre ... I was wiping the sweat from my forehead and trying to sound normal ...'

Angela giggled but quickly composed herself. Her heart went out to her innocent victim. But, tragically, she could only talk about the CD. 'All right, the CD is in... so tell me another good customer story in the meanwhile, Neil.'

Neel looked at the supervisor's console. His phone was still not being monitored by the quality control folks. 'Well, there was this lady who thought that the mouse was something like the foot pedal on her sewing machine, so she was pressing away on it and assuming that it was the power button. Without much success, I'm afraid,' Neel added drily.

'You're kidding me! You're making me fall off my chair!' Angela said, bursting into laughter.

'Any inadvertent injury caused by humour evoked by a call centre agent's experiences is not covered under the insurance warranty you have for the computer, Ma'am,' Neel said, making Angela laugh out loud again.

'Why are you working in a call center? Go to Broadway, man! Go to one of those stand-up comedy places! I'm sure you'll make way more money!' Angela said.

Broadway. Hmmm. Neel was sitting in New Delhi, thousands of miles from Broadway.

Some ten minutes later, Angela's printer was working fine. She took some test prints, and everything seemed in order.

'Hey, thanks so much, Neil... before I hang up, tell me one more.'

'One shouldn't have too much of a good thing,' Neel said in his famously sexy Bryan Adams' voice.

'Aw, c'mon. I know you have a treasure trove. Gimme one for the road. It'll make me look good with my friends!'

'Well, here's one of my favourites. This happened three days ago. A young man called to say he was on the computer and eating pizza when he got a call, so he put the pizza slice on the tray. Then he accidentally pressed a button and the piece went inside the computer. The tray got jammed; the computer was not working and all he could retrieve were some onion rings.'

'What tray? My computer does not have a tray,' Angela said.

'Neither did his. He had placed his pizza on the CD drive!' Neel said.

'I don't believe this! You made this up! God, it was really nice talking to you, Neil ... you are funny ... may your tribe increase ...'

'Amen to that, and I hope you sizzle on the ramp...'

Angela paused, but only for a split second. Then she blurted out what she was going to regret for a substantially long time. 'Yes, thank god. I am getting some good assignments. Might get to do the London Fashion Week in two months, if I am lucky. And of course, Miss America is coming up.'

The wise elders say that you should not tell one lie because you will have to tell a hundred more to defend it.

Now that she had done it once, Angela was going to find herself falling deeper and deeper into her little deceit.

LOVE, VIRTUALLY

Angela woke up late the next morning very angry at herself. Why on earth did she make up all those lies to Neil Patterson about modelling and stuff? A phone prank was one thing. But this was becoming a habit. God. How could she do this? And — more importantly — how could she undo this? What if he really became her friend and came over for coffee one day and found out she was not a model? How about that, eh?

It was a Saturday morning. Angela decided to have a long hot shower, pamper herself with pizza for lunch, and then do some shopping in the afternoon to distract herself. There, that would fix her and she would be normal by evening.

Hardly.

When she turned on her computer there was a mail waiting from Neil Patterson.

Hi Angela:

How is your computer feeling? ... Just writing to say that I'm sort of hoping it will act up again ... so we can talk again at leisure sometime soon.

Neil

What? What does he think of himself? One or two phone calls and a little small talk and we are friends? What does he think of himself, mailing me like this? Why the hell should I write back?

Pause.

Well, I might as well just write a polite reply. Why antagonize these people? Who knows, if my computer packs up again, he might come in handy. Yeah, that's right, that's the mature approach.

Dear Neil:

Thanks a lot for your mail. It was great hearing from you again.

Thanks 'a lot'? Why 'a lot'? What for? He's just doing his damn job, sister! And why is it 'great' to hear from him again? Are you a desperate spinster staring at your email inbox, waiting for Prince Charming? And even if you are why show it? Hah. Oh yeah, and why 'dear' Neil? How did he suddenly become so 'dear'? Delete, delete, delete, delete. New sentence.

Hi Neil:

Thanks for curing my computer. It's working fine for now, but you never know! Talk to you soon ...

Angela

Ouch. Why did she say 'but you never know' and 'talk to you soon,' she asked herself the moment she pressed the send key. It was like holding open the door and inviting him in with a red rose between her teeth.

C

Across the continents, Neel was preoccupied as he dressed for work. For once he was not thinking about America. He had been behaving like a stupid teenager lately. He pictured Angela, saw her as one of those *haute* models on the catwalk of Fashion

TV, and shook his head thinking she was so out of his league. Yet he shaved extra carefully before going to work that night and splashed on the best cologne he had, as if getting ready for some sort of a virtual date. Perhaps he thought she would even be able to smell him over the phone. When he knew his parents were not looking, he went to the puja room, took off his shoes and walked in. It was a room he had never gone into before. He sent up a quick prayer, flicked some rice and roli at a picture of Shiva and darted out. He had prayed for divine intervention to ensure that Angela Cruz's computer would never work properly for more than a few days. (I doubt Ganesh would agree, and Durga Mata would probably give him one tight slap.)

When he got into office, the first thing he did was grab a coffee from the cafetaria and call home. He had started doing this for some days now, ostensibly just to say hi and all before his parents went to sleep, though the real reason was that he wanted to get the low-down on his father's mood from his Chief Spy, his mother, so that he could steel himself for any nasty surprises in the morning before he went home.

'Your father is on that trip again,' Narmada said on the phone in a hushed voice.

'What trip? Marriage? But I thought he had gotten over that when he talked to me the other day?'

'Yes, he had. For a day or two. But yet another of his colleagues gave him a wedding invitation today. Now he says we urgently need to find a girl from a good Brahmin family. I think he is going to talk to Meenal's father too.'

'Ma, can you please tell him not to? Meenal likes someone else.'

'What? Why didn't you tell me? I was warming up to the idea ... hai bhagwan, you always get me into trouble, Neel ...'

Neel smiled. He knew his mother would be able to handle it.

'OK, he is coming. Promise me you'll find yourself a good Indian girl soon, OK? Bye,' Narmada whispered, and quickly hung up.

A good Indian girl. Hah! — That's what all Indian parents want their daughters-in-law to be. Indeed, that's the kind of woman all Indian men want their wives to be.

Sure, at parties, in college canteens, and in restaurants, the Indian male loves the kind of woman with a kind of, you know, zing. The sexy woman. Who wears 'sexually suggestive' clothing. Who bites her lower lip in a certain way when she talks. Who runs her tongue over her lips for no reason and shares a cigarette with sensuous, carefree abandon. Who knows dirty jokes. Who is 'open-minded' — which means she will dance with you at parties and let you hold her close though she knows you have a girlfriend. Who knows that 'balls' are not just used in cricket and 'hump' is not just an undulation on a camel's back.

Of course, that is not the woman he wants for a wife. *That* kind of woman? Dear, dear. What will his parents say?

No. Ideal Indian wife material is a woman who does not swear, does not smoke, or drink, or dance with other men, or use sexually explicit words. She makes breakfast, goes to work, takes care of the kids' homework, cooks again, and sinks into bed at night, holding her chin (and breasts) aloft, heaving and enjoying the moment as the husband, who has just gotten up from flipping television channels for three hours, lives out his carnal desires. The ideal woman has never had anything to do with a man before marriage except the odd crush. She takes care of the house, loses weight, looks sexy for her man, doesn't laugh too loudly before the in-laws, does not watch sex shows by herself, looks perfect all the time, does not have stretch marks or eye bags or blackheads, if she works she turns down invitations to office parties because the men there make her husband jealous, and she knows exactly where her husband's underpants are when he can't find them in the morning. The ideal woman knows how to make a five-course meal after coming home from an eleven-hour work day, has perfect bathroom habits though her husband is permitted to splotch toothpaste in the basin and leave pubic hair in unexpected places. She never needs to have sex unless her husband wants it. She never feels aroused or makes the first move; she never finds another man good-looking on TV, in a magazine or at a party, though her husband will swoon and sigh over the waitress at the Italian restaurant, the air hostess on the flight, and her own best friend.

That's the good Indian girl for you.

However, Neel was yet to be tested on all this. He had never had a real girlfriend, though he did write and receive a lot of cards and letters from the girls around. Like all good Indian boys he grew up having crushes on a lot of women, but never had the courage to take it past making eye contact. One of them was a voluptuous older neighbour, married but separated and very aloof from the rest of the world. She had, as all women have, a sixth sense. She seemed to know what Neel wanted. She invited him once to her home for coffee and he just sat there for one hour, barely managing to look at her because she was looking oh-so-sexy in a cotton kurta. Neel just kept talking about the weather. The coffee went cold. Something in the woman did, too, I guess. I wouldn't blame her.

The second crush was on this same neighbour's young and doe-eyed maid. After some years of throwing come-hither glances at Neel when she passed by his window each morning to do the dishes, she eventually ran away with a painter two days after he whitewashed the neighbour's house. After that, there was the girl who went to the same mathematics tuition class that Neel attended. He'd finally drummed up the courage — and cash — to buy her a birthday card but, apparently, she was hitting on the tutor. She tattled on him to the tutor and he ensured that Neel flunked in the second term examination, which needless to say did not please Neel's father, who told Neel a few things he did not want to hear. Then there was Meenal herself, once upon a time, but you know that she, um, went on a different path.

And now there was Angela.

❀

Neel logged on to Instant Messenger and checked if Angela was online. She was.

'Hi Angela, it's Neil.'

'Oh hi ... the comp doc ... how are you?'

'I am good ... and your computer?'

'Fine, thank god. Are you at work?'

'Yes ... just wanted to say hi online. We are not supposed to be chatting on the Internet at work, but sometimes they make an exception. How's your day been?'

'Pretty good ... I should get to work too, soon.'

'Got to strut your stuff?'

'God, no. Preparing my... uh...portfolio. Have to go for another photo session with this famous photographer, and then I have to meet a school band.'

'Which photographer?'

'... um ... Paolo Bertolucchi ... I was lucky he agreed to shoot me.'

'Oh, wow ... well, best of luck, and will you send me one of your autographed snaps when they are done? That way, when you become Miss America I can brag to everyone ...'

'Ya ...right!' she said.

'So what do you play?'

'What?'

'An instrument. Do you play an instrument? You mentioned a band ...'

'Oh, that! I wish I could! No, actually it's about these kids at our local school, they are so exceptionally talented. They have qualified this year to play at half-time at the Orange Bowl, but you know what? They don't have money to pay for their trip! So I try to do what I can to help them, we are trying to raise money …'

'Oh, wow, great going! You must know a lot of celebrities, and I'm sure you must have done a celebrity fundraiser … you know, those $150 a plate dinners …'

'Yeah … something like that … Those kids mean a lot to me… So you work at this time every day? Mornings?'

'Yup, same time … I am working to save money to study next year.'

'Cool … what do you want to study?'

Long pause. 'Interior designing. I like taking grotty little spaces and turning then into airy, beautiful things.'

'Oh great! I love make-overs.'

'Yeah redesigning, re-inventing stuff is my forté… oops, there goes my buzzer, I need to get back to work … talk to you soon!'

'OK, happy dealing with grouchy customers!'

⟡

It was a Sunday morning on the wide Ossining Avenue, the main road of Upper Plymouth Village, and the parents of Angela's twenty-four had assembled to set up small counters to sell fruit, posters, juice and T-shirts to raise money for their children — the members of the Plymouth County School band. Angela's enthusiasm had infected the parents as well. Though they had been reluctant to join her at first, she had gone to each of their homes to personally request them to assist her. She made a speech. She used emotional one-liners. She played on their guilt. It worked. After some persuasion, they had all agreed. All, that is, except for Juanita's parents. When she had knocked at her door, it had been opened by Juanita herself. Even though it was late in the evening Juanita was alone at home. Angela asked her where her mother was but the poor girl looked so upset that Angela quickly stopped probing. Is there no joy invented for a six-year-old's sadness, she had thought.

Now Angela was at the fair making sure that every thing was in order, going from counter to counter. She was treated as nothing less than a VIP, and normally would have enjoyed it. But she was preoccupied. Mark had just told her that he had seen Juanita crying. She was looking for her when someone tapped her shoulder. 'Hey! Remember me?'

Matthias Baldenburp was a cop with a crew-cut and an irritating habit of caressing his close cropped pate every seven minutes. He would have been better suited to a career in streetfighting than crime fighting but, as destiny would have it, he had got a job with the police department. Everyone took an instant dislike to him. Maybe he was frustrated because he had such bad luck with the ladies. And then, some months ago, just when Matt had managed to finally get some grudging attention from the woman he had been hitting on for three years, his mother had walked up to him, stroked his bald head and said: 'How's my Mattie? How's ma baby?' Unknown to Matt, a photographer of the *Upper Plymouth Journal* was standing nearby, and he snatched out his camera and took a picture of Matt, in full police uniform, having his cheeks pulled by his mother. The picture was on the front page in four columns the next day. Within about a half hour, Matt became the laughing stock of the entire town because of the story titled 'Baby Cop'. When he had gone to the office of the *Upper Plymouth Journal* to protest, Angela Cruz was the only one to come out in his defence. So perhaps he was predisposed to fall in love with her.

Now, I do not recall whether it was something about the weather on that sunny afternoon. I do not remember if there were more clouds drifting lazily through the skies than normal, or a balmier breeze, bringing in the fragrance of the ocean, or a harsher sun, melting the heart of the cold-hearted police officer — but that moment, that very moment, had a magical impact on Mattie's heart. He stood transfixed, gazing like a buffoon at Angela's face, moved by the incredible beauty of her flushed cheeks and expressive eyes.

'Hi, Matt!' said Angela. She stopped, but just for a second, and then kept walking on.

'Angela, can I talk to you?'

'Matt, I am sorry … I'm looking for one of the kids…' Angela looked around worriedly.

'I can help…I'm a cop…'

'No, she's here somewhere…' Angela walked briskly away leaving Matt staring at her as she strode past the small crowd and headed towards the deserted community centre building a few hundred metres away.

The building was a beautiful red brick structure, one that had stood there since the days of the Great Depression. Once upon a time, there used to be a soup kitchen here for the desperate, out of work, young and old of the county. They used to line up here, unshaven, in their loose trousers and dirty jackets, on the spacious stone gallery where Angela was walking now — stockbrokers, traders, merchants and dreamers, all trying to make sense of the overwhelming tragedy that had swept through their worlds. The loneliness of the building evoked awe and respect and fear.

She knew where the loo was and quickly walked towards it. She entered the room now marked UNDIES, the first two letters defaced and replaced by some pervert. But even that pervert had a sense of fairplay; some distance away, the GENTS room had been renamed with the addition of three squeezed-in letters, making it GENITALS.

Angela pushed open the door of the ladies restroom. Little Juanita sat curled under a sink, shaking in fear, and sobbing helplessly.

'Honey, what's the matter? Sweetie, tell me, you know I will help you...'

'You can't ... no one can,' the little girl sobbed.

'Let's try, honey ... Just tell me what's wrong, will you?'

'My mommy had to go away suddenly, she's sick, but she doesn't want anyone to know, she said she got sick 'cos she was poked by a dirty needle and now her blood is full of poison.'

'O my god, poor baby.'

'She said to stay home real quiet otherwise the police will come to take me away and then she'll never see me again...I don't want to lose my mommy but I'm scared to be alone...' Juanita cried.

Angela gathered the little waif into her arms. 'You don't have to be alone, sweetie, you can come and stay with me till your mom is all better.'

Angela held Juanita by the hand, it felt so small and precious and Juanita looked up at her with eyes so full of trust and gratitude that Angela felt her heart would break.

❦

Neel's father was unexpectedly cheerful when he came home from work that day. He had heard a credible rumour about him getting a promotion and moving to the Prime Minister's Secretariat. That would mean not just a raise, but a zooming rise in his professional standing. When Narmada walked in a few minutes later, Ravi had already changed into a white kurta pajama and was looking at himself in the mirror, settling his hair. Narmada giggled. Ravi turned around, in embarrassment. 'Why are you laughing, Narmada? Is it only a woman's right to gaze into the mirror for hours?' he asked with a smile. He walked over to the bed and lay down, and Narmada sat decorously beside him, setting down the tea-tray on the bed.

'No, it isn't. Shall I put a separate mirror here so that both of us can gaze into the mirror together each morning?' They both laughed; it felt like they were laughing together like this after a long time.

Ravi looked up at his wife's face, still glowing in the way it had in her youth, so many years ago. 'When Neel gets married, who will believe you are a mother-in-law? You still look just the same as when you got off the car after our wedding, all puffy eyed with crying. You soaked my hanky in no time,' he said, tracing his finger down her cheek. 'Thank god, we don't have a daughter ... you would have soaked your sari in tears when she went away after marriage,' he smiled.

'Yes, I would probably die of sorrow ... it is so tough ... but someone else will go through the same feelings.'

'Who?'

'The mother of our daughter-in-law.'

'Ah,' he said. 'That's when you let me find a daughter-in-law. I found Meenal, but you don't seem to find her good enough.'

'I do. I think she will make the perfect wife and daughter-in-law. I really like her. Unfortunately, she does not want to marry Neel. She likes someone else. Now, promise me you won't go around talking about this to her father. He'll give her a hard time.'

'What? You mean another man? When did girls from good Brahmin families begin to get trapped into this ... love thing? I am shocked! They are all getting it from the films, I tell you. Meenal's father should find out who the man is and have him beaten up. And no, I won't talk to him about this. Why make him ashamed?'

'Ashamed? Why?'

'Why not? That man, whoever he is, is corrupting the poor girl!' Ravi said.

'They are both adults and can do what they want. They are mature enough to know what's good for them.'

'Now, now, Narmada, don't you go on about this love marriage thing. It's been imported from America and England, it's not right for our country. Boys and girls are not mature enough to decide for themselves. A man can never think straight if all he is thinking about is a woman. Do you know how many divorces they have in America and how many small small girls become pregnant?'

'That's bad, but because of that you can't say falling in love is bad.'

'It is fine. As far as it's not my son doing it. This is all I hear in my office these days ... all the fathers and mothers are just complaining about this love business. Rotten minds. It's all this disco culture.'

Narmada decided it was wise to change the topic before things got out of hand. 'So, all of them must be very jealous of your promotion, eh?'

Ravi took the bait. The tension-laced arches on his brow disappeared. He smiled. 'Yes. They all look so constipated these days. I will become their boss! They will have to apply to me for leave!'

'But that will mean your job will get even more stressful, right? Will you spend longer hours in the office?' she asked.

'Sometimes. Not always. But it will be a prestigious position. Personal Secretary to the Private Secretary to the Prime Minister of India,' he said grandly.

'I am glad something in your office interests you after such a long time. Otherwise, you always came home so tired and unhappy ...'

'I know ... I also know that I am often grouchy ... but the office makes me so. My shoulder hurts so badly from typing all day. My eyes hurt. Plus the tension of this high pressure job. One mistake and you could be fired. Now, I could be getting my own secretary! Can you believe it?'

'I hope it's not a woman,' said Narmada, instinctively.

'You will get jealous, eh? I like that!' Ravi was thrilled.

'Why should I be jealous? Show me your shoulder. Is it still hurting? OK, just turn over and lie on your stomach,' Narmada said.

'What?'

'Just do it ... I will give you a massage. And then I will give you a facial that will make you feel so fresh.'

'A massage? A facial? Where did you learn all this?'

'You don't know so many things about me ... you are the same old forgetful man I knew in college,' she said, smiling as she began caressing his shoulder muscles with the strong thumb and finger movements she had learned the previous week. Then she coaxed Ravi to close his eyes and let her place two cold cucumber slices on them as she smoothed a special sandalwood paste on his face. When the face mask and the cucumbers were taken off, Ravi felt like a new man.

'Vah! What was that? I feel so good ... Tell me, honestly, where did you learn all this?'

'I learnt ... from a friend,' she said, thrilled at the effects of her massage and facial.

'No, you are really good. I don't think those trained beauticians in the beauty parlours can make a person feel as good as you can ...'

Narmada thought the time was opportune for her to make her confession. 'Um ... Ravi ... there is a company that gives training and assistance for housewives who want to become working women and open their small businesses —' she stopped abruptly because she could see that her husband's face was changing colour. His eyes had that look, that glazed, steely look that Narmada was most scared of. The effects of the facial and massage evaporated. The crease on his forehead was back in place.

'So?' he said. Zen was then. This was now.

'Do you think that I can also open a small ... beauty parlour? They will give a loan at a very low interest ...'

'*What*? I can't believe you are saying this! Am I dead that you have to work? Do you feel we are so short of money? And opening a ... beauty parlour and rubbing sandalwood on people's faces every day? That's like being a waitress in a restaurant ... It's such a lowly job! Narmada *never* talk to me about this again!' And he stomped out of the room, roughly pushing aside the plate with the cucumbers and the sandalwood paste.

Narmada lifted the tea-tray, the bowl of sandalwood herbal paste and the cucumber slices and walked back slowly to the kitchen. The prisoner was back in solitary confinement.

☉

It was a question that Angela would ask herself repeatedly in the coming days: why don't little girls come with instruction manuals? Juanita was so quiet and withdrawn sometimes that it was unnerving. Angela had taken time off from work to get Juanita settled in, but sometimes she felt that she just couldn't reach her.

First off, they had gone to meet her mother who turned out to be even more malnourished than her daughter. She took just a few minutes to tell her story: She had AIDS. Now she had signed up for a clinical trial program. Meaning, a revolutionary treatment, as yet untested, that, as human guinea pig, she could get for free. It was a system imported all the way from India. Something called Ayurveda, Juanita's mother explained, lifting herself up from the hospital bed with some effort before holding Angela's hand and adding, 'Please, don't let them send my baby away to a home. I know I will get better. I just need a couple of weeks, I'll be out soon and be able to look after Juanita...'

Angela promised, 'Juanita will live with me until you are ready to come home. I'll make sure that no one takes her away...'

Juanita who had been standing solemnly by her mother's bedside all along, lay her head on her mother's chest and held her hand against her heart: 'I've told God to look after you. And he's promised. I love you, Mommy. Please don't be sick any more. I love you so much.'

That night, as she tucked Juanita into bed, Angela thought that if anyone ever asked her what the most inspiring moment of her life had been, Juanita's assertion of love for her mother and the conviction with which she spoke would be tops on her list. Childhood was a lifetime in itself, Angela realized, and she was revisiting hers thanks to Juanita.

Over the next few days, as Angela the working woman suddenly became Angela the foster mother — her punctuality dedicated not to racing off to the subway to reach an interview on time, but ensuring that she was home on time to help Juanita with her homework and serving her something warm and wholesome for supper — her priorities, and her pastimes, seemed to change completely. She didn't mind in the least not going out with her pals on Friday night, or declining Matthias Baldenburp's advances, preferring to take Juanita to meet her mother as often as she could and witnessing the healing power of a six-year-old's love. Then, at the practice sessions of the band, she would watch mesmerized as the same little girl, who would otherwise barely utter a word all day, transformed into a tiny diva, her voice carrying through the tennis court, resonating in the heart of every single person who heard her.

Three weeks later, when Juanita came home from school she hugged Angela spontaneously and pulled out a picture she had drawn. Three stick figures of a little girl holding the hands of two women. 'My two mommies,' she said and then started chattering animatedly about her day at school. Angela had never felt more complete in her life.

But Angela's friends told her to think twice about what she was doing; she was becoming so attached to the little girl, how would she cope when Juanita's mother recovered or the social service people took the child away to a foster home? She knew that her friends had genuine concerns, and she agonized over their questions. But most of all, she agonized every night over how her father would react when he learnt about Juanita. Angela had not told her parents about the little girl because she knew that the first thing her father would think of was her race. She wrote to Neil, seeking his advice.

❦

Hey Angela,

Juanita is a doll! I am not really a children person but even I am excited! You saved her life, I'm sure she'll kiss you for it some day...You know, I know you better than you think... you're going to feel real low when Juanita goes back to her mom, but you've got to listen to your heart... don't feel scared of letting a little love into your life...If you feel lonely, just write me or call me ... I will fill up your loneliness with stupid call centre jokes.

Meanwhile, there have been no complaints from you or your computer for weeks. I am very upset. Please drop your machine on the ground so that it breaks and you can legitimately call me.

Neil

Hi Neil:

Thanks, for the tip. I think my friends have all given up on me. They can't understand why I'm with a six-year-old. My dad will go ballistic when he finds out. You know, there was once a time when I wrote long letters to him, and gave them to him when he came back from work. I used to tell him about my day, and about my friends, and say sorry for things I had done, or gossip I had spread, which mom said I shouldn't have. He wrote me replies and put them under my pillow when I was asleep, and told me in the morning that the postman had come to my window at night. It was a secret between my father and me – which everybody in the family knew, by the way! At dinner, we would talk casually, nothing about any letter, and then, when I woke up the next morning, Bingo! Another letter under my pillow.

But he has changed. We are not the same father and daughter now. I think having Juanita in my life has made me realize what I once shared with my dad...

Angela

P.S. By the way I'm 'letting the love flow'.

Hey Angela,

I'm thrilled my advice has come in handy! Meanwhile, don't let your dad get you down. I wish someday your father will understand you...but until then just chill... you are making choices that make you better understand yourself...Is temping as a mom affecting your work? Can you still go to the London Fashion Week?

I hate to admit it, but you have been so much on my mind (especially images of you sashaying down the catwalk!)... those stories you told me about you and your father in your childhood ... and your failed first date ... I was thinking about all that and smiling to myself when I was watching TV last night ...

Neil

Hi Neil:

I still haven't decided about London Fashion Week. It will all depend on when Juanita's mom comes home. That's another worry. If something happens to her mother, Juanita will be devastated. And when she goes home to her, I think I will be. God, you don't know how much I will miss her. Enough about me. How have you been? Tell me more about yourself and your life. I was thinking about you too, especially when I wanted to entertain Juanita with some funny stories!

Angela

Hi Angela:

Here is the rundown on my life ... My boss is a crook. My co-workers keep stealing my food. My neighbour plays loud music at night. He also has a dog who barks like a cannon at odd hours. It sometimes seems my other neighbour has a real cannon, but it turns out that he is going through a difficult digestive period in his life. My friends call me in the middle of the night to have long discussions about their sex life, or mostly the lack of it. That is a cruel reminder of my own such grievous lack. My neighbour's cat knows how to open the refrigerator and drinks all the milk when it can. A punk groped me on the subway last night. There is a kleptomaniac prowling around our building taking away bottle openers, golf balls and condoms. My landlady thinks I am that klepto. I want to go with her on a vacation to the Grand Canyon and come back alone. Otherwise my life is full of laughter and sunshine.

Do tell me more about yourself ... More of your funny stories about your silly high school dates ... Kidding ...love to Juanita...
Neil

Hi Neil:

I cracked up reading your mail and almost woke Juanita. What a life! Hope you and your landlady and your neighbour and everyone else are back on peaceful terms now, otherwise your life is going to become very chaotic soon ...

You know pretty much all there is to know about me ... There's just one new development this week ... I might be moving to a bigger apartment where I can see the sunshine and hear the birds in the morning ... I am like that, I don't want big cars or a lot of money, just a nice home and sunshine and the moon to look at during the night, not the fire escape of some ugly apartment complex ...

Angela

Hey Angela:

Sorry I haven't written (not that you complained!) I have been trying to prepare for my interior designing exam, and though I always kept telling myself at the back of my mind that I must write to you, I just couldn't.

I hope you and Juanita and your computer are all well, although your computer's ill-health does mean that I get an opportunity to talk to you. It's like what docs must think all the time – if all the people in the world were healthy and well, then they would be jobless!! I want to write so much – but sometimes I'm not sure where to begin...and my mind thinks up a thousand things when I imagine the day I will tell you about them. That's also probably the reason that I won't tell you about them. You sound like such a genuine, warm, sincere person. And I feel I can just pour my heart out to you, say anything I want, however outlandish, and that you will understand...I know I am rambling. I know you don't mind.

I've been a bit messed up lately because of things at home. We are a close-knit family. Though I haven't had such a great relationship with my dad either, I respect him a great deal for what he is, and for the fact that he is a hardworking honest man who has given me many of the values that seem old fashioned to many of my friends. My mother is a sweetheart. But lately, one thing or the other seems to be making them fight all the time, and I don't know how to deal with them. I want them to be happy. I feel helpless that I can't do anything about it. I hate it when my parents fight or sulk or don't talk to each other. I just wish our parents would grow up.

Neil

☙

When the dreaded phone call from her father came, Angela was fortified by Neil's letters. She braced herself for the onslaught.

'How could you do this, Angela, are you nuts?'

'Excuse me?' Angela said.

'What's all this about adopting a child? You cannot keep that kid in your house any longer. Who knows who she is? Which part of the world she's from, maybe she's carrying a disease ... Go put her in an orphanage or something.'

'Dad, you know, I have a very strong urge to hang up on you.'

'Don't talk to me like that.'

'Well, there might be many things that you do and others don't like, I hope that thought does cross your mind sometimes.'

'What did I say to offend you so much? I just asked you not to pick up strange kids from public bathrooms. There are disease issues. You know. Health issues. You should have just informed the cops and let them take care of her. Why did you bring her home? This is like abducting a child. It could be illegal, you know. Don't try to be Mother Teresa or whatever that old gran's name was, OK? Don't go around picking up street children like her.'

'Bye, Dad. I am hanging up now.'

☙

Neel was also beginning to feel boxed in. As a child, his parents had taught him to always speak the truth, because (as you know

now) if you tell one lie you have to make up a hundred to protect the first one.

And Neel had fabricated an entire person for Angela. Initially, he did it because it was part of the job requirement, but now he was doing it because he did not have the power to disable the monster he had created. He had to sustain the existence of Neil Patterson and feed it new depths each day, because his friendship with Angela depended on it. For something told him, deep in his heart, that Angela, his faraway telephone friend, could well be someone special for him, a woman after his own mind, a woman who would evoke his love and admiration. Since he did not have it in him to tell her the truth about himself, he knew that over the coming months he would be sucked deeper and deeper into his life's greatest moral dilemma.

But Neel naively believed that love conquered all. That if he wanted to, if he felt strongly enough, or cared passionately about a woman, about a girl like Angela, he could deal with any obstacle — distance, lies, racial differences, timezones.

How he would do so, however, Neel couldn't say.

☾

The grainy television screen flickered noiselessly in a corner of the room. Narmada had a cup of tea in one hand and the remote control in the other. Her fingers pressed the buttons on it mechanically, like a robot in a sari, even though all the channels were blank — there was a power failure in the cable company. Narmada should have been in beauty class, mastering the next level of intricacies of the fruit and honey facial for dry to moderate face types, nudging the woman on her left for answers to a question the instructor was asking, and nervously wondering whether her husband was calling at home while she was out trying to become a working woman. But she was at home, in a baggy nightgown, with no intention of going anywhere.

The severe yelling that she had gotten from her husband the other day had broken her spirit. She had barely spoken at home since, talking only occasionally to her husband when he wanted his shirt or complained about less salt in the curry.

Narmada looked around the home that she had lovingly created over the years. The wall hangings. The beautiful but wobbly glass stool with one leg slightly shorter than the rest. The framed paintings of Krishna and Radha from the Kishengarh school. The dusty Buddhist miniatures from Bhutan from an exhibition in Pragati Maidan to which she had dragged her husband. The red and cream hand-woven curtains. The brown teak table the side of which Neel had once chipped with his cricket bat. The expensive Kashmiri carpet that she had bought and agonized over ...

Then she looked out of the window. Two housemaids, illegal refugees from another country who spoke in a strange language and dreamt of their homeland, were walking to their homes after cleaning and scrubbing several homes in the apartment block. They had the ends of their saris tucked in their waists, a few glass bangles on their wrists, an old plastic bag of wrapped-up leftover food in their hands, and an eternal sadness in their eyes. What was the difference between them and herself? At least they did not live a pretence. She did exactly what the housemaids did every day– made sure the house was clean; that the two men of the house had what they needed; that the food was cooked. She was nothing more than a maid-servant in this house, she thought. It made her want to cry, and she tried to, curling her lips and narrowing her eyes in preparation for the tears. But they did not come.

As always, when she was angry with her husband, Narmada thought of the day, many years ago, that she could not forget – a violent, terrible day when she had almost walked out on her husband. Ravi Pandey had often yelled at his wife but it was the first time in their marriage — and the last — that he had raised his hand to hit her. That day Narmada had told herself that she was not going to take it any more. She was leaving with her son. It was a memory that had been covered up by the weight of the unstated love between husband and wife. But there had been no love that afternoon. After the one erotic encounter with the village teacher in her youth, that day had been only the second time in her life that Narmada had rebelled against the seen and unseen forces that controlled her life. That afternoon was now once again suddenly coming alive before her eyes, that afternoon when she had flung her wedding ring across the room —

She yanked it off her finger, sending tiny arrows of light shooting from the three precious stones studding the gold ring — like the mythical quiver of the Sun God. Then, she sent it spinning and somersaulting, directly at her husband.

The glimmering missile struck Ravi Pandey on his face, and then fell with a clang on a small glass stool. Ravi closed his eyes, arched his brows and winced. It hurt. He knew his wife had been an ace markswoman in college, winning medals now stuffed away with old family albums in a dusty wooden cupboard. But she had proved her talent only now. Ravi's harsh character, ill temper and mood swings had simmered for years. They were vapour now, filling the bedrooms of their apartment. Today, there was a cloudburst he had never anticipated.

Neel had just joined school and spent the rest of his busy after-school life either at his silent, contemplative best or at his hyperactively destructive worst. Narmada, friendless and lonely because of her husband's unpredictable mood swings, had made her son her friend and confidant. When she was not with her son, she went to the temple, walked in a nearby park, stared silently at old family albums, conjured up stories of dragons and kings and lions for her son, and wept silently. Little Neel shared a deep, indescribable bond of loneliness with his mother.

When they were together, they were like two young children getting to know each other, or two old friends sharing a park bench, or two convicts sentenced to a life-term in the same cell.

It was around the time Ravi had just landed his job in the Prime Minister's Office, and often spent long hours late into the night proving his hardworking capabilities. Narmada craved for her husband, for their togetherness, for their innocent afternoons, playful evenings and eventful nights. She dreamed of having warm cups of tea with him on the balcony, watching the July rain. She had loved him for years. But that love was dwindling. Ravi was no more the man she had first met in college.

She had suffered insults for so long but couched them in the love she had for her husband. But he had raised her hand to hit her today, stopping himself before he actually did. Even so, Narmada felt as if she had actually been slapped across the face ... In a second, tears were soaking her cheeks, temporarily dousing the burning pain in her heart but stoking an even greater fire.

Narmada had decided to walk out of his house, carrying with her only two suitcases, years of memories – and her self-respect.

'Thanks for everything, Ravi. That was my parting gift to you,' she said as he sobbed, looking at him straight in the eye. It was that look. She barely moved. It seemed she barely breathed...

That afternoon was now many years old but Ravi Pandey had not been able to shake off memories of it either. Narmada had left him, and had come back only after a week, when Ravi went to her parents' house, broke down and apologized. Neel had said the most heartbreaking things about not being able to see his parents fight. That afternoon had had a searing impact on Ravi and it had made him think hard about himself. Over the years, though his temper occasionally flared, he had tried to make himself less hurtful.

Narmada had forgiven him long ago.

And it scared him to think that this time she might not.

©

Night fell. In another neighbourhood not far away, a young woman kept glancing nervously at the clock as she packed some clothes, CDs, and books into a small suitcase. Last of all, she put in a family picture. Every three minutes, she walked to the first floor window and looked down at the empty driveway. Her parents were not home yet. She had been under a sort of undeclared house arrest for days. Today was the first day that her parents had slackened their grip, leaving her alone at home while they went for a wedding.

The woman quickly dialled a number. The woman at the other end had been expecting the call, and picked it up on the first ring

'I have packed. I am leaving now,' the woman in the room whispered.

'Are you sure about this?' the other woman whispered back.

'Yes, I am. I love you.'

'I love you too. Come quickly.'

The woman in the room locked her suitcase, looked at herself in the mirror to check if she was looking all right, and wrote a note with a thumping heart.

Dear Mummy and Papa,

I love you. I am sorry I am having to do this. I will be back when you accept me as I am. I will never be far from you. Please take care of yourself.

Meenal

With that, she walked out.

Meenal Sharma had left the building.

Rock in the Dock

For several months now, the main door to Rocky's two-storey office had been shut with a huge padlock covered in sticky red wax and sealed with a government seal to make sure no one attempted to mess with it. The narrow lane edged with a smelly open drain that lay in front of the building was empty. Only confused goats, foul-smelling chickens and lost children wandered through the street which ran along the back doors of the lower-middle-class quarters. Every few days a police constable in khaki with a long bamboo truncheon walked up to the door from the nearest police station, holding his nose with one hand and the bamboo stick with the other. His job was to ensure that everything was all right, that the house was still sealed, that the wax-coated padlock was still in place, and that no suspicious men were found loitering about. Then the policeman went back to his table and included his observations in his long weekly report to the Station House Officer, the top man in the police station — who was so senior that he had been given a mobile phone by the government.

Sometimes the constable got imaginative and added some colourful details in his report, which should, ideally for government documents and as per government regulations, have been boring, circumlocutory and impossible to understand. He described the vegetable vendor at the opening of the street and his activities; the women peeping from rooftops; the garbage collector who, it seemed to him, lurked suspiciously about and the ragged scrap-selling children. Soon, however, he got lazy and did not always come to inspect the sealed house. On such days he merely took the previous report, changed the date with eraser fluid and gave it to his boss.

Today was one such day. So it was just the right day, and the right hour, for a phone call to be made by Rocky's mole (yes, the cop's hunch was absolutely correct, it was the garbage boy!). Within fifteen minutes, an old stolen car and a noisy, smoke-belching motorcycle screeched to a halt outside the door. Rocky had come prepared with the mild-mannered local locksmith who added to his meagre income by moonlighting as a petty thief. But, one must add, there was nothing petty about his craft. His skills were legendary and his only tool was a six-inch-long aluminium pin. He scraped off the wax from the padlock and assessed it with nimble fingers like a doctor palpating an infected appendix. Then he began twirling the aluminium pin with the grace and poise of an orchestra conductor. In his other pocket, the thief — sorry, the maestro — carried a fake government seal and a small glass bottle of molten wax. When they left the building, he would heat the wax with his cigarette lighter and smear it on the padlock to seal it back again. That way there would be no proof that anyone had come here and taken anything.

Voila! The lock opened in ten seconds flat. Rocky Randhawa, the visa conman, and his assistant, the little runt with the extraordinary voice, had come to their office for the first time after the police had raided and sealed it. (In darkly brooding moments of doubt, The Voice had even seriously considered abandoning his boss and going back to one of his former businesses — frankly, a far more lucrative option right now - i.e. standing near the exit door in Delhi Transport Corporation buses and picking the pockets of exiting passengers by slitting them with a tiny razor.)

It was a sombre moment. A moment of reflection and introspection.

The two brothers-in-arms, tied together by a deep bond of lawbreaking dreams and instant-money-making ambitions, had come to an important crossroads in their life, and they would have to make a tough choice about which way they went from here. Their office had been shut down, their loans were mounting, and their monthly income, which earlier ran into lakhs of rupees every quarter, had dried up like roadside public taps in the summer. After their release, they had tried to work out of their homes, but who could possibly dream about an American or British visa, sitting in a one-room flat, in a congested, filthy neighbourhood? It was like promising pearls from the swirly depths of an ocean while squatting in the middle of a puddle.

The only clients they got were poor tailors and poor carpenters and poor masons who wanted to break free from the endless squalor of their lives and fly away to the oil-rich Gulf states — to work as rich tailors and rich carpenters and rich masons. Or, there were murderers and robbers, rapists and swindlers who had set out to become politicians but ended up in the wrong political party and, therefore, on the wrong side of the law. These were people who didn't mind coming for a business talk in the dead of night, or sitting on rickety chairs, or being offered no more than tepid tap water. They were desperate to go abroad; they were willing to sacrifice a bit. But the trouble was, because of the uncertain nature of their careers, Rocky and his assistant rarely got to hear from them again. Most ended up at Rocky's previous address: *Tihar Central Prison, Jail Road, Hari Nagar (New Delhi)* — before the second sitting.

Things were bad — really, really bad. The worst blow had come when the city's most notorious men — its black market moneylenders who worked like slimy toads somewhere in the seamy underbelly of the city – had refused credit to Rocky. It was as if the world's best credit rating agencies had suddenly given a C-minus-minus rating to a rich nation. That was it – it was the worst thing that could happen to a crook who had fallen on bad days. The refusal of black money credit marked the lowest one could fall and it was factored into everything – business deals, birthday invitations, bar brawls and contract-killing negotiations. In the bustling stock market of crime, Rocky's share had nosedived.

Not that there was much stock to take, they realized within minutes. Rocky's once plush office was empty – there were no chairs, no tables, no sitars, no carpets, no picture frames, no water coolers. 'Where is my stuff? Who stole my office?' Rocky said in a loud, hysterical whisper.

'Who took our stuff?' The Voice echoed looking abjectly at his boss with baffled puppy eyes. 'I am feeling very emotional, Boss-ji. I think I want to cry,' he mumbled and slumped against a stripped-bare wall, once adorned with a beautiful picture of the Statue of Liberty and large digitally-altered pictures of Rocky with diplomats from different countries. The sense of loss was so deep, the two men felt like sitting down and beating the floor with their hands. The sadness was deeper than Rocky had felt at any funeral, or after any gambling defeat, or the loss of any customer.

'I know who did it!' a confident voice boomed suddenly.

Rocky and The Voice turned around, expecting a fourth man who had suddenly crept up the stairs. But it was only the locksmith, who had suddenly discovered a deep warrior-like voice because he had something important to say. He had, as journalists would say, a scoop.

'First, what's with that voice?' Rocky Randhawa said. 'And second, so who did it?'

'The police,' the locksmith was convinced.

'The police? Why? But why? Will my chairs and tables be counted as evidence?' Rocky bellowed. There was something erupting inside him.

'Head Constable Paramjit Singh Arora's daughter was getting married. So he told the other men that he needed to furnish his home for the guests, and that they would bring it back later.'

'What? Well, at least it will all be back,' Rocky said, confused whether to be glad or sad.

'No.'

'Why?'

'He liked the quality. He gave it all away as his daughter's dowry.'

'*What?*'

'Yes. And the groom's parents were very surprised to find a lot of office stationery and office furniture in the dowry, but they took it to mean that the bride's family was very well educated. They are happy. They sold it to scrap dealers and made some money.'

'They sold everything? Even my revolving chair?'

'Yes.'

'And the cracked almirah?'

'Yes. But cheap.'

'And my favourite teak cabinet?'

'No, that they kept. Good stuff.'

'I thought giving or taking dowry was illegal?' Rocky said, rhetorically, not expecting an answer. 'And there were about a hundred and ninety chairs in this building, and so many tables, and much else. That bloody constable gave it all away in dowry?'

'No, the police people only took away eighty or so,' the locksmith said.

'See? There is some honesty still left in the police force. Very good. *So where is the rest of my damn stuff?*'

'Someone in the police force called up Babban.'

'Babban? That skinny little rat ? Babban, who used to serve tea in my office?' Rocky asked. He was becoming hysterical. It was not tears now, but a heart attack that seemed to loom in the distance.

'Yes, the same Babban. He says you are his inspiration.'

Rocky's chest puffed up automatically, like the flotation device that the air hostesses promise will open on its own in case of an emergency. 'Well ... I did try to encourage him as much as I could. So what does he do now?' Rocky asked like a defeated general, savouring a small moment of pride in the middle of a rout.

'He is a thief.'

'Huh?'

'He has one of the biggest gang of thieves in Pandavnagar and this building comes under his terrain. The other gangs respect this,' the locksmith said.

'So, when someone in the police tipped him, Babban ... you mean to say *my* Babban, then —' the grieving Rocky could barely complete his sentence.

'— Then Babban brought a jeepload of men and a truck one day, and they took away everything except the stools. They said they didn't like the stools,' the locksmith said.

'The little bastard! Bastard! I taught him everything, I gave him his bread and butter, and ...'

The Voice looked at the stools. He took to heart the fact that the stools had been discarded by the thieves because they were not considered any good. He had personally chosen them after a four-hour recce in Karol Bagh market. 'They are nice stools. I wonder why they didn't like them, Boss. This is pure teak, for god's sake. They must be illiterate not to realize its value,' he said morosely. *Khote de puttar*. Sons of donkeys.

Rocky ignored him. He sat down on one of the prized Karol Bagh stools with a deep sigh. Like a betrayed father stabbed in the back by his own greedy son. The stool had a loose nail. One leg of the stool had, in any case, been planning for a long time to come off, and it chose this sacred moment to do so. The stool disintegrated with a loud noise, and Rocky went crashing onto the floor, creating an even louder one. Because Guru Nanak Dev Ji was looking out for Rocky, his bones were saved. But because Guru Nanak Dev Ji had chosen to end his jurisdiction just where the inner seam of his trousers began, Rocky found himself sprawled in the centre of the room, with a huge hole ripped in his pants in the region of his posterior.

Rocky did not want to make a spectacle of himself before his men. He put his right hand over his, you know, his behind; acted as if nothing had happened, and carried on the conversation with a straight face and a mooning bottom. Despite the backstabbers that surrounded him, despite the massive setbacks that had crushed his life under a sort of elephant of problems, Rocky was not one to lose heart. He was a valiant from the great land of the Punjab, where the word 'problem' was not permitted a place in the Punjabi dictionary. He turned to The Voice. 'We have lost everything we had,' he said stoically. 'We will have to think of something if we do not want to end up taking the next Punjab Mail and going back to Jalandhar and working on the farm.'

'Shall I go to the railway office to check if the Punjab Mail goes to Jalandhar, Boss-ji?'

Patience was the chief virtue of the great, and Rocky ignored his assistant's idiocy yet again. 'Go to the secret location and see if our records are still there,' Rocky said. 'The time has come to revive our old contacts. We have to play some big, big game.'

The secret hideaway was actually the toilet on the second floor, where Rocky, in a moment of genius, had built a secret cupboard in which he had placed a complete list of his most valuable contacts. This was a sort of concealed, ceramic-covered compartment built on top of the cistern. Despite the marauding double invasion from both the police and Babban the Bandit, the treasure trove of Rocky Randhawa's little empire was untouched. There was still hope. The Phoenix would rise from the ashes.

The Voice opened it and took out five big plastic bags full of visiting cards, pictures, letters and other papers. Then he went downstairs and upturned the contents in front of Rocky.

Lying before the three gentlemen was a lifetime of names and numbers of people they had met and dealt with. There were hundreds of business cards, torn pages from notebooks, photographs, picture postcards, and even some numbers hastily written on stolen restaurant napkins. When a man's got to give his number to his friend at the dinner table, he's got to do it, you see, even if it involves lifting the dainty white skirt of the lady at the next table and scribbling on it.

Rocky went down on his haunches, suddenly overcome by a curious mix of emotions − a deep melancholy, a poet's romantic longing, an embarrassing homesickness, and a sharp pain in his cellulite-solid, rarely-exercised legs. He sifted through the papers and finally picked up one card.

'My boy, I think our troubles will soon end,' Rocky said.

'Yes, Boss,' The Voice bleated.

'Bring me my cell phone.'

'Sorry, Boss-ji, you sold it two hours ago to pay this month's phone bill,' The Voice said.

'Ah,' Rocky sighed. 'Don't worry, those days will soon be gone. I think our day has come, my boy. Let us go to the phone booth.'

'Where do you want to call, Boss-ji?'

'America. I will call my old friend Matthias Baldenburp. He had asked me to call him anytime I wanted. And this is that time.'

℀

Matthias Baldenburp and wisdom shared a turbulent past. They had never stayed together in a room long enough to get acquainted. Matt had visited India years ago as a backpacker, and on an evening when he was particularly distraught, he had run into Rocky Randhawa in New Delhi. They had met at a local coffee shop and Rocky quickly made friends with him, using his newly-acquired knowledge of broken English. Matt was in trouble. He had just returned from a once-in-a-lifetime whitewater rafting trip with some hippies in the remote Kashmir Himalayas, where he had gone tumbling down the frothy Zanskar River beyond the Kargil region to experience the thrill of his life. Unfortunately, and due, equally, to his inherent stupidity, Matt had gone tumbling in the aforementioned frothy waters of the Zanskar because he was constantly rubbing his bald head with his right hand instead of holding the bloody oar. He had been saved by the police, but put instantly in prison after drugs were discovered in the bags of the group. He was produced before a local judge and was granted bail, and Matt had taken the first bus from Ladakh to Kargil and Srinagar and then a bumpy flight to come to New Delhi, all to escape punishment for a crime which he, god promise, had not committed.

Still, as he was technically running from the law and jumping bail his passport had been impounded by the grouchy judge back in Kashmir. Just when it seemed that Matt was about to become a fugitive, or be arrested, or be tried for drug peddling or worse, the God of Passports manipulated things in such a way that Matt ran into Rocky. Now good old Rocky had become sort of an expert in his trade by this time. Being the quick learner that he was, he made Matt a new homemade U.S. passport and stamped it with a brand new, unsoiled Indian visa.

Unknown to Rocky, Matt had since crossed over to the other side of the law. He was a police sergeant in, you guessed it, Upper Plymouth village in Upper Plymouth county, a suburb of New York.

C

Hi Angela,

Sorry I couldn't mail you for a week. I was away holidaying on the West Coast with some guys. We drove all the way – it was the best time of my life! I was thinking of you ... I wanted to talk to you, but on the day when I was about to call you, the guys pulled me away to watch the game at a friend's ... I just lived like a caveman and didn't shave for days ... How's Juanita?

Neil

Hi Neil,

That's fine. The Yankees scored over me, I guess.

And what's with the caveman stuff? I know men think it makes them look sexy. But god help me I prefer my men shaven.

Juanita is doing well. Her mother has responded dramatically to the Ayurveda treatment. Agony begins now.

Angela

PS: I was also watching the game!

Angela, my sweet:

Heyy, hang in there. You can go and see her any time. I'm sure her mom and she think of you as extended family now. So this is for the best.

Regarding the shave, I wish I had a girlfriend to tell me how she preferred me. Single and intending to mingle right now. Though even if she was there, I still wouldn't have shaved on a Sunday. A man's got to stand up for his rights sometimes, you know...

What about you? Do you have a hunky male model in your life?

N

Hey N,

No males. Just emails.

Forever online,

A

THE STATUTE OF LIBERTY

Ravi Pandey had been sharing the same bed with his wife since the day of their big showdown, but it would be quite safe to say that, mentally, he had been spending the night on the couch.

Narmada had been civil to him, passing him the pickle at the dining table, giving him the sports page when she was reading the newspaper, and bringing him his ironed shirt when he was getting late to work. But she had made little attempt otherwise to make any conversation. She stirred her tea and listened to his harangue against office when he came back from work, but never offered any comment. She brought sweet prasad from the temple and put it in the stretched palms of her son and the maid, but asked Neel to give it to the waiting Ravi. She hummed songs from old Hindi films in the kitchen, but stopped when Ravi passed by. She stopped talking about the things Ravi loved to hear her talk about most – the saris she liked, their son's job, and their shared dream of a lovely Indian girl as their daughter-in-law.

Narmada's love had always been unconditional; free-flowing like the river that she had been named after. Ravi's love was like the rocks that the river flowed through – jagged with his ego and taking for granted the shimmering waters that went past every day. It wasn't as if Ravi had been unmoved by the events that had happened that day and since. He had not been able to apologize to his wife because every time he wanted to and every time his heart made him step towards Narmada, his ego came in the way. When he tried to smile at her, she just lowered her eyes and walked away. She had begun reading the *Bhagwadgita* more than she ever had before. Reading it brought peace to her agitated mind. Like dousing her head with a mug of cool water in the middle of a scorching afternoon. Standing in the midst of a deadly battle that had killed tens of thousands, Arjun had said something that was so true of love, of relationships and of the bond that Narmada shared with her husband:

Na chaitvighnah kataranno gareeyo
Yadwa jayem yadi va no jayeyuh ...

(We don't even know what is better for us,
Winning them over; or their winning over us.)

She was reading the *Bhagwadgita* one day when the bell rang. Ravi was home early. He had started looking very tired and overworked after his promotion. Today, too, he'd had a rough day at office because Republic Day was approaching and there were a lot of VIP requests for passes and invitations to process. But more than the physical work, Ravi was crushed by the mental load he was carrying on his mind. He could not remember the last time he had seen his wife smile. The guilt, the silence, and the distance between him and his wife deeply disturbed him.

'I'll make tea,' Narmada mumbled, walking towards the kitchen.

Ravi loosened his tie and walked behind her. He stood leaning against the kitchen door, fixing Narmada with a helpless look as she measured out one-and-a-half cups of water. Narmada could feel his gaze on her back; it was disconcerting. But she worked on, silently picking up the container of tea leaves and the sugar.

'Narmada?' Ravi finally said.

'Hmm?'

She picked up a stump of ginger from the vegetable basket, washed it under the tap and began grating it. Everybody in the family loved ginger tea.

'Will you please look at me for a second?' he pleaded.

Narmada collected the ginger, put it into the boiling water, and turned around as it simmered. She folded her arms and looked him straight in the eye. 'Fine.'

But Ravi's eyes could not meet hers. He looked at an aluminium pot in the corner of the kitchen. 'I don't know what comes over me sometimes. Can you ... forgive me? I will never be like that again. I will try, honestly.'

That was all that this silly woman wanted to hear her husband say. She smiled weakly, and with relief. She also wanted a gracious end to the days and days of sullen moping that she had begun.

'I forgive you, Ravi ... let's go have tea,' she said as she handed him his cup, deliberately letting her fingers brush against his hand.

'And will you give me that massage again, please? It was magic,' her husband said, holding her close.

☾

Hi Angela,

Been wondering what you look like....Since we don't look like meeting anytime soon, why don't you describe yourself to me ...

Neil

Neil:

Be nice to me and I shall send you my picture soon.

Also ... you said the other day that there was something about you that I don't know, and that it kept you from opening up to me. What's the hitch?

Are you married?
Are you gay?
Are you a woman?
Angela

Hey A,

None of the above. I am quite single, quite straight, and quite male. Actually, quintessentially male, if you know what I mean.

Thinking about you,
N

Yo,

I am quite relieved to hear that. I don't want a woman to have a crush on me. My ultra-conservative dad would flip.

Have another small recital for the band tomorrow. The cash flow is as meagre but the music improves everyday. I think longing for something adds depth to their emotions... wish you could hear them...

Angela

Yo back,

Hope all goes well.

By the time you return, you will find a thousand mails in your inbox.

Wish I was there too.

Love,
Neil

C

If there hadn't been a turbaned Sikh in the group, you could have mistaken it for a Gestapo meeting.

In a small, dimly lit room filled with slow moving shadows and silent whispers, an inscrutable Rocky Randhawa sat at the head of a derelict wooden table. A skinny boy in a torn brown shirt holding a large kettle and a tall column of piled-up glasses from the shop across the road placed a glassful of tea before each delegate. Then he cleared his throat, waiting to be paid. No one reached for his wallet. After standing about for a while the boy slunk out, realizing that this was one of those influential groups of customers who drank now and paid later.

The Voice sat motionless for a change, embedded at his boss's side but safely out of reach of Rocky's freewheeling whack. The boss had called a meeting of his trusted lieutenants for a crucial strategy session. Rocky had a Plan that would catapult him from the cluster of small-town wheeler-dealers to the league of far bigger players who operated across borders, smoked cigars and stayed in five-star hotels. There was a little problem, though. Rocky's personal intellectual capital matched the finest in the business, but his manpower comprised the scum of the city.

None of his rag-tag bunch of goons could utter even a few straight sentences in any language. They swaggered, they chewed paan leaves and spat out generous amounts of reddened drool where they stood; they stared down women's breasts and winked at teenaged girls and old women; every sentence they spoke was embellished with abusive incestuous accusations regarding sisters and mothers. In short, not the kind of people Rocky would like to take along for a swish business meet at the Taj Mahal Hotel. What these men had were rippling muscles and a bravado that could send business rivals scurrying into their wives' laps. But at this stage of his career, Rocky did not need lap-snatchers. He needed business executives. Who could speak in English and floor visa officers and scamsters in America with glib talk about India.

'So ji what is the plan, Boss?' said The Voice.

Rocky began his speech, determined to sound optimistic and making no mention of the great human resource issue looming before him. He cleared his throat. 'As you know, boys, we have reached a difficult stage in our business. We have had our office raided, we have lost our money, we have been robbed by our enemies and betrayed by our friends. It is a situation that no one would ever wish even on one's enemy.'

'I would,' quipped The Voice. Rocky ignored him.

'Now we must think of some good ideas to make money with guaranteed returns,' he said.

The harebrained gathering piped up:

'We can kidnap the food minister's son. He is very rich,' a gruff voice spoke up.

'The food minister was earlier the area head of the Billa gang. He will kidnap all our children and then take ransom from us in return,' a caustic voice to the left retorted. It gives one so much pleasure to give the boot to a good idea.

'We can become pimps for male prostitutes. That sort of thing is also becoming quite common now, Boss-ji,' said a poker-faced bully.

'Irfan's gang is already into that. Irfan himself tests all the men first,' the same voice on the left interrupted.

'We can sell kidneys.'

'Who eats kidneys?'

'Not for eating, you donkey, but taking them from poor people for 10,000 rupees and selling them to rich, kidney-less people for five lakhs! Simple!'

That's where Rocky, who had been hearing all this in silence, drew the line.

'Enough, you owls!' he shouted. 'First, I will never get into any business which involves cutting people up, either to get their kidneys or to take out their hearts. We will not hurt people like that.'

(That was one of the reasons, admittedly. It was true that Rocky did not want to stoop so low. But another important reason was that he could not stand the sight of blood. He had fainted at the sight of the first slippery frog he had been required to cut in his biology class in school. He was carried out of the classroom right behind the frog, and both were kicked out of the course. Of course none of this would make it to the minutes of this important meeting.)

'Secondly,' Rocky said, 'you morons can just not think big. You will always remain small-time chain snatchers and pickpockets and fake beggars. I am fed up of these small small games. I am going to play big this time,' he said, picking up the bag retrieved from the secret location the other day. 'I have been in touch with a friend in America. He is a very powerful person and has agreed to help us out in the next big Plan. He has even given me a few ideas, though they are not as brilliant as mine,' Rocky said, laying out Matt's letter on the table.

The Voice tried to pick up and read the letter. This earned him a rap on the knuckles. 'I wrote back to him, and we have now decided the exact Plan. There is a very big chess tournament in New York in six or seven weeks. The World Youth Chess Olympiad. There will be teams from many parts of the world. But there is no entry from India.'

'Why?' someone asked.

'Because they do not have a sponsor,' Rocky explained exasperatedly.

'What's a sponsor?'

'Someone who pays so that you can have fun.'

'Oh, wow! I would like a sponsor for myself.'

'So what does all this have to do with us? Do you want to play and become the champion and make a lot of money, Boss-ji? But there is no entry from India, and you can't even play.'

'There is going to be a team from India.'

'Really? Whose?'

'Rocky Randhawa's,' Rocky said.

'*What?*' his cronies chorused.

'You people will bring in customers who want to go to America. You will get 25 per cent commission. Since we are talking about America, the rates will be much higher. So we charge about twenty lakhs each. Then we take them as members of the chess team. When we reach there, they will play a game for the record, and then become part of the Great American People before anyone knows what's happening! Even if the police people come to know of this, my contact, who is a very senior officer in the police force there, will tip us off. Simple.'

'Then?' The Voice asked in an excited whisper.

'*Then* we will come back as respectable citizens. *Then* we will go back for next year's tournament. *Then* the rate will be 40 lakhs per player.'

A stunned silence fell over the delegates. They had never heard a better Plan. They had never imagined so much money.

The Voice gave action to his feelings. He rose to his feet and kissed Rocky's hand. 'Boss, this is a VIP idea! This is a super idea! This is a Monday Jackpot idea. This is more super than any idea you have ever had before,' The Voice rambled on idiotically, his voice trembling with emotion.

'So you all like the idea. Good,' Rocky said. 'But there is a problem. You see, to look like a chess team, we have to have some person who can wear a suit-voot and pant-shant. Who can shake hands with the foreigners without trembling. One who can eat their food with a chhuri-kaanta — what do you call it? A knife and fork. We need someone who can speak in English...'

Four hands went up. 'Myself speaking English,' each one of them said.

'You sons of donkeys, there are more words in the English language than "thank you" and "mention not". You are not going to America. Your only job is to get me customers, OK?'

Rocky fumed. 'Tell me, what happened to the English teacher we had hired for the visa interviews? We can take him.'

'He resigned,' The Voice said.

'Why?'

'He said he wanted to study more.'

'Why?'

'Because he failed the exam in college.'

'What exam?'

'English.'

The Voice cautiously moved a few steps away from his boss's seat, out of the range of his ruthless hitting arm, and then spoke, 'Boss-ji, I have an idea,' he said.

'Save it,' Rocky said.

The Voice continued, nevertheless. 'Why don't we call that man who came to us ... he looked like a suited-booted gentleman...'

'Who?'

'The one I had trapped at Mandi House?'

'Who?'

'Neel Pandey.'

SWEET LIES AND PHONEY LOVES

Hey Angela:

Thanks for calling. I have a separate extension now – 34294 – so you can call me directly without going through the board.

By the way, is that your real laugh? Because it reminds me of butterflies fluttering in a dreamy garden on a summer evening ... Your voice paints a picture of a calm, placid lake where birds are flying ... Your words remind me of the whisper of a fairy in my ear on a dew-soaked morning. Your words are like the gentle murmur of a mountain spring, like the uninhibited flight of the gazelle, like a rabbit gazing into the eye of the rainbow ...

Neil

PS: I stole all of that poetic stuff from the Internet. Does your boyfriend ever say anything like that to you?

Hey,

Never.

How far do you live?

Me

Next door if you close your eyes and think of me ... but three light years away if you count the train and walking time ...

I am going through some rough stuff at work ... our work is being evaluated and we are being trained for a new client ... need to focus if I want to keep my job and become a team leader by next year. Plus there are some problems of my own that I am carrying around with me.

God, I really really want to meet you, and I think we should when I am through with all this …

N

I understand. Another time.

You said you are having some problems. All well? Need a shoulder to cry on?

A

Hey Angela:

I certainly like the idea of your shoulder (!). In fact, I like the idea of all of you. With me. By my side. All the time. And we will meet someday, I promise. I'm a great believer in destiny. In life's crazy coincidences and cosmic set-ups... So if we are not able to meet for some time, there must be a reason for that as well,

until then,

N

C

It had been several months since Neel and Angela had started their virtual flirtation. Angela had an image of Neil in her mind — a sensitive face with a prominent jawline, black hair, full sensuous lips and soft brown eyes — a guy whom you could actually take to meet your parents; as well as pin down on the couch! He seemed like a nice fella. He loved the small things, he treasured the tiny moments, and understood her need for Juanita in a way her other friends could not. He wrote to her about his vacations with his grandparents on a farm, cultivating mushrooms and laying awake all night watching the stars and listening to the sounds of the night. He told her how he loved country music and how he would stare outside the window as raindrops washed up against the glass and the cars became a blur of metal and light, giving a feeling of living out a tiny moment of peace even as dizzy life passed them by...

She spoke to him of her life, her childhood, the prejudices she was surrounded by in her growing-up years, her first crush, how she tried smoking the first time and hated it, and all those things she would never have imagined sharing with a man she had never met. She told him of her dreams, of how she sang in the bathroom all the time, how she loved her father but could never understand his ways. She told him she wanted to learn the salsa. Did he? Of course what she really wanted to know was whether he would hold her close as they danced the night away ...

They began talking for long hours on the phone. Neel told her he could not talk freely at home because of his roommate, so he would mail her when he was at work, and that he would call her after his shift was over. They always avoided geographical references in their descriptions. Where in Upper Plymouth was her modelling school? Where was his grandparents' farm ? Where was the sky in his story? It was all incidental. Sometimes they made up entire stories, but then felt guilty and didn't write to each other for days. But then he couldn't resist, and she couldn't either, and they would begin writing again.

It was as if both Angela and Neel held a mirror before themselves and talked to their own reflections. When they spoke to each other they were actually articulating their own fears and nurturing their own fantasies and living out a world that sparkled when they described it. Nothing else mattered. Not even the fact that they so often had to put aside the truth when they exchanged confidences. They were conjuring two fake personas when they talked. Ironically, the love of these fake people was true.

She adored his voice, the simple way he put things, his sense of humour and his down-to-earth romantic ways.

And he adored simply everything about her.

Neel was deeply drawn to this woman across the Pacific who seemed so much like him – but there was no way he could tell her the truth about himself. No way he could tell her he was an Indian working in a call centre with a fake name and a phoney accent, pretending to be from Manhattan. No way he could break away either; because he was captivated in a way he had never been before.

Neel didn't know what to do. He had assumed a dual identity, and he had started inhabiting the skin of his workplace identity more than his true self. Neel Pandey was slowly beginning to feel more and more like Neil Patterson. He knew that he was getting sucked into a Bermuda Triangle of emotions, where he could only hurt Angela. But he could do nothing to stop it. He was helpless. He was so scared to lose Angela that he fell deeper and deeper – into his own trap, and into love.

That night, Neel logged on to the Internet and sent Angela an email.

I am sending you my picture. I am not half as nice looking as you – you are a model, after all! – but here I am, warts and all.

Neil

©

When Angela opened her mail the next morning her heart skipped a beat. It was as if they were meeting face to face for the first time. She clicked on the link and the attachment began to download. It took a while – long enough for her to imagine a hundred faces, some dreadful, some charming, some naughty, some ugly, some flirtatious ... but all with a lovable smile on their faces, all of them unrefusable if they came with the soul of Neil Patterson. She downloaded the picture.

What a pity, he was not ugly at all.

The picture of a handsome white male slowly assembled on her computer screen. Neil Patterson was before her. He looked out of the picture with an arrogant smile on his face, an arrogance that many women would find alluring. Angela didn't quite like it at first, but she reminded herself that it was the arrogance of Jane Austen's Mr Darcy. One would be misled by this arrogance in the beginning, but in the end he would turn out to have a heart of gold.

She wrote back impulsively:

Hey:

Let's meet. I am not sending you my picture, so that I can recognize you and you can't recognize me … That way I will feel in control! I would not want you to think I'm throwing myself at you...Since tomorrow is Sunday and your day off at work, you have no excuse and I will not take any. I will meet you at Lil' Jo's, on the 38th and 5th at 6:30 tomorrow evening.

Oh, and there's something about myself that I have to tell you when we meet!

Me

C

Neel sat in zapped silence before his computer. Angela had ordered him to meet her. Oh, what a beautiful mess.

Neel took a deep breath and had some water. Young men and women were buzzing around him. Phones rang. The room buzzed with fake accents. In a corner, a team leader was having coffee and flirting with a sexy new trainee. Neel was finally being forced to confront the question that he had been scared of all along: why did he have to lie to Angela? Well, in the beginning, he had to because call centre employees are not supposed to reveal their location. But, later, when he became Angela's friend, why didn't he tell her then? Neel had deceived a woman who had fallen in love with him without even seeing his face.

Neel raced down the hall to a small room on the rear side, where a black phone on the conference table with international dialling was his only hope. He needed to tell Angela who he was, and why he had lied to her, and most importantly, that he truly loved her despite not being truthful. The room was closed. He walked across to his manager, a friend, and explained to him that he urgently needed to make a call to the U.S., it was an emergency. It was an unofficial favour he was seeking; no one except top managers were allowed to use this line. Six minutes later, the room was opened.

Neel had Angela's home number in his wallet. He closed the door behind him and dialled, his palms sweating. He heard Angela's voice, and his heart nearly stopped.

It was the answering machine.

'Angela ... it's Neil ... This is an emergency ... please take the phone if you are still there ... I want to talk to you urgently ... I won't be able to make it this evening ... O god ... Angela please pick up ... Please don't go to Manhattan, you won't find me there ... I am far away ... so far away...'

Big Apple Hang Up

On a busy Saturday evening, the train pulled into Grand Central at 5:15 p.m., and Angela Cruz stepped out, a bit nervous, a bit shy and more than a bit happy. She was finally going to meet her mysterious lover. Two days ago, Juanita's mother, looking frail but happy, had come to collect her daughter. The mother and daughter were so delighted to be going home together that Angela could say nothing. Her house was empty again, she missed Juanita terribly and Angela needed Neil more than ever.

Angela wore a sleeveless cream silk shirt and black trousers. She had gone the previous evening and shopped for the right perfume, the one that the shop-girl assured her would make men follow her like dogs. She didn't want a lot of that happening, so she bought a small bottle. She would have men following her like puppies.

The station was crowded. She walked from her platform to the sprawling, brightly-lit main hall that she always found fascinating and stood for a while by the ticket windows in the centre, pretending to look for a timetable, but actually just standing there and soaking in the crowds milling about. She had deliberately come early for her 6:30 appointment. She would first meet the city, she thought. Then she would meet the man who was her closest friend in the whole world.

Angela loved New York. But she didn't have many friends here. In a way, that was good, because when she came in from the suburbs, she didn't have to spend her time watching some boring film with a girlfriend or lending her a shoulder to cry on as she shed copious tears over a lover who had just walked out on her.

Angela joined the throngs walking on the streets. A bearded Asian taxi driver slowed down and looked at her expectantly. She smiled and shook her head. He smiled back and gave her a 'have a nice day anyway' thumbs up. A well-mannered New York cabbie? It was a sign, Angela told herself.

Angela cautioned herself to walk slowly. She was probably walking too fast. The chatter in her head was getting louder. Slow down, woman, slow down. He won't be there yet. There is still a half hour to go, and he will probably be late anyway. What will he wear? What if he's a terrible dresser ? Nah. He is not a geek. What if he is married? What if he is gay? What if he is a spy set on me by Dad to test me? What if he burps? What if he is a slob? What if he is already there, waiting for me, looking at his watch repeatedly, about to go home to eat, belch, sleep and snore?

'Hey, there, Jo!'

'Hello, Angela, how are you? Long time ... Sorry your favourite seat is occupied, it'll just take a few minutes, the customer is just paying his bill.'

'No problem, I'll wait ... Sweet of you to remember.'

Is he here? Look around. Who's that man over there? Naah, he has a round face. Or that man with his back towards me? Oh shoot, that's a woman ... Darn ... maybe he is in the loo ... Does he have good loo manners?

'Who can forget you, Angela? Your beautiful smile is your ambassador!' The old rascal Jiang Guangmei used the same line on every female customer who came to Lil' Jo's diner which he'd started thirty years ago after migrating from China. Since Americans have difficulty pronouncing names easily pronounced in the rest of the world, Jiang Guangmei had changed his to Jo. 'Are you alone or are you expecting friends?'

'Um ... just one more person, Jo.'

'All right. Would you like to have something while you wait?'

The bathroom door opened. Angela looked up, with a ready smile on her face. It was a charming woman in her forties. Angela suddenly felt quite stupid. 'Shoot ...'

'Anything wrong, Angela?'

'What? Oh, no, nothing, Jo, just remembered something I forgot at home. I think I'll have a coffee while I wait.'

It was a beautiful evening. Angela looked out of the window as she sipped her coffee and gazed across the road. She always noticed the children first. Some ran down the pavement, their exasperated parents telling them not to. Some walked obediently, like disciplined soldiers walking obediently alongside their colonel. A double-decker bus full of gawking sightseers drove by, with a group of foreign tourists with baseball caps and Statue of Liberty hats laughing and waving to no one in particular.

'Some more coffee, Angela?' Joe asked.

'Um ... in a bit, Jo.'

'Your friend's delayed?'

'Yes ... he must be caught in traffic ...'

❦

Hi Angela:

I don't know where to begin, because I am scared where this will end.

I am at work, but I can't think straight because I can think of nothing but you. I have just been severely reprimanded by my boss.

He said the kind of mistakes I am making today could cost me my job. I don't care. All of that is insignificant in the face of what I could lose if I lose you. When you reach the end of this mail, you might wonder why we met at all – if not physically, at least in the mind ... you will wonder why I came into your life and turned it upside down ... It's hard to explain to you how I am feeling right now – so horrible, and guilty, and desperate.

As I write this, I know that you are in Manhattan, waiting for me. But I won't be there. When you read this mail, you will probably already hate me but I just want you to hear me out.

I have often written to you that there is something about me that you don't know. I want to tell you today what that is because I have resisted telling you the truth for a long time.

I won't be at the coffee shop because I don't live in New York. Or in America. I live far, far away ... in India, in New Delhi. My name is Neel Pandey. I am a middle-class guy who had finished college and was looking for a job. I love America, I wanted to go to America and live there. I even applied for a visa, but it was rejected. So I joined a call centre. We have lots of them coming up in India these days, and all the calls that Americans make to numbers in the U.S. for their computer problems, and phone bills, and their tax returns, are routed to these call centres. I joined one and I was taught, like all of my other colleagues, to speak with a phoney American accent and affect a phoney American way of life – I was even given a fake name.

So Neel Pandey became Neil Patterson.

Then you called me one day, and we became friends. The more I talked to you, the more I realized that you were special, so right for me. I was scared that you would reject me if I told you the truth. I got pulled deeper and deeper into a friendship, which turned into love. I think of you all day. I admit I told you stories that were fake, but only to the extent that they did not happen in America, but in India. Yes, I do have a neighbour who hates me. Yes, I used to have a roommate in the hostel who was all the things I told you he was. And my father is a difficult person, he is hung up on marrying me to a high-caste Brahmin girl ... I was desperate to remain in my make-believe world, because it was a virtual world that I had created for myself to escape reality. I began to believe that this make-believe world was real, and that I was indeed Neil Patterson, and that I live in New York. And that you loved me...

Whatever you think about me, please know that I love you, and I will always love you from the depths of my black heart. I swear I have loved no one like I have loved you. It's strange that my feelings for you are so deep – because we have never even met, but what the heck, people fall in love chatting on the Net these days, at least I have your voice to cling to. This invisible romance is real, Angela. I am real. I might not be what I told you I was, but all my love, all of my feelings, are for real.

I don't know the future logistics of this relationship, or whether it will have a future at all. But I want to make it happen – because I know that it is right, and that we will be happy together. I might have lied to you in the past, Angela, and I apologize to you for that. But this is the truth – I will make you the happiest girl in the whole world. Just give me one more chance.

Please make this invisible, faraway romance real.

I don't want to lose you. I love you. That's all I know.

Please make me yours.

Neel

Attached to the email was a picture of the real Neel Pandey, with a stupid smile on his face; a smile that had since disappeared.

C

Twenty minutes had passed. Thousands of miles away, at Lil' Jo's in Manhattan, there was no sign of Neil Patterson.

'Some more coffee, Angela?' Jo said.

'Yes, please. I'll just go to the ladies.'

Twenty more minutes. Angela was getting irritated now. No one had ever stood her up before. Especially someone who said he loved her. But she was putting on a brave face. She even smiled back at Jo, who was smiling at her from across the restaurant for the seventy-eighth time that evening.

Angela was losing hope that he would show up. She stretched her legs under the table. She looked at the cosy couple on the next table, huddled together and whispering god knows what to each other. She played with the napkin holder. She looked out of the window. She walked to Jo's counter and picked up a few magazines. She looked at her watch. She flipped some pages in a magazine. She gulped some coffee. She made a face because it had gone cold. She put it aside. She looked out of the window yet again. She flipped pages. There was a long story on pharma companies working on some new, revolutionary ways of waxing. She flipped another page. And froze.

Alongside a short profile on him, Neil Patterson's face stared from the magazine at Angela with the same arrogant look. Unknown to Neel, the face of the white man that he had sent Angela after a blind search on the Internet belonged to Mark Ferrara, one of the most swiftly rising male models in New York's fashion business. Angela looked at the picture for several minutes, unable to decide what to think of it. This man was not listed as Neil Patterson. This was someone else. So who was Neil Patterson? And who the hell was Mark Ferrara?

She began to read the article.

'Ferrara's spectacular rise on the New York fashion circuit has been matched by his soaring personal popularity. He is known for his swooning female companions, who say they adore him for his charm, humour, a hint of arrogance — and his great practical jokes.'

Practical jokes?

She took a few seconds to make sense of the developments of the evening — Neil Patterson must be a friend of this Ferrara fellow, and when Neil told his friend about the whole affair, the Ferrara fellow must have decided to play a prank on her.

Practical joke, eh? A prank on the queen of pranksters? *Right.*

Her cheeks were flushed. She was suddenly very angry. 'Um, Jo, can I have the phone directory, please? Oh, and if someone comes for me pour this coffee over his head, will ya?'

Angela pulled out her cell phone and spent some fifteen minutes talking and gesturing, looking visibly upset and angry. Angela was calling up the advertising agency, and struggling with the man on the phone to get the address of Mark Ferrara. She wouldn't let him get away so easily. Angela used argument, flirtation, persuasion, prodding, pleading, cajoling and threats. She got the address.

And then a broken-hearted Angela Cruz began walking to the station for the short ride to Greenwich Village, where Mark had a studio apartment.

❦

Angela:

Where are you?

I have been checking my email every ten minutes. I've tried your home phone and your cell phone so many times … You didn't take my calls. More than three hours have passed. I thought you would be home by now. Please tell me where you are, what you are thinking. Are you so furious that you won't even acknowledge my mails?

Are we still together? I love you I love you I love you … I love you so much … I can't think straight, I can't even think. Please mail me, even if it is just to say that you hate me … but please don't give me this silence and this vacuum.

Please talk to me Angela ... I did what I did only because I loved you and because I was scared that if I did it any other way, I would lose you ...

Somehow I think that I already have ...

In torment,

Neel

❦

Mark Ferrara was a ladies' man who had given himself to understand that women were a commodity useful only to grace the bed and the kitchen. He presumed — wrongly, may I add — like Mel Gibson in 'What Women Want', that the surefire way to make a woman happy was to disrobe her and engage in the carnal act. All of his women blamed themselves for getting pregnant because he did, indeed, include the word 'protection' among the many words he huskily whispered into their ears during the elaborate and well practiced foreplay that he specialized in. But many abused, and hence abusive, women had also surmised after their inevitable break-up and gynaecological examination that Mr Ferrara had some sort of a tie-up with abortion clinics and shrinks and that they paid him a commission on each client he got them. Ferrara, you see, had brains as well as an accompanying set of balls — and that, you would agree — made it a deviously explosive combination.

That evening, the unsuspecting Mark was using this combination to full effect with a female colleague — a blonde bombshell who many said was tipped to become the next Miss Universe. This may or may not have been true, but he was currently shaking up the universe of the aforementioned beauty, who moaned and screamed and asked for more as he rode the waves of the storm, if you know what I mean.

That's when the bell rang. Not once, but several times.

'Damn. One minute, honey. We'll start over. I promise it'll be even better,' he whispered into the ear of his queen for the night. Mark slipped on a pair of shorts and went, bare-chested, to answer the door.

There, he found a woman of exceptional beauty, breathing hard from walking too fast, adjusting the strap of her bag on her shoulders, with a few strands of hair falling on her face making her look even more beautiful. He just looked at her in puzzled silence for a few seconds.

'So you are the one, huh?' Angela screamed. 'How could you do this to me? You lowly bastard. Where is Neil Patterson?'

Mark Ferrara didn't know what to say. 'Um. Why don't you calm down first, lady?' he said, reaching out to touch her shoulder. Any excuse to touch this beauty was good enough.

'W-w-ho are you?' Angela shouted, beside herself with anger.

'Who do you want me to be?' Mark said, putting on his charming Greek God look. Bad move.

'*Fuck you!* Gimme a straight answer! *Who are you?*'

'Mark ... Mark Ferrara, honey.'

'Yes, I know. But how do you know Neil, and why did you do this?'

'Why did I do what, lady?'

Just then, the unsatiated soon-to-be-Ms-Universe emerged from the bedroom — with just a sarong tied around her waist.

Angela looked at the woman, then looked furiously at Mark. '*You b-b-a-s-t-a-r-d!*' she shrieked again and slammed her knee into Mark's groin. Then she yanked her bag off her shoulder and took a wild swipe with it, whacking him across the right side of his face before turning around and running out of the building in angry tears that she could no longer control.

Staggered at this sudden assault from a woman he had never met before in his life, Mark Ferrara collapsed on the couch.

'What did you do to her, you son-of-a-bitch? Did you give her a baby too? Huh?' The beauty queen was all fired up by Angela's fury and angrily snatched up her things. She too had something to add before leaving. She took her bag off her shoulder and complemented what Angela had done by slamming her genuine snakeskin Gucci purse into the left side of Mark's face.

'Men!' she said, and stormed out, leaving behind a bewildered Casanova.

☺

The lone customer in the 24-hour cyber café sat holding his head in his hands, staring blankly at the screen. Three empty cups of coffee stood on the table. A set of headphones lay on one side. On the wall facing the man, was a large clock painted in the tricolour of the Indian flag. 8 a.m. Indian Standard Time. A haggard and devastated Neel Pandey clicked the mouse to press 'send' on his email for the umpteenth time.

Angela?
Your answering machine won't even take any more messages now. Please don't do this. Where are you? Just call me once to say you are safe. Please. And if you can, just tell me that you forgive me.
I have never felt so desperate in my life. So far away.
Neel

Angela:
This is my tenth email to you today. My head is about to explode. Please write to me. I cannot take this any more. I have been up all night. I don't know what to do. I want to bang my head against the wall.
I love you.
Neel

Within thirty seconds, an icon popped up and a message said: 'You have one new mail.'

Neel hurriedly pulled his chair forward and clicked the inbox. 'Undelivered mail. The recipient inbox is full,' it said.

Neel stared for a few seconds at the message, then banged his fist on the table and deleted the email. He logged off, shut down the computer, and turned around. 'O! You! Bhaisahib!' he shouted at the young man in the crumpled shirt and pajama who was on the overnight shift at the cyber café.

The man, who had dozed off, woke with a start. 'What? What is it?' he shouted back, clearly in a foul mood.

'Can I have one more coffee?'

'There's no milk. You used up all of it.'

'Can you go get some?'

'I don't have money. Don't you have a computer at home? Can't you do all this at home? I normally sleep all night, there is no customer. But today you kept me up all the time.'

'How much do I owe you?'

'One minute ... you have used the Internet now for ... seven hours. That will be two hundred and ten rupees.'

'Won't you give me a discount?'

'OK, give me two hundred,' said the sleepy man, eager to get rid of the customer.

Neel paid up. 'Have you ever been in love?' he asked.

'Huh?' the attendant looked at him with a sneer.

'I said have you ever fallen in love?'

'Don't talk nonsense so early in the morning. Only mad people fall in love.'

❦

The woman whom Neel was trying so hard to contact was standing by a roadside in Greenwich Village, New York. She had tears in her eyes. She wiped them with the back of her hand, and wiped the back of her hand on her black trousers.

Angela's mascara had melted away. Her cheeks were soaked and smudged. Her feet hurt from the amount of walking she had done that evening. Her head pounded. Something was banging against the walls of her arteries; something was smashing inside the ventricles of her heart.

Why did Neil play this trick on me? Why didn't he send me his own picture? Who is this man? Does he have a face? How dare he play this prank on me. How dare he. What kind of a jerk would do something like this?

Angela felt dizzy and leaned against a parked car for support. The street was deserted. After taking control of the emotional rollercoaster she had just boarded, the cruel logistics of the night dawned on her. It was past twelve. She had walked on, unmindful of the direction, and was now in an isolated corner of the Village. She looked around. Nothing, except the odd car speeding away, a few men and the long shadows of the utility poles shining under the lonely neon lights. There was no taxi, none that would stop for her.

One-and-a-half hours later, she had reached the end of her slow and tortuous walk. She was on 42nd Street, walking into the lofty entrance of the Grand Central Station. A few people walked behind her. Some ran, wobbly and shaky after that one martini too many. Two women in precariously high heels tried to totter briskly past but then took off their sandals – and ran. A man wheeled a big suitcase past her, panting hard and almost falling twice on the exquisite marbled floor. On the stairways on the sides of the hall people sat morosely, perhaps those who had missed their trains or those who had realized – like her – that their journey, and their destination, was not what they had imagined.

She walked up to the chart. There was no train to Upper Plymouth. The last train had left fifteen minutes ago. 'What?

This can't be happening!' she said loudly, as a guard walking nearby turned around, smiling at the disappointment and outrage he heard each night at this hour.

Minutes later, an announcement boomed on the public address system, echoing across the hall. 'It is 1:30 a.m. This station is closing now. Please vacate the premises. The station will reopen at 5:30 a.m. We are sorry for the inconvenience,' the voice said.

What? Grand Central closing at 1:30? How could that be? They said this city never sleeps! Police officers began walking from passenger to passenger, requesting them to leave.

Angela heard the announcement wearily. Perfect. It was just in keeping with the rest of the day. The people on the stairs got up, all swearing under their breath in their respective languages, and began walking off. Angela got up too, her legs hurting so badly now she could barely walk a step. She walked into 42nd Street, with no idea of what to do next.

Out of nowhere, opportunist private taxi drivers appeared, probably used to waiting each night for the 1:30 a.m. kill.

'Upstate! Westchester!' a taxi driver shouted.

'Connecticut! Upper Plymouth!' another joined in.

Angela opened her purse to see how much money she had. One hundred and fifty dollars. She considered her options, and then walked up to the man headed to Upper Plymouth in a beaten-up limo.

'How much for Upper Plymouth, please?'

'One-eighty dollars for the beautiful lady,' the Chinese driver said.

'What? I could have reached home in six dollars!'

'Before 1:30, lady. Now there's no train, no bus, no nothing. Take it or leave it ... Connecticut! Upper Plymouth! Upstate!'

'One-twenty-five? That's all I have,' Angela said.

'OK, one-twenty-five it is for the beautiful lady,' the driver agreed and stretched to open the rear door for her.

Angela hopped in, put her bag on the seat, kicked off her shoes and closed her eyes.

An invisible sadness was filling up the dark sky.

ROCKY STRIKES BACK

Many of you would agree it is unseemly to call someone at six-thirty in the morning on a Sunday — unless one's house is on fire and a bucket is needed (or a pen, to write a dying note). However, it is downright criminal, if the person being called happens to work in an Indian call centre where he works all night, hasn't eaten in two days, is suffering from blood pressure so low that the BP machine shuts down and refuses to start, and the woman of his dreams is imminently poised to dump him.

But those rules don't apply here. Rocky Randhawa, the person calling, was not one sensitive to Sunday morning etiquette.

In the faraway farmlands of Jalandhar's suburbs, you see, slapping a man on the back with a ten-pound arm and then guffawing heartily when he gasps for air is a form of greeting. Lifting up an entire tandoori chicken by the leg and tearing it apart with one's teeth (while the poor fowl's soul winces in Poultry Heaven) is the preferred form of consuming it. And a robust belch afterwards is just a musical note in the overall Fifth Concerto of life. Rocky had the teachings of that rugged school of thought coursing through his veins.

After the second night that he didn't go to work and spent awake, Neel was finally catching up on some asleep. He had dozed off two hours ago after sitting up all night chewing his fingernails, and I suspect, some part of his fingers as well, waiting for Angela to write. That was part of the reason why he wasn't eating properly these days. Fingernails will be considered a dietary supplement someday.

'Neel? Neel? Wake up, beta, there's a call for you,' Narmada, unaware that her son hadn't slept all night, shouted in his ear.

His eardrums didn't so much as quiver. His face didn't register a single ripple, no sign whatsoever that he had heard a syllable in that sentence. He seemed in Love Coma. He was sleeping after selling his horses, as the phrase goes. Only the boom of a battle tank, the blast of a nuclear explosion, or the roar of a lion could wake him now. Or, perhaps, the whispering of a certain name.

'It is someone called Rocky Randhawa,' Narmada said.

Like one of those 'Hit Me' toys with a red nose and a powerful spring somewhere in its posterior, Neel bounced awake. '*What?*' he said. 'Where is he? Is he at the door? Why is he here? Ma, why don't you say something?'

'I did, Neel. I have been telling you for five minutes. There is a phone call for you. He's on the line.'

'Why didn't you tell him I am asleep?'

'I did. He said it was urgent.'

'O my god. O my god. O my god.'

'What's happened, Neel?'

'Nothing. I am just remembering god. Early in the morning.'

'Neel don't talk rubbish. You shouldn't keep a gentleman waiting like this.'

Neel was in half a mind to explain that the inventors of the great English language, particularly of the word 'gentleman' had obviously not encountered Mr Randhawa and that the word might suit a roaring man-eating lion, not the person currently on the phone. But he saw from a corner of his eye that his stern father was still at home. Any suspicious activity on his part would arouse his father's curiosity, his questioning and perhaps his reprimand, and thus, taking a look at the larger picture, it seemed that he was better off dealing with the brutally vicious Rocky Randhawa than his father, the silent killer.

Neel slowly walked to the phone. 'Hello,' he squeaked.

'How are you, Pandey praaji? Do you remember me?' said the growl at the other end.

'Of course, how can I forget? I am well, Mr Randhawa. I am sorry I could not return your calls all these days. You see, I work at a call centre now and I keep very odd hours. I hope you understand. I hope you are well. How is your assistant?'

'You must be thinking that I am calling to abuse you or threaten you. I am not. I am calling to tell you about a Plan that will be of great interest to you. And I am calling you despite what you did to me. You stabbed me in the back, Pandey, despite the fact that I have severe spinal problems,' Rocky said.

Ah. The raw nerve. Just the bloody nerve that Neel was trying bloody damn hard to avoid. 'Look, I was just coming to that,' Neel said. 'And let me clear this misunderstanding once and for all. I had no role in the raid that took place on your office, Mr Randhawa. So I hope that that ends the bitterness between us — mostly from your side, because I still hold you in the greatest esteem. I did not tip off the police.'

'Really? Then how do you know about the raid? You think I am a bloody fool?' Rocky snapped.

'No, I don't think so at all. I know it because it was in *The Delhi Today.*

'No, it wasn't. I had got my men to straighten out the crime reporters of the three main dailies.'

'Well, my father read it out to me.'

'Shall I straighten him out then?'

'*What?*'

'OK, Pandey, OK. I will give you the benefit of doubt ... One crime reporter was in the loo when my men went in to silence them and they must have bashed up the sports reporter by mistake. I did wonder why there was no sports page that day... anyway, about your father ...'

'No, please, let's keep him out of this. He works in the Prime Minister's Office.'

'OK. Give him my regards. Tell him that if anyone in the Prime Minister's Office needs any consultancy related to foreign travel or immigration assistance, we will be most happy to serve. In fact, if the Prime Minister himself has difficulties in foreign travel due to any economic sanctions or such restrictions, we can always provide him help, on subsidized rates of course in the national interest. A Cheap U.P. trick ... hahahahaha,' Rocky said.

'Right, Mr Randhawa.'

'About the plan. I would like to see you to discuss this plan, Pandey. Today.'

'I'm afraid today will not be possible, Mr Randhawa. In fact this whole week looks difficult,' Neel said.

'Pandey, I come from a land where they know how to get things done. But you need not be afraid of me. I promise you that I will not hurt you. My men will not hurt you, although they believe that you are the one responsible for forcing them to go to banks to take loans, rather than to rob them. But I promise I won't beat you up.'

'Thank you, Mr Randhawa, but as I said, this week will be imposs—'

'—I am not done yet. I promise I won't beat you up if you come. However, if you do not come, my men will come there and make you realize that if you want the no-claim bonus on your health insurance policy this year, it is best to not mess with Rocky the Ferocious Randhawa.'

'Any time today will be perfect, Mr Randhawa. I am totally free all day.'

☾

If Einstein or one of those other brainy scientist types had ever invented a machine to measure bad vibes, it would have shattered from the intensity of the readings on that sunny day. In a restaurant in the bylanes of Old Delhi, flanked by the huge red sandstone Jama Masjid, it was an impending tsunami of bad vibes.

Neel Pandey sat across the table from Rocky Randhawa in an isolated corner of the Nanhe Miyan restaurant. Both stared at the onion rings on the cracked quarter plate. Both stared at the dirty surface of the table. Both took deep breaths at regular intervals.

Nanhe Miyan, famous for its kebabs and mutton rolls and chicken preparations, was chosen by Rocky because it was located inconspicuously in the heart of Old Delhi, in the cobweb of lanes and bylanes that seemed to begin everywhere and end nowhere. Police rarely raided this area. If they did, it was very easy to slip into one of the sidestreets and keep walking on past the faceless devotees, oil massage men, shoeshine boys and vendors of religious books who roamed these streets or set up stalls there. It was the favoured rendezvous of Rocky and his men for business meetings. Besides, the owner of Nanhe Miyan owed Rocky; his nephew had gotten a fake visa to the United Arab Emirates many years ago through Rocky and had since earned and sent home many lakh rupees. In gratitude, the owner had offered Rocky a lifetime of free biryani, his rice speciality. But Rocky had too much family pride and self-respect to agree to that sort of offer. He had insisted on nothing less than Nanhe's famous tandoori chicken.

Outside the restaurant Bollywood film music blared from small radio transistor sets across the street. Children hung around the sweets shop, watching with fascination as the halwai made convoluted jalebis in a large pan of boiling oil. From a room somewhere inside the centuries-old mosque towering above the lanes, the muezzin chanted Islamic chants on the loudspeaker to beckon the faithful to the third namaaz of the day. Bicycle riders meandered through the lanes. Streetside Romeos took puffs from cigarettes laced with psychedelic powders, hastening their visits first to Heaven, and later to Hell. A horse trotted along the narrow street, grumpily pulling a huge tonga with three sleepy passsengers. The tonga owner took turns shouting at the horse and those on the road blocking the passage of the majestic coach, the kind of which had trodden on Delhi's streets since the Mughals horsed around here centuries ago.

Life trundled on outside the restaurant. What would those poor souls know of the matter of transcendental importance being discussed on table number four?

Neel had never imagined himself voluntarily meeting Rocky again. Still, here he was. It was not so much because he was afraid of Rocky and his muscled men. (That was one reason, but he could always ward Rocky off by hiding perpetually in the bathroom.) The main reason was the faint glimmer of hope that this could be about going to America, legally. Rocky's call had come at a time when he was desperate to be in New York, the city where Angela lived. He was staring at the shattered pieces of an unnamed relationship that he had built across the oceans, and he was desperate to put it back together, to meet Angela and convince her of his love. He did not know how he would do it, but at this point, the only person who could help him was Rocky. So, unknown to each other, both the men were equally desperate to meet each other that afternoon.

Rocky cleared his throat. Neel stopped playing with the onion rings and looked at the three other men at the table. One was, obviously, The Voice. The other two looked like crooks, and I don't want to be falsely judgemental – I say this only because of they way they stroked their stubbles. They had typical big-time-crook stubbles.

'Shall we begin?' Rocky asked.

'Yes, Mr Randhawa,' Neel said meekly.

Despite Rocky's assurances to the contrary, it was clear that the raid on his office was an unwritten item on the agenda. Rocky had built that office with his savings over many years – money accumulated after moving the most formidable mountains and executing the most devious Plans. There were so many – a thousand, perhaps – respectable citizens in countries around the world who were earning dollars and pounds and liras and dinars on foreign soil as masons, drivers, electricians and mafia sharks thanks to Rocky's ingenuity. His had been a sprawling industry. The bread and butter of so many crooks and policemen. But in one cruel swoop, it had been destroyed. Someone needed to be blamed. And Neel it was.

Still, the gang knew that it would be foolish to confront Neel. Even if he had caused them damage of many lakhs, he could help them now in an operation that would earn them ten times more. They could have Nanhe's delectable tandoori chicken for a hundred years, if they lived that long after eating it.

'Pandey, you and I have had a turbulent relationship, despite the very promising start that we had on the first day. However, I want to let bygones by bygones. We should start afresh. We have called you here to discuss a business proposition,' Rocky closed his pudgy ringless fingers around a glass of sweet and salty lime juice that the waiter had just served up on a steel tray. 'What I am proposing to you is a perfectly legal project that involves nothing unlawful, and will give you great returns.'

'What do I have to do?'

'It's like this. There is a Youth Chess Olympiad being held in which we want to take part. We have a team that will participate in it. We are the travel managers for the tour. You know, the guys who basically run the show.'

'And?'

'The players, you see, are from different parts of the country and they have limited knowledge of the English language. However, it will reflect very badly on our great nation if no one in the team speaks English. Fluently. We would like you to be part of the team. As the captain. Your only job will be to play however best you can and to speak with the organizers in English and keep them in good humour.'

'What? A *chess* tournament? This is really not the sort of thing I can focus on right now, Mr Randhawa. I am very distracted and I am going through a difficult ti –

'The tournament is not in India, Mr Pandey.'

'What?'

'It is in the United States.'

'Exactly. I was saying that I am very distracted and I am going through a difficult time and this is just the kind of break I need... wait a minute... *In the U.S.?* Where in the U.S.?'

'In a city called New York.'

Neel almost leaned over and kissed Rocky in excitement. 'And you are saying ...?'

'We are offering to send you to New York, pay for your ticket, pay for your stay and also some sightseeing, if you do this little thing for us. Would you be remotely interested?' Rocky said pursing his lips dramatically and tapping the grubby, oil-stained menu card with his thick fingers.

Neel watched Rocky like a beggar would watch a five-hundred-rupee note being offered to him by the man in the car at a traffic light. Like a struggling actor would watch the pen offered to him to sign the contract for the next big blockbuster. Like George Bush would have watched a stack of weapons of mass destruction in Iraq.

'And you are saying that this is perfectly legal, and it does not involve a fake visa?'

'Not at all, Pandey, this is a perfectly legitimate visit. We are not the kind of people we used to be. In fact, we did the Vaishno Devi pilgrimage too, to atone for our sins. Plus there will be many people going. And it is impossible to make so many fake visas together.'

The Voice took that as an insult to his skills. 'No it's not. How is it impossible, Boss-ji? In fact —'

Rocky kicked his assistant hard under the table. The Voice revised his sentence. 'Boss-ji, in fact, I was saying that how is it impossible? I ask you, how is it just impossible? It is not only technically impossible, but it is also morally impossible, religiously impossible, and constitutionally impossible. Thank you, Boss-ji,' said The Voice, looking victoriously at Rocky.

'So that's the deal, Mr Pandey. We take you to New York and you make us look good. Wear you best shirt and your best cologne, and comb your hair real hard,' Rocky said.

'I will be happy to work with you, Rocky-ji,' Neel said. 'But how will I get a visa? Isn't there a bar on not being able to apply so soon after being rejected?'

'Sports, Pandey, sports. We have already sent copies of your passport to the U.S. Embassy and done some preliminary enquiries. The U.S. consular officials have studied your case. Of course they had all other details about you in their database. And you will be happy to know that they said they will waive that rule in your case because they believe that they should spread the cause of sports around the world. Chess is just an excuse; the real motive of this majestic tournament is to spread brotherhood — and sisterhood also, of course — to let people break borders and meet, and to foster cooperation between the members states of the United Nations,' Rocky said, puffing out his chest. 'Apart from the War Against Terrorism, the War For

Sports is the other great objective of the United States...' Rocky turned his head to the right and he found his assistant gawking at him with his mouth open, experiencing total awe at the scintillating speech his boss had just made.

'Yes, yes, of course, Mr Randhawa, I am very, very interested. When do we leave?' Neel said.

'Right away. Give us your passport, and you shall be on a plane in a week. Like I said, the only condition is that you will have to go as the captain of the chess team and talk in English with all the American officials so that they or the members of the media can never get to interview the other team members,' Rocky said.

'But why is that?' Neel asked.

The Voice interrupted. 'Because they have never seen a foreigner before. They are farmer —'

Rocky kicked him under the table. His assistant shut up. 'Because they are *former* champions and accomplished players. The distraction could affect their game,' Rocky said. 'I have a liaison officer there, a very capable man by the name of Matthias Baldenburp, who shall be assisting me at every step in our visit. You can talk to him in English and I will watch TV and have expensive American beer.'

'You are also coming? That's fantastic!'

The Voice announced: 'Boss-ji will also find his love in America.'

'Oye! Shushh!' Rocky shouted.

"No, Boss-ji, let me not keep anything in my heart, let me speak. Your pain is my pain. Let me tell you, Pandey, there was an American woman who took away my Boss's heart, many years ago when he was a young boy in Jalandhar, and in return left only her visiting card. Boss-ji is looking for her, and she said she is in New York State, but only Wahe Guru knows where she is. It is a great pain that Boss has in his heart. He remembers her most when he sings Mukesh and Kishore Kumar songs. Sad sad ones,' The Voice's voice quivered with emotion.

All eyes turned to Rocky.

For the first time in his life, he was blushing.

C

Neel:

You said you don't know where to begin, because you don't know where this will end. But our relationship has ended, Neel, before it could really begin. I realized after letting go of you that I was in love with you. But not any more.

I don't entirely blame you. I did something lousy as well, and I am paying for it by losing the one relationship in a long, long time that I thought could have worked. It wasn't just you who pretended to be someone else. I did some phoney stuff too.

I am not a model, I was never famous. I wanted to be. Maybe that's what made me invent all those stories. I am a journalist. My folks live in Jackson, Mississippi — that is in the southern part of America and a very race-divided region (I know you know much less about America than Neil Patterson). I work for the *Upper Plymouth Journal* in the Upper Plymouth county outside New York. I have for a long time had this strange habit, a kind of game that I play, of assuming false identities and calling up people. I mean no malice. It is just for fun. I have also made some strangers my friends in the process.

You were one stranger I really wanted as my friend. But I screwed up — as did you. I played the game for too long. I should have told you. We have both deceived each other. We don't deserve each other, or our love. I am sorry for what I did to you, and I will never forgive you for what you did to me.

I waited three days before I could type even a single word to you. I just could not bring myself to write. You don't know yet what happened to me over the weekend, but here it is in a nutshell. The picture — the fake picture — you sent me turned out to be that of a fashion model. I waited for you for a long time at the coffee shop, making a fool of myself. Then I spotted your picture – I'm sorry, the picture of the man you had sent me – and I thought that you and he were in this together. So I went to that guy's house and slapped him.

Neel, talking to you made me happier than I had ever been before. It made me dream. I was so content. The amazing thing – and now it seems tragic – was that though I had never touched you, I felt so like a woman.

But some other questions too have been coming to my mind over the past three days. I told you why I lied to you, and why I kept lying. But why did you lie to me? When we started getting friendly, why didn't you tell me you were in India? You know, I like the idea of India. I had South Asian studies as a subject at NYU. I do yoga, I have seen Richard Attenborough's *Gandhi*, I have two Indian friends. I've always wanted to go to India some day...

Maybe you're right. This might never have started if I had known that you are thousands of miles away. I don't know, looking back, whether that situation would have been better than this ... Perhaps, as you people say in India, this is destiny. And perhaps all that happens, happens for the good. I don't know what good there is in this deep, throbbing pain that I am experiencing now, but our coming together was good while it lasted. Still, I just wish things had been different. I wish you had sent me your real picture. I wish I had not been so immature, and had told you the truth about myself, maybe that would have encouraged you to tell me the truth about yourself.

I have to say bye now. I had a great deal of anger inside me for three days; I had it even when I started this letter. But writing to you has been a sort of catharsis. What a rollercoaster we have ridden, and what an amazing story we had, Neel ... I keep reading all the time in the papers here about outsourcing to India and all that, and I never realized how closely it would touch my own life. I never realized I had outsourced my heart ...

I am fighting racial prejudices at home. I hate people who pretend to be all progressive in the workplace and at the restaurant table but are just racist pigs under their skins. I would have taken you as a lover – and perhaps even my husband – for just the warm, caring, funny, intelligent guy you are. Nothing else would have mattered, Neel. I would have loved you just the way you were – but I don't want our relationship to be built on the edifice of a huge lie.

I realize that you must have had your reasons to react in the way you did. You are such a mature and sensible guy, you must have a compelling reason for it.

I have not opened the attachment with your real picture. I don't want to see it. Let this failed romance remain faceless.

I don't want to fall in love, ever again. I feel betrayed and I am heartbroken.

I am crying as I write this, and my tears are falling on the keyboard. Maybe it will stop working now. But I will never call the call centre to fix my broken computer. As I will never call you to fix my broken heart.

Angela

CHECKMATE

'Neel, why didn't you tell me before? Why? I feel so horrible ... why?'

Neel had finally mustered the courage to tell his mother, from whom he had been hiding the most important development of his life for months and months now, about his feelings for Angela. He had often wondered why he had not confided in her earlier, because his mother was his best friend. Perhaps, because he thought that Narmada would advise him to not get too close to Angela because there was no future in the relationship; it was logistically impossible. Plus his father would never, never agree. 'I don't know, Ma. I was living in my own world. I'd created a whole new world for myself. It wasn't real. A new name, a new identity, it was just ...'

Neel and Narmada were talking in his room as a gentle evening breeze blew in from the open balcony door. Their tea was getting cold. A chilling sadness was seeping in through the door. And his mother was surprising him again. 'It *is* real, Neel. The love is real, but everything else about the relationship is not, beta,' she said.

'What would you have done if you had known?' Neel said, sipping his cold tea.

'I would have asked you to tell her the truth.'

'But what if she had just hated me?'

'Hated you? Because you are from another culture? That's rubbish, and you know it, Neel. She is not that kind of woman. She doesn't sound like that. She is not like your father, or her own father. They are the people who believe in all these things – high caste, low caste, blacks, whites, browns, reds – but maybe they will also realize one day that there is more to people than skin tone. This girl is so different from the environment in which she grew up. I like her just from what you have told me about her. What she played on you was just a prank that went out of control, but what you did was born out of a deep inferiority complex. Or maybe because you have no pride in your own country.'

'You mean, you wouldn't have objected to my falling in love with her if I had told you earlier?'

'Look at me, Neel. You think I would have done so?'

'No.'

'Then? I would have supported you with all my heart, baba. I would have told you to tell her the truth. And she should have done the same. Even if you had told her two months ago, she would have been shocked for a while, maybe she would have gotten upset with you for not telling her earlier, but she seems to me to be the kind of adventurous woman who would love to have an across-the-world romance.'

'But it would never have worked. It had no future,' Neel said, looking out of the window.

'That's ridiculous. How can you be so pessimistic?'

'What do you mean?'

'I think there is always a future for a relationship when two people reciprocate each other's love. The very fact that you fell in love with her means that there is a future destined for you. I know this Rocky guy is shady, but he is taking you there at his own expense. It's a sign from god. I will sell my jewellery and give you money as a back-up if he ditches you there or something. Go, beta ... get her. Go and win her back.'

Neel held his mother's hand and tried not to get too emotional. 'I hope you know that you are the best,' he said softly.

'OK, stop flattering me. We have work to do.'

'What work?'

'We have to pack. And I have to teach you some chess!'

'What? You know how to play chess?'

'Let me tell you a little secret, Mr Pandey. Your grandfather, that is my father, was the chess champion of the district and had won many medals. But only one person could beat him.'

'You? I don't believe it!' Neel said, laughing in disbelief.

'Indeed! He and I used to go to the orchard outside our village, with a chess-set that he had won in a city tournament. And we would spread out a sheet on the ground, sit under a tree and play for hours. We took water in a clay pitcher and some salted peanuts. And that was all we needed. Sometimes ripe mangoes would fall from the trees and we would eat them. Or we would ask one of the village kids to shimmy up the tree and get us a few raw ones. Game after game, game after game! We weren't father and daughter, we were just friends out to fool my mother and enjoy every moment of it ... God, I miss those days ... and I miss Baba. I wish you and your father shared that sort of relationship, Neel,' Narmada said, wiping a tear in memory of her father.

'So, what do you think my old man will say ...?'

'We will not tell your father why you are going to America. We will tell him your office is sending you there. Then, when you come back, we will tell him the truth. A lie spoken for a good cause is forgiven even by the gods. I will pray to Lord Krishna tomorrow. *He* is sure to understand... '

℃

The phone rang. Neel picked it up. It was Meenal. This was the first time that Neel was hearing from her since he had joined the call centre. 'Heyy ... how are you?' Neel said, as Narmada walked out of the room to start her evening cooking chores.

'Neel, are you alone? Can you talk?' Meenal asked.

'Yes, now I can. Where have you been? I was hoping you'd call me.'

'Uh... did you know that I've run away from home?'

'What? Wow. I wish I had your kind of guts! But where have you been staying and all? And how's your girlfriend?' Neel asked with concern.

'She's fine, but I'm not. My father is furious. The maid is acting as my mole in the house. She calls me every evening, when I switch on my cell phone for half an hour just to receive her call. It seems my father had picked and finalized a guy for me to marry and they have had to tell his parents that I've gone away for a conference and will be back in a few days. When I didn't return they cooked up a story about my going away on a vacation after the conference. Anyway, the guy broke off the marriage and made some shitty comment about more and more girls running away with their boyfriends. So my dad is thoroughly pissed right now. I have shattered family prestige, he says. But he knows that he can't be mad at me for a long time, so he is directing all his anger at Sonia. My maid informed me that he was talking at dinner yesterday about filing a police complaint against her, claiming that she has abducted me. And I know that he will do the worst he can through his PMO contacts and get an arrest warrant issued for Sonia. So we have decided to split up for a while and then meet after a few weeks and get married. Sonia is going away to Bombay to be with some friends.'

'What? Wow! Can you do that? I mean, get married? Forgive my ignorance.'

'Actually there is a law in India under which people of the same gender can be arrested and jailed for seven years if found having sex. It's the same law under which you can be jailed for having sex with animals.'

'Oh my god, that's primeval!'

'Yeah, exactly. But there's no law that actually prohibits people of the same gender from marrying each other. So we just have to find a pandit or marriage court clerk who will do it for us,' said Meenal. 'But I need to lie low for some time. Once the police complaint is filed, they will look for me everywhere. I am running out of money and there are very few places I can go to.'

'Is there any way I can help you?' Neel asked.

'You were the only person I could think of ... but I don't know what you can do ...'

Neel thought in silence for a few seconds. 'Hey, Meenal, do you play chess?'

☽

Later that evening, Neel told his father he was getting a chance to go to the United States. He said it was a trip sponsored by his company for advanced training. Ravi had just come back from work, and was taking off his shoes. Narmada placed three cups of tea on the table.

'What sort of training?' Ravi asked.

'It is ... to upgrade my communication skills, Papa.'

'How many days?'

'I think about ten days or so. But it could be extended.'

'What do you mean you don't know how many days? This is a strange visit. Haven't they told you how long you are going for? And where will you stay?'

'They have made some arrangements, Papa. Don't worry, it's an ongoing program, people go all the time.'

'Hmmm. So how much money will you need?'

Narmada interrupted: 'I will give him some money, you don't worry about that.'

'Where did you get money?' Ravi asked her, puzzled.

'I saved. I do so many things behind your back, you know!' she said, smiling.

'I can never understand the plans that you mother and son make ... Look, Neel, you know my dislike for the United States. But I don't want to stop you. I only want that we should have a final talk about your marriage before you go.'

'Final talk?' said Neel, alarmed.

'Final talk?' said Narmada, amused.

'Yes, I think before you go to the U.S., let's decide on a girl so we can have the engagement right after you come back. I am an open-minded person, I am giving you full freedom. Look at the other people in my office — they just decide who their son should marry and that is it. Done. But I am not like them. I still cannot understand why you don't like Meenal, but chalo, OK, I will go by your decision. At least choose some other girl! Did you show him the girls' pictures I gave you, Narmada?'

Neel stiffened in his seat.

'Listen, we can talk about this later,' Narmada said. 'I promise you, we will talk about Neel's marriage when he comes back from the U.S.'

'Narmada, our son is getting spoilt because of you. You are the one who always keeps postponing this. Mark my words, if our son remains unmarried any longer, people will start talking. "What is wrong with Ravi Pandey's son?" That's what they will say. What face will we show to the world then?'

(

The phone rang for a long time in the large living room before it was answered. Martha came out of the wash room drying her hands on her apron.

'Angela!' her mother exclaimed. 'How are you, honey? How is the fund-raising work going on?'

'I am fine, Mom. Work is fine. How are you guys?'

'We're OK ... And we have a surprise for you.'

'Has my father pledged me away to a tattooed man on a motorbike because he is white?' Angela said coldly.

'Angela, please don't talk like that ... your father has his ways, but he only wants the best for you.'

'Where is he? Doesn't he want to snatch the phone and give me his sermon on racial relations?'

'He's gone to work.'

'What? Mother, I am so happy! I'm sorry for what I said earlier about him.'

'Oh no, honey, I agree with you on most of that ... and especially about Juanita ... I mean, I also was a little, you know, uncomfortable, when I first heard about her, but, honey, she's changed you, you're a whole new person ... I am so happy, and proud of you, honey, for doing what you did ...'

'And Daddy? Have his views changed in any way?'

'He doesn't say so, but I think they have. Plus, you know, I am hoping that getting this job after so many years will change him. It will make him busy and I think he will be less cranky. What do you think?'

'I think so too. This is such great news, Mother. But how did it come about?'

'It was kind of strange. You remember the company that had put your father out of business? Taj Mahal? They are expanding in Mississippi and some other areas, in fact your father was in a really foul mood the day he read about it in the paper.'

'Oh, I can imagine that,' Angela said.

'And one day a big car pulled up outside our house and who should be there but the owner of the Taj Mahal company!'

'What?'

'He said that he was looking for someone to head his operations in the whole of Mississippi, and he couldn't think of another person with as much experience, who would be so right for the job ...'

'O my god, and what did Dad say?'

'Well, he hemmed and hawed and finally said yes. It's a great job, he has a big staff and a nice office, and everything ... I keep knocking on wood all day, sweetie. When are you coming, home, Angela?'

'I was planning to come soon, but now something's come up. I am going to get real busy for some time, Mom.'

Angela had just lied to her mother, but what could she do? She had decided to shut out the pain of heartbreak by shutting herself to family, friends and emotions, and immersing herself in her work.

C

Neel was going to America and his father was coming to see him off. He had never thought this day would dawn. The rest of the group would meet him at the airport, and Meenal – a last minute addition thanks to Rocky's largesse – would come much later to make sure Neel's parents, and heaven help her, the police, did not notice her slipping out of the country.

Neel sat on the front seat of the taxi, his parents at the back. His mother clutched the rudraksh necklace that she had brought back with her from a pilgrimage to the Gaumukh shrine, near Uttar Kashi.

Narmada rarely ever took the beads out of her little temple at home. They had sat there for years, moving out wrapped on Narmada's wrist only once to the hospital when Neel, then an infant, had been very ill. Today was also one such occasion when the protection of the gods was needed for her son. She clutched the beads hard; their pointed edges pierced her fingers and she winced with pleasure. Pain was hugely satisfying to a devotee.

Narmada pressed the beads harder in her hands and silently muttered a Sanskrit mantra from the *Bhagwadgita* that her mother used to recite when Narmada went to write her exams.

Karmanyevaadhikaaraste ma phaleshu kadaachan
Ma karmaphalheturbhoormaa te sangostvakarmani
Yogastha kuru karmaani sanga tyaktva dhananjaya
Siddhayasiddhayoh samo bhhotvaa samatvam yog uchchyatey

(You have only the right to do your duty and deeds, but you are not the claimant of what is derived from them.

Do not regard yourself as the result of your deeds, and never involve yourself in not doing your deeds.

Set aside the lust for victory or defeat, and do your duty with equanimity.

This is the true yoga.)

❦

As the car turned into the airport, Narmada's face was momentarily lit up in the glow of the passing streetlights. Ravi saw his wife's lips move, whispering the words of the mantra, her entire being centred on the communion between herself and her almighty. He felt deprived. He also wanted to proclaim such selfless devotion. He also wanted to submit to a power that he knew was greater than him. Narmada's faith was about a two-way communication with her gods — she asked them and they told her. It was like a conversation in a private window in the chaotic buzz of god's superbusy Internet chat room. But Ravi's faith was only about the rules that the doorkeepers of his almighty had conveyed to him.

Ravi envied his wife. He wanted to have the same liberating, freeflowing faith that did not tie him down unconditionally to customs made in an ancient era, moulded to the logic and circumstance of hundreds of years ago. Why was he so desperate for his son to get married to only a certain sort of person, live his life a certain way, and have a certain outlook? Was it because Ravi was a concerned dad? Or was it because this was his way of adhering to his faith — and the social mores handed down for generations in his dogma-steeped family? Perhaps there was a logic in that era for women not to go to temples when they were having their period. Perhaps it had to do with hygeine. Clean napkins with and without 'wings' were not available then, nor were there any chemist shops. Maybe that was the reason. He didn't know. He was just guessing. The laws of that era must have been fashioned by the circumstances of that era ... But why was he shackled to them now, Ravi wondered.

Why does the keeper of the knowledge not want you to question it? Why is the questioning of faith a sacrilege? After all, faith as it stands must also have been created after questioning and rejecting some other sets of norms and beliefs. These were thoughts that had often drifted into Ravi's mind, but they were churning now, and the vortex spun faster and faster as the taxi neared the airport. For centuries, the Hindu religion encouraged its followers to question and debate their faith and not accept it blindly. There were thousands of seers and sages who had done it in ancient times. But now, many pandits and their followers had regressed to a position where questioning was not welcomed by the torchbearers of the faith. They clammed up on religion because it suited them to be unquestionably in power. And followers like Ravi Pandey were left with the same set of values that their forefathers had stuck to, with no space to question it. The oppressive caste system had little to do with religion, and yet it had become part of the whole package, and people like Ravi were not brave enough, or enlightened enough, to see through the charade.

So what was true faith? Was it in conforming or defying? Why do we call a dog faithful? Because he follows the master mindlessly? Why does one have to be following someone, or something, to be faithful? Why isn't a leader faithful?

There was a sense of urgency in these thoughts. As if Ravi wanted to reach the destination of his mental journey before the taxi stopped and his son started out on his own real life one.

His wife was more devout than he. She kept a fast once a week for the well-being of her husband and her son. She went to temples. She observed all the religious customs taught by her mother and mother-in-law. So she was a faithful. Yet, she was the one who didn't mind even if her son never went to a temple or kept a fast like her, and she had forgiven him even after he left the sacred yagyopaveet thread in the bathroom after an eight-hour long religious ceremony. She wanted her son to follow his dreams, to do what he wanted, whether or not it was in consonance with religious norms. In that sense, she was a rebel. If her son chose a so-called 'untouchable' Dalit woman — whom no one in the family would accept, Ravi knew that his wife would be the first one to break the walls of taboo and offer her water and her love.

And at that moment Ravi saw that loving someone, like being faithful, meant unshackling your hold on them. Withdrawing. Letting go. Letting fly. Ravi had always wanted to fashion his son after himself; to make him pursue the dreams that his own father had for him, and to live the life that his father thought was fit for him. But Ravi knew today that he needed to let Neel drift in the stratosphere of his mind the way he wanted to, and for as long as he wished. Watching Narmada letting her son pursue his dreams, with just a protective prayer on her quivering lips, Ravi realized that his wife had a religious maturity that he had not achieved or experienced in the rigid world of ancient rules he had strictly enforced.

He reached out and did something very unexpected: he held Narmada's hand in his right hand, and placed his left on Neel's shoulder: 'I'm proud of you, Neel. Be good and be safe.'

They had reached the airport.

Seated in the rear seat of the rickety Ambassador taxi, Ravi Pandey had made a mental journey that he had not been able to make for more than twenty years.

And, in doing so, had made his son his friend.

☾

Wheeling his trolley towards the X-Ray machine at the airport, Neel noticed a man moving towards him with a small crowd trooping behind. The man wore a snappy black suit, a trimmed Van Dyke beard and a cocky self-assured expression on his face. He walked with a kind of swagger. As the man closed in on him, Neel grew alarmed thinking he was about to attack him. The next moment the man was all over him, ensnaring Neel in a bone-crushing hug with the gusto of a just-married gay partner. It was Rocky Randhawa, now unrecognizable in his smart attire, minus sunflowers and golden streaks.

'Pandey! Yaar! We are going to America!'

'Rocky! Man! You look so different! And so smart! And in such a good mood! And hey, thanks so much for helping out my friend Meenal. She will come in later because of, you know, the situation.'

'Oye, no problem, I can do anything for love. I can get her a visa to any country as a refugee any day, my friend, you just have to give me a signal!' Rocky jabbed an elbow into Neel's side. 'She will be our team psychologist. That's what we wrote on the visa form. Brilliant, isn't it? And maybe she can help me find my girlfriend!'

'But our documents are all legal, right?'

'Legal, yaar of course it's all legal ... why do you keep asking? Oye, why do you worry? Come, let's meet the team!' Rocky said.

He waved Neel to a group of men some twenty feet away. Like half-excited, half-nervous teens on their way to their first summer camp, thirty grown-up men darted about the check-in lounge of the Indira Gandhi International Airport, exchanging notes and comparing ticket prices.

Neel took one look at them. They didn't look like chess players. They looked like ... truck drivers. No offence to truck drivers, but you know the type: hardy, uncouth, muscular — not the soft edges and refined intellect that chess players reflect. They were all freshly-shaven, with a clueless look on their faces, as they looked around dumbstruck soaking in the sights.

Neel shook hands with a few. These were not the nimble, artistic hands of chess players. These were the hands of boxers, or hired assassins. 'These are ... chess players?' he asked Rocky incredulously.

Before Rocky could say anything, the tallest and the most muscled in the group — a man who could easily have torn apart anyone in a WWF ring — spoke up. 'Oye, any doubt?' he said flexing his biceps menacingly.

'No, no doubt. No doubt at all,' Neel hastily reassured him. That was the last time he spoke to any of his team-mates.

'Boss-ji! Sir! Rocky Sahib!' The shouting of a man from the entrance caught their ears. All of them turned around. It was

The Voice. He had been waving frantically for the past ten minutes, waiting for someone from the group to notice him. Now he was becoming desperate. What if they all went away without even looking at him? He was blowing kisses now. He was banging his boots on the iron railing at the entrance. He shouted Rocky's name.

The entire group waved back. This seemed to satisfy The Voice and having got the acknowledgement he wanted, he walked away slowly.

'Isn't he coming with us?' Neel asked.

'Both he and I are required to show our face at the local police station every Monday and he will continue to go. I have sent in a letter saying that my grandmother is dead and I have to rush to her funeral. I also sent in the postcard I had received from my village informing me of her death due to a heart attack. Plus I had to drop him to accommodate your "friend" Meenal,' Rocky wiggled his eyebrows suggestively at Neel.

'We are just good friends,' Neel said exasperatedly, '... and I am sorry to hear that.'

'What?'

'About your grandmother. She must have been very old.'

'Yaar, Pandey! You are such an innocent! My grandmother, god bless her soul, died when I was six. I have been living off her death ever since. Wahe Guru bless her.'

THE LAND OF HOPE AND GLORY

Neel Pandey was soaring over New York like a seagull — and for once it wasn't in a dream.

It was a beautiful sunny day. The plane had been circling over the city for the past half hour, waiting for permission to land. Passengers craned their necks and greeted the city with silent smiles or wistful stares. Children waved at tiny buildings below. Lovers cuddled as they peeped out of the windows. Flight stewardesses hastily remade their faces and readied themselves to smile.

This was the moment that Neel had dreamed of for almost ten years now. But it was a truncated victory. It came laced with heartbreak. The dream of coming to America would remain incomplete without the woman whose faraway companionship had become his lifeblood. That companionship stood at a funny crossroads right now — because the two persons who had fallen in love with each other were imposters. The two real people who remained, had to figure out where they stood.

Nowhere, as far as Angela was concerned. The emotional upheaval had been too much for her, and it had come just when she thought she was ready for a real relationship. She was heartbroken and angry, drowning her grief in work; slogging day and night to ignore her wounded heart in an attempt to nurse it. Being with Juanita had taught her that trust and commitment in a relationship was all that mattered. More than being furious at Neel for his deceit, she was bewildered that something like this could happen to her, the expert prankster. The wildest inventor of stories and falsehoods had become the victim of a huge prank played on her by love itself.

Neel had no escape planned out. He wanted to heal her hurt and his own, doing whatever it took — quackery or charm, voodoo or the rope trick — to win her back.

They had been approaching a moment and now that moment had passed them by. He wanted to hold on to it, however lacerated with lies and gored with deceit that moment might have been. They had to heal it, and they had to heal themselves. Everything was pinned now on one simple question that many others had faced before them — would they be able to transcend borders, race, religion, caste, doubt, deceit, anger, hurt and heartbreak to come together?

Would their love have the strength to leap over this wall of fire?

Neel looked down from his plane window at the ships lined up on the West Side pier, majestic and aloof. The waters of the Hudson shimmered in the sunlight, and the ferries looked like toy boats in the distance. Skyscrapers jutted out into the sky like tall children gazing at the horizon, asking for things they knew they would never get. But they still didn't stop asking for them. They didn't stop dreaming. There were thousands of people inside those skyscrapers, all chasing their tiny and big mirages in a sprawling desert — some wandering hermits at the Great Palace of Desire, some charlatans trying to grab more than the fistful of dreams they were destined to get. Perhaps Neel was also trying to reach out to grab more than he had been ordained by the great powers that ran his life. Perhaps he was being greedy too, flying from his small-town destiny to this dazzling metropolis in search of love.

Destiny, Neel thought, as he looked at Meenal and Rocky, sleeping peacefully after a night of one-sided conversations, is a funny thing. It was bizarre that the man who was so after Neel's life at one point, and a source of most of Neel's nightmares, would himself chaperone the lover to the land of his beloved. It was destiny's way of rewarding these two men, so hungry to succeed. It was destiny's sense of humour.

Rocky was propelled not just by greed but the undented belief, that, whatever the world might think, there was a bizarre form of creative satisfaction in what he did for a living. It was the love of life itself that drove this crazed man. He could have made almost the same amount of money back in Punjab in the real estate business. But he had the spirit of a buccaneer. That is what prodded him into a business that he had elevated to an art form. He took pride in the fact that he had transformed the lives of thousands of people and their families, helping them get better lives in faraway countries. Pity they were all illegal immigrants. Pity Rocky was on the wrong side of the law and was probably about to land up in jail.

Neel turned to Rocky and smiled. The two were finally hitting it off. He was beginning to sort of like this guy. While Neel and Meenal had tried to grab some shut-eye, Rocky had jabbered on through the night – about his village, about Punjab, about their travel business, about his father, and most of all, about the American woman who had taken his heart away. At some point, after downing all the drinks the stewardess would allow him, Rocky had produced his most treasured possession from his wallet. A business card, slightly frayed at the edges but otherwise crisp: *Susan Blair, florist, Queen's Avenue, Saratoga, New York State.*

Meenal had been mostly quiet during the flight, preoccupied with thoughts about home. This whole thing was quite a rollercoaster for her – all she knew was that she was getting a free trip to New York, away from possible arrest by the police, and it was all thanks to Neel and his kind-hearted friend. In return, she would have to talk in English on behalf of the chess team, perhaps play chess if needed, and counsel the players and make them feel better if they felt homesick. She had no idea that she was going on a fake visa designed and manufactured by Rocky's gifted craftsmen back in Jalandhar.

After the storm settled down, Meenal planned to go back to India and reclaim her life. No one could take her life away from her; not the police, not her parents, and certainly not her cowardice. 'I miss Sonia,' she said wistfully as she looked at Neel in the seat next to her.

'I miss Angela,' Neel said. They both smiled understandingly at each other and Meenal gently rested her head on his shoulder.

Rocky, only partly awake, looked at the both of them and winked at Neel, as if saying, 'Way to go, man! One girlfriend in the city and one on the plane! Wahe Guru is great!'

At last the cabin crew asked the passengers to straighten their seat backs, tighten their belts and fold their tray tables.

'New York!' Neel whispered as the plane began its descent.

'Yes, we are going there only,' Rocky Randhawa muttered sleepily.

©

'What is the purpose of your visit to the United States?' the blank-faced immigration officer asked the first chess team-member he encountered.

'Chaaass,' said Gurpreet Singh proudly. You couldn't blame him for the way he pronounced the word. After all, he wasn't a privileged student of Ms Lily at the BPO Axis call centre.

'Sorry?' said the immigration officer.

'Chaaass.'

'Jaaz? What about jazz?'

'Play,' said Gurpreet, expansively. He was getting a sick feeling in the pit of his stomach. Had Gurpreet ever been to school back in Jalandhar, he would have known that this was the kind of feeling one got when lining up to receive one's report card after the final examination. As it was, he thought it was yesterday's farewell meal of three butter chickens asserting itself.

'You are a jazz singer?'

'Chaaass. Play ... Kartaaaar?' said Gurpreet, turning around and helplessly calling out to the man behind him, his best friend Kartar Singh Dhillon, also from Jalandhar. This was turning out to be a bit different from the mock interviews that Rocky had set up for them and Gurpreet wanted some help.

'Kartaar?' Gurpreet said again, looking at his friend. Kartar was himself clueless.

But the immigration officer had already understood the whole story. 'Guitar ... So you are a guitar player in a jazz band from India and you are in the United States to play at a show?'

'All right, thank you, Mr ... Singh?'

So Gurpreet did as he was asked. He began to sing.

'Taai din na jawaani nad chaldi, kurtee ... malmal di!!
Patli kurti de pichhon di/Roop chhatiyan maare
Ang ang tera ... tapda renhda/Noo Noo kare ishare
Jutti khal di maroda nahion chaldi
O Jutti khal di maroda nahion chaldi
Kurteeee ... malmal di'

(When she grows,
Her muslin shirt becomes tight in two-and-a-half days,
The thin fabric clings to her body,
Showing the beauty of her breasts,
The transparent linen

Reveals her curves.
It is alluring ...
And her leather shoes break
Unable to keep pace with
her stylish walk...)

The immigration officer looked at Gurpreet in complete awe. He dropped his pen. In the twenty years of his experience, the biggest names of rock and jazz had passed through this desk, but this, believe me, was new.

'This way, Sir,' said the immigration officer, respectfully showing Gurpreet through the green channel before he broke into another song.

C

An hour later, they were all seated in a bus, headed uptown to a New York hotel where they had been booked by the organizers. It wasn't the Waldorf Astoria, and the thirty-one men had sixteen rooms between them, but at least they got to sleep for a few hours, and the food was paid for.

On another day, Neel would have been spellbound by the sights on the way from the airport to the hotel. This was the city he had grown up dreaming of, after all. He had read about these avenues and streets in books, seen them in the movies and walked on them in his dreams. He had imagined himself a thousand times, walking down these roads, soaking in the dazzle of the most wonderful city in the world. But the city of his dreams seemed empty today. He could only enjoy it with Angela by his side.

Being team captain and psychologist respectively, Neel and Meenal had got separate rooms to themselves. Neel put away his suitcase, made a quick trip to the loo, and then rushed to the phone. He had to dial a number in Upper Plymouth.

The phone rang several times at Angela's home, and then Neel ran into the all-too familiar answering machine. He dialled again. This time Angela picked up after two rings.

'Hello!'

'Hi, Angela?'

'Who's this?' she said, and then her voice changed as she recognized the caller: 'Neel?'

'Yes, it's me, Angela — '

She hung up even before he could take her name a second time. But she didn't go away. She knew he would call back. Maybe she wanted him to call back. He did.

'Angela —'

'Look, Neel, why are you making this difficult for the both of us? It is over. In fact, it can't even be over because it never began. Non-existent people don't fall in love, Neel Pandey ... I am going to hang up again now.'

'Angela, please listen to me ... Don't give up on us, I am trying to make this work.'

Angela was speaking through her tears. 'And I am trying to make this go away! Go away, Neel, find a nice young woman in India and get married to her ... I cannot confront this relationship again, I invested all I had in it ... I have nothing more to give ... I wish you well. Don't call me again. Long distance calls cost a lot, you know, like long distance romances.'

'Oh — I am not in India, I am —'

But Angela had already hung up.

Neel quickly dialled the directory services. He needed to find out Angela's address. 'I'm sorry, Sir, it is an unlisted number,' said the woman at the other end.

'Oh damn ... could you then give me the number of the *Upper Plymouth Journal*, please?'

It was no use. Angela hadn't come to work. And no, they could not give her address.

Unless the God of Home Addresses did something pretty soon, Neel Pandey had hit a dead-end just hours after embarking on his American journey.

☙

Rocky Randhawa and Matthias Baldenburp stood facing each other in the hotel lobby, and the entire world ground to a halt.

'Matt, my brother!' Rocky shouted, stretching his arms and stepping forward to give him a big Punjabi back-slapping hug. Matt knew that sort of behaviour could transform his image from a macho police officer to an icon across the gender divide. He sheepishly stuck out his hand and poured a big bucket of water over Rocky's sublime enthusiasm.

'Rocky, how are ya, pal? Nice to see ya again after such a long time,' Matt said. Then he paused and looked at Rocky's paunch. 'Boy, have ya prospered,' he said, laughing.

'Why not, Matt ... I get a steady supply of the purest homemade butter every month,' he said. 'And how is it with you, my friend? Found a woman?'

'Um. Right. Let me show ya the city, pal.'

'Oh ... why, she ditched you? Who can ditch a macho man like you? Yeah, we'll see the city, first let's go to the room for a bit, I have brought you some gifts. My friend Neel is talking to the guy at the reception, it'll take just a few minutes. His girlfriend also ditched him,' Rocky said, looking at Neel's back and leaning over the granite desk at the reception. 'So did you have trouble finding the hotel?'

Neel walked back to join them near the elevators.

'What, are ya kidding? I know Manhattan like the back of my ass ... I lived uptown for donkey's years before moving to the suburbs — Hey, pal, I am Matthias Baldenburp. You must be Rocky's friend.'

'Neel, this is Matt. My very old and very close friend. Matt, this is Neel,' Rocky said.

'Hi, I am Neel Pandey. Rocky talks about you all the time.'

'Upper Plymouth. Thirty-minute train ride from Grand Central. I'm sorry, Neel what were you saying? We are all talking at the same time.'

'Matt, did you just say you are from Upper Plymouth?' Neel asked.

'Yeah, that's where I live ... you guys should come over some time,' said Matt.

'Yeah, I certainly will. I have to meet a very dear friend. But I don't have her address and I can't contact her,' Neel said, stepping out of the lift.

'Really? Well, maybe we can help you find her ... is she the one Rocky says you are pining for these days?' Matt winked at Neel and laughed.

'Ha ... actually yes, you could say that ... Rocky here is very perceptive,' Neel said, smiling.

'So what's the story, pal? You wanna tell me?' said Matt.

'It's a long story. You see I work for a call centre in India ...'

C

There were three pizzas laid out on Angela's kitchen table and seven children sat around them without reaching out to pick up a slice. Angela stood by the table, holding a tray of drinks watching the kids with a rueful smile. 'Why isn't anyone eating?' she asked. No one responded.

Their band had run out of hope just as suddenly as Angela's romance had run out of luck. They had both been tantalizingly close to their deadlines – now the Orange Bowl organizers had already sent a gentle reminder once, saying that if they didn't pay up within the next ten days, the band members could watch the extravaganza sulking in their beds, not in the stadium. It didn't need an Einstein or Ramanujam to figure out that the battle was lost. Nyasa Okri, the trumpet player, had called Angela the previous night and finally mentioned the unmentionable: they should perhaps return the money that people had donated them. Angela had heard her out in silence. Nyasa had started sobbing.

Angela knew what Nyasa and the rest were going through. Wasn't she going through the same sense of loss, after all? She had just declined Neel's love. The enormity of her loss was a realization that had plagued her through nights of talking to Neel in her dreams, screaming at him, hitting him, asking him why he had let her down so badly and then throwing herself into his arms and saying she loved him. But when the sun rose and she had to show her face to the world, she would clam up the hurt. When the world started buzzing around her, Angela Cruz knew that her vulnerability could not be disclosed. Specially now.

Angela had begun to drown herself in work. She went to the office and stayed there to do story after story after story and then she volunteered to help with making the pages. She took on assignments no one else wanted to do — she would go to a conference on organic farming or a lecture session on meditation practices or the findings of a new study on the mating-calls of rats.

'Hello? The pizzas are getting cold!' Angela said forcing herself to be bright. Angela had to do a lot of pretending and smiling to get through this lunch. Heartbreak sucks.

'We are not hungry,' said Juanita solemnly.

'Do you know we have not practised for three days? It just seems so worthless ...' said Jo Brown, the young cello maestro. 'After all that you did for us...'

Angela sat down, placed the lemonade and cola glasses before her guests, and looked around at the woebegone bunch. 'No it's not worthless, Jo, and I'm really disappointed that you would even say that. And to me. I am the one who believes in you the most — even more that you kids believe in yourselves. So don't do this. And don't kid yourself into thinking I have done something extraordinary for you. We have come this far only because of your talent and hard work and belief in yourselves. Because you are an extraordinary bunch of kids who are pursuing a dream. That's it. There will be people who will try and help you. All the way. But those people are not doing you any favour. They are doing themselves a favour ... OK, so where do we stand on the money?'

'Just where we were when we last met,' said Chang, blinking worriedly from behind his thick glasses. 'About twenty-five grand short.'

'What about the last story I did? Did that get in something? And the nice words the mayor said about you guys at the annual ball the other day?' Angela asked, taking a bite from a pizza.

'We got letters, more greetings cards, some that were hand painted by children. A Tibetan monk sent us some holy scarves. Some people sent prayer beads. We got a lot of free lunch coupons, and a free annual subscription for the *Journal*. It was all very sweet. But there's hardly any money. Just letting the love flow instead of the cash...' John said.

But Angela was not listening and though she tried hard to blink them back her eyes were suddenly brimming with tears. Then the kids were all around her, hugging and kissing her, trying in their childlike way to soothe her troubles away. 'What is it, Angela, tell us, we can help you...'

'I ... lost something very precious. I am trying to deal with it.'

'Where will you find it?'

'Nowhere. I will never find it again.'

'Then why are you looking for it?' Nyasa said.

'I'm not.'

'But your eyes say that you are, Angela...' Juanita the Oracle said.

'Maybe you will also find what you are looking for, Angela.'

Angela's phone rang. A welcome diversion from the route the conversation was taking.

'Excuse me. Office beckons,' she said, hastily wiping her eyes.

'Hey, Angela, it's Hema.' It was her news editor and best friend. 'Listen, I am sorry I am bothering you on your day off but it's kind of urgent.'

'Hey, Hema... Oh, that's perfectly all right, go ahead.'

'Actually, the sports desk needs your help ... I know you have done some sports stories before and they all say you are a natural, besides I thought it might help take your mind off everything,' said Hema Easlay, also hoping to flatter her into doing a story for which there were no takers. 'They are swamped tomorrow and two reporters are on leave, one sick; the other's getting married ... Could you please do an assignment for them tomorrow? And when you are done hating me for that, I have another easier assignment for you!'

'Tell me,' she said quietly

'Look, honey, if you don't want to that's OK. First Juanita and then that Neil chap, I know how you feel...'

'Ha! Hema, what's with you? I am fiine! OK, tell me what I'm supposed to be covering.'

'Aw, nothing much ... a chess tournament ... an international Youth Chess Olympiad. And I'm making up for it by sending you on a special junket afterwards – to LA! I don't need anything too technical, just have fun with it, do some interviews, write a breezy, funny piece, I know you will do it really well. The chess tournament is in Manhattan, you got a pen handy? Let me give you the address ...'

Matthias Baldenburp's right arm slammed a solid punch into the wall, a show of extreme anger that sent him yelping around the room like a bleating pup. He loved slamming phones and breaking door handles when angry; he always yelped later. The blow toppled a picture which landed on Neel.

'Owwwww!' Neel said, holding his head. Matt had reacted in this mindlessly violent way the moment Neel had finished telling him his story.

'Owwww! What the fuck was that?' Neel shouted.

'You bugger, are you trying to tell me that you're in love with Angela Cruz?'

'Matt ...' said Neel, trying to get up now. He nursed his jaw with one hand, and opened the fridge to get some ice. Neel was sure his jaw was broken.

'Shut up! I would have killed ya right now if I wasn't a cop!'

'She loves me too, Matt. I am sorry.'

Matt was in the middle of trying to throw an ashtray across the room. He froze, as if someone under the chair had said 'Statue!' With his mouth open, he gaped at nothing for a few seconds, then threw the ashtray on the floor, buried his face in his hands, and began to whimper. It was a strange moment between two men in love with the same woman. This moment had to happen. I am telling you, Matthias Baldenburp and Neel Pandey came into each other's lives because they were entwined by the illusory forces of destiny.

Invisible tears rolled down Matt's eyes. He wiped them with an invisible hanky. Matt felt as if his heart had been ripped out and pricked like a large balloon. Pricked by a tiny prick from India! He would show him. He would have Neel and his rustic band of grandmasters deported in ten days, he thought.

Matthias Baldenburp turned suspiciously noble. 'OK, you can have her,' he said.

'And her address as well? ' Neel asked shamelessly.

℃

The sunny day was dissolving into an evening of a thousand hues. Angela had come to the riverfront for a walk. She needed some quiet time.

Tomorrow was going to be an extremely hectic day. First there was the chess tournament (ugh). Then she would have to rush back to office to file the story, go home again to pick up her suitcase, and race down to the subway just in time to catch the 2:45 bus upstate for a weeklong, multi-city junket — a tourism story. She would be exhausted by the time she got back, but Angela did not mind the physically draining journey. She needed time to be by herself. She wanted to reflect on her life so far — and the emotional whirlwind of the last year — as well as her life that lay ahead. She thought she had escaped the sad life her father was pushing her into, escaped towards a cool lake of love and happiness and freedom, surrounded by lofty trees. But there was no lake. There were no trees. It was a mirage. And that dreamy world had disappeared in the snap of a finger, leaving her standing desperate — and alone.

Angela wanted to cry, but it would serve no purpose. Plus the man next to her on the bench had spoilt the moment by loudly blowing his nose.

She looked at him. He was an old man with a lonely face, holding one end of a fishing rod as it rested on the ground. Like her father would be in twenty years, she thought.

'Hi,' she said. The man turned around, a bit surprised at being spoken to. It seemed he was surviving only on his loneliness. 'This is a late hour to come fishing, don't you think?'

'Ha ... oh the rod... well I came here in the morning, actually. I have been sitting here on this bench for a long time, watching the kids and the young people, having fun and being happy. It's nice. Makes me feel like them.'

'Did you catch anything?'

'Oh no, not even old sneakers! I don't hope to catch anything when I come here, honey. I just pretend to be fishing when I come here... I'm alone now...'

'And your wife?'

The old man took out a picture from his pocket, a frayed black and white photograph eaten away at the corners. 'See this?' he said. 'It's me and my wife, ten years ago. It was taken right here, by that railing you see by the tree. I had come here with my wife Nellie, and she and I were having a picture taken by a stranger. She was all childlike and leaning into the river. I was yelling at her not to do that but my eyes were on the camera. Then the man photographing us started to shout and I turned around and saw that Nellie had gone. Just like that. She had suffered a cardiac arrest and had collapsed into the river.'

'*Oh my god!*' Angela gasped.

'She was so happy that day. This is the spot where we had first met sixty years ago. This is the spot where I proposed to her. I found her here, and I lost her here too.'

'How did you two meet?'

'On a blind date. Life is a blind date, honey ... there is nothing more blissful than falling in love with a perfect stranger and discovering the magic that slowly works its spell on you...charming you with new depths and yet-to-be discovered secrets everyday...'

THE UNITING STATES OF AMERICA

The dimpled Nyasa Okri, trumpet player of the Plymouth County School band, slumped onto her couch after a day of all sorts of painful paperwork. She was the most accounts-friendly band member, and had been given a tough task: making an inventory of all the money that had come to the band over the past months, from the big payments to the one dollar bills to the dimes and quarters. Every donor had given whatever they could, including the tiny children in the neighbourhood who could never understand what the fuss was about, but knew nevertheless that this was something really important. Nyasa was also making a list of all the equipment that the band had loaned from the school, down to the last drumstick.

All this was for a purpose. All of it had to go back where it had come from. The band was finally splitting up. Angela's last minute plea had been no good.

They were still twenty-five thousand dollars short. The children had decided to take the honourable way out at their meeting the previous night. They would return all the money to the donors, and all the equipment to the school. A small note would accompany each cheque — 'Thank you for believing in us. We could not make it. But we will, another day.' Each note would be signed by a band member on behalf of the rest.

Some members had started to cry at that meeting. But most of them just remained silent. A dream was dying. Why create a spectacle?

Nyasa's mother called her for dinner. But she was mechanically flipping through her notebook, reading the names of the people who had spared their time and attention and money to support the dream that the children had seen. With Angela's support, the children had come within striking distance of their target. Almost.

Nyasa's mother called her again. She put aside the papers and was going down when the telephone rang, startling her. She shouted, 'I got it!' walked back in and took the call.

She wasn't her usual pleasant self when she began the conversation. She was actually edging on the curt. But after she said yes, it was Nyasa Okri speaking, and as the person on the other end started to talk, she went into a shocked silence. Then she softly whispered a dazed thank you, sunk into the soft couch and hid her face in a cushion. Her mother was calling her again. But Nyasa didn't hear any of that. The only words that were ringing in her ears were those of the man on the phone.

A stranger had just told her he was donating the last twenty-five thousand dollars to the school band. They were going to Miami, to perform at the Orange Bowl, after all!

❦

Neel and Meenal sat at a table on the far end of the small, open- air coffee shop. It was part of the sprawling building where the chess tournament was to be held, in the ballroom of an old colonial hotel that had once resonated with the dazzle and music of evening soirees.

Neel was talking with his parents on a phone he had rented for the trip. Meenal looked at him curiously, as she played an aimless tic-tac-toe with the salt container.

'Yes, Papa, the training is going well. Yes, there's a nice place to stay. Oh yeah, all to myself. No no, I have enough cash, and there's my credit card also. Yeah ... can I talk to her?' he said, his tone changing the moment his mother came on the line.

Narmada cleared her throat and said: 'So, did you meet your big boss?'

'No, Ma, she is furious with me. She doesn't want to meet me at all. She hung up on me the other day. I got her address from a guy who knows her, so I'm going there right after the chess tournament. Yes, that's now. But I don't think this is getting anywhere. If she refuses to see me, I will come back on Saturday. Friend? Who, Meenal? What happened to her? She left her home? O my god! I hope she's all right ... Anyway, I have to go, Ma, the championship will begin soon. Yes, yes, I remember how the bishop moves, Ma!' Neel hung up and winked at Meenal. They laughed. Then he gave her the phone.

'I think you want to make a call. I'll go away while you talk, and then we will go in to watch the chess. I think it will be fun!' Neel said as he started to get up. But Meenal held his hand and asked him to stay. How could she hide anything from her might-have-been husband?

Meenal dialled Sonia's number and began talking, looking straight across at Neel, her elbows resting on the table. As she held it to her ear and waited for the phone to connect, she made a face at Neel and reached for his hand. The phone was busy. She tried again.

Neel put his arm around her and ruffled her hair.

Meenal and Neel smiled with satisfaction at the secret about them that only they knew. But the customer on the next table watching them rolled her eyes in disgust. 'Stupid lovers,' thought Angela Cruz bitterly. She couldn't stand the breed any more. Especially the men. She looked the other way in disdain.

Meenal first spoke to her detective at home — her maid. 'No, I am not in Delhi. Tell me about the police thing. When? And what does the complaint say? ... Yeah, yeah I know, but didn't you hear anything while they were having dinner? ... Yes, what was he saying? ... OK, keep me informed. I'll call you again tomorrow, same time,' she said, squeezing Neel's hand.

Angela heard the entire conversation although she pretended to be enjoying her scrambled eggs. Eavesdropping on the next table's conversations had been something she had always looked down upon. But today, she couldn't help herself. They were lovers and they looked Indian. She realized she was jealous. She got up and walked out.

Nobody likes scrambled eggs on a broken heart.

❦

The chess team from India had registered and had been assigned its tables; the burly-looking members of the Indian team proudly pinned the badges of the World Youth Chess Olympiad on their lapels and loudly slurped their hot coffee. Before they went in, Rocky had decided to give his Punjab lions a pep talk.

Neel and Meenal stood next to him. The rest of the team stood silently, their hands folded and their minds begging the one question: We had asked only to be brought to the U.S.A., and we bloody well paid for it. Why put us through this test of fire?

Like a true leader, Rocky spoke first. They heard him out. 'My friends, although you all have been confined to your rooms since you came, welcome to America,' Rocky said. 'I trust you have all slept well and adjusted your body clock to this country.'

'Sir-ji! Please, I have a complaint. I didn't get a body clock in my room. I only got shampoo and a shower cap!' one member said.

Rocky looked around. Everyone else was raising their hands. They too had not received their body clocks.

'Stupid villagers,' Rocky said, gnashing his teeth, as Matt sniggered behind him. 'Get your Punjabi asses out there and prove that you have drunk your mother's milk,' he said.

Like terrified rats, the men slunk in one by one into the huge hall that seemed to swallow all who walked into it. As Neel began walking in towards his table, Rocky stopped him. 'Neel, my friend, I must say bye to you now,' he said.

'What? Why?' asked Neel taken aback.

'Matt has not taken the news of your romance with Angela well,' Rocky said, looking the other way. 'He is planning to have our whole contingent deported. I must leave now if I am ever to go to Saratoga to find my lost girlfriend... and if I am to escape the anger of thirty incensed farmers! I will catch up with you when you return to Delhi. Bye, Meenal, Neel's a good man but he has his eyes set on some American beauty, you should look somewhere else.' Then he suddenly turned serious, 'You don't have much time, Neel. Wish you all the best with your love-life, yaar...'

'Rocky, thanks a lot for everything, for bringing me to America, for helping with Angela ...' Neel was overwhelmed.

'Chhad, yaar. What are friends for? Leave it, you're making me emotional ... I can't handle it, yaar.' Then he squashed Neel in a huge Punjabi hug, straightened the creases in his shiny blue suit, and was never seen again.

❦

And now the moment had come for Neel to walk in for his date with the World Youth Chess Olympiad. Twenty-nine other troopers — Rocky Randhawa's valiant men — walked in front of him, all dressed in suits stitched by a local tailor in Jalandhar who had never quite got over his fixation for the look inspired by the Indian cinema of the Seventies. It was the first time most of these poor farmers were wearing suits — a parting gift from Rocky — and they stumbled into the tournament in their generously flared trousers, double breasted coats with many buttons and big, loud, broad ties.

A large banner at the door of the hall read: 'Chess is the Gymnasium of the Mind — Blaise Pascal.' This enthused many of the Punjab farmers, since they worked their muscles more than their brains. They whispered to each other that there was a gymnasium at the site as well; they would do push-ups after the game.

It was getting crowded now. Participants and some spectators — mostly the players' friends and cousins — were walking in. Angela walked right past Neel, and headed to the media registration desk. She signed the registration form and gave them her business card.

The sprawling hall was full of tables, each with two chairs facing each other. On each table stood flags of the Chess Olympiad, digital and manual clocks, and bottles of water. This was the knockout round. Those who won here would proceed to the round robin matches, and then to the quarter-finals. The excited hub-bub of voices slowly died down. A hush fell over the huge hall.

The games had begun.

Sheroo, the most educated of all the farmers, had sat up all night to study from a chess primer. But he went into a daze even before the game could begin, when his opponent, a curly-haired, straight-faced British woman, said: 'Just to inform you, this is a forty-minute, sudden death game.'

'Sudden death?' Sheroo asked himself. 'I never realized this game is so dangerous. Wahe Guru save me please, I will offer a saropa and a golden kirpan at the Akal Takht.' The sacred vow, and the thought of his bull back home, of the same name as his, gave Sheroo courage, like a last-minute pre-race steroid shot. He made the first move. In a manner reminiscent of the way he had dealt with his high school examination years ago, Sheroo had scribbled his key moves on his palm. So he would make a move, then bend down in his chair, ostensibly to tie his laces, read his next move, and get up and play. His style of play was very unnerving for his opponent, who was puzzled when she realized that none of Sheroo's moves were made in response to her own. It was a dangerous sign. Clearly, her opponent was building some grand attack that she could not figure out. It was very unsettling. She retired after the 34th move.

Ram Lubhaya, Sheroo's teammate had black pieces and he had come up with a brilliant trick. He just did exactly what his opponent did. His opponent – the champion of Maryland University, a white guy with thick glasses – moved the pawn to e4; Lubhaya moved to e5. His opponent moved the bishop to c4; and Ram Lubhaya moved the bishop to c5. The Maryland champion moved the queen diagonally across to f3; so brother Ram didn't waste a second in moving his queen right opposite to f6. His opponent was flummoxed. This was a style of play that he had never encountered before. This hide-and-seek went on for 26 moves, when the Maryland champ took a deep breath, and offered a draw.

Ram Lubhaya accepted, mainly because he did not understand the question.

But I would say the best game of all was between Kartaar Singh – the man who had charmed and scared the immigration clerk with his singing – and his Pakistani opponent, Mohammed Ali, whose parents had named him after his country's founder, Mohammed Ali Jinnah. The two opponents were both from Punjab – Mohammed Ali from the Pakistani side of the province and Kartaar Singh from the Indian side.

After one move, Mohammed Ali muttered a swear-word in Punjabi that seemed to indicate that he wanted to fornicate with Kartaar Singh's sister. Interestingly, Kartaar wasn't the slightest bit offended. Firstly, his sister was already married and in Gurdaspur, far far away from New York and out of Mohammed Ali's reach. Secondly, her husband was a local daroga who had been a wrestler before joining the police force; he would settle all accounts with aspiring fornicators. Thirdly, Mohammed Ali's words were actually quite fascinating to Kartaar — he had never imagined he would hear the sweetly familiar sound of curse-words that he and his friends uttered all day back in the village — so far away from home, in the land of foreigners. He responded in kind, muttering under his breath a Punjabi phrase that conveyed his heartfelt intention of having sex with Mohammed Ali's mother.

That was it.

That was the last straw. The Pakistani looked directly into the Indian man's eyes with his own bloodshot ones and uttered the words that can charge the blood of any Punjabi across the world. 'Are you Punjabi too, Brother?' said Mohammed Ali.

'Yesss, Brother! O my god! Wahe Guru is great!'

'Oye, Allah is great!' said Mohammed Ali.

'Oye, Jesus Christ is great too!' said Kartaar Singh. He was from a secular country, after all, and why not show that off among firangis?

Both men got up and gave each other a massive hug, with Kartaar actually lifting Mohammed Ali a few inches off the ground. The rest of the room thought it was a groping break in an Asian gays-only match, and went back to their games. Meanwhile, brotherly love was erupting fast and thick between the two men separated by history and borders. Both now began insisting on losing the game to the other. Neither agreed. Finally, they decided to settle for a draw after six moves, and to celebrate later over two tall glasses of lassi with thick malai at the first dhaba they spotted in New York

Kartaar Singh decided to make a confession. 'Brother Mohammed Ali ...I want to tell you something. Swear you won't tell anyone.'

'I swear on Allah the Merciful, peace be upon him, tell me, Brother Kartaar Singh ...'

'I don't know the ADPC of chess, Brother Mohammed Ali,' Kartar Singh whispered.

'You mean ADBC, Brother Kartaar Singh? Same here, Brother.'

'And I haven't come here for the chess tournament, Brother Mohammed Ali.'

'Same here, Brother Kartaar Singh.'

'I have paid twenty lakh rupees to get a fake visa and I came here, Brother Mohammed Ali, pretending to be a chess player.'

'*What?* I paid *thirty* in Rawalpindi, Brother Kartar Singh! What a bastard! He cheated me! Son of a donkey!'

C

Angela watched the proceedings from the press gallery, where the other reporters were busy making elaborate notes on the matches they had shortlisted. One of these tables would make a small two-column headline on the sports page the next day. She sat sipping her coffee, her legs crossed, looking around with a glazed look of polite interest. Covering chess was a new assignment. But it was hard to keep her interest alive after the sounds died down and the ticking was only in the contestants' minds. Angela looked at the massive hall before her with its chandeliers and frescoes, its stained glass windows and ornate pillars – and drifted in and out of reverie and gloom. She imagined a sunny day with no trace of the dark clouds of despair currently enveloping her sky. She saw music. She saw happiness. She saw herself clinging to her lover and dancing to the soft notes of a piano at a ball. She could feel the pulsating rhythm of that evening and the thump of her own heart — the same rhythm that she had felt when she had walked into Lil' Jo's on that emotion-filled evening. She smiled, faintly.

☾

In another part of the hall, Neel was also looking up at the same ceiling, gazing at the same frescoes and carvings and the chandeliers, and weaving his own dreams. That's the great thing about falling in love. All the beautiful things remind you of your lover, especially when they are not there to share them with you.

'Shall we begin?' said a voice across the table.

Neel's opponent was Karl Dostovsky, a young man of Russian origin who liked to imitate his idol, Anatoly Karpov, in the way he dressed and walked.

'Oh hi — I am Neel Pandey from India,' Neel said, trying hard to concentrate and shut Angela out of his thoughts.

'Oh, you are from India? I am a huge fan of Vish-wa-na-than Anand ... I think he's really the best player in the world right now, though I am a greater fan of Karpov. It's so good to have a worthy opponent like you. I am Karl Dostovsky. My father was born in the USSR.'

'Right ...' Neel said.

'I've been the NYU champion for two years now. And you? I understand you are the team captain. Are you the Indian university champion?'

Neel gulped some water. His lips still felt dry. 'Ha...well, some thing like that,' Neel said, laughing. The laughter was deceptive. Actually, he wanted to sink onto the floor and howl. What the hell was he doing here, at this chess tournament, with Karl Dostovsky, the champion of NYU? He would make a fool of himself! He should have been out, at Angela's door, doing the job he had come here to do. Strange are the ways of destiny; two weeks ago, there was no way he could have imagined that his shattered, defeated life could undergo such a dramatic transformation and take him to the doorstep of the woman of his dreams. Now that he was on her turf his heart told him he could still win her back — if he tried hard enough.

Where is Angela right now — right this instant, Neel thought. What is she doing? What is she wearing? Is she thinking of me? Does she still love me?

'Your turn,' Karl said.

Neel made his move. She didn't sound too happy with me yesterday on the phone, he thought, but then she didn't know I am here, that I have come all the way to win her back. Hope that will tell her something about what I feel for her.

'Your turn,' Karl said, hitting the timer knob.

Neel thought of home, of his street, and how Angela would walk on it when they went together to visit his parents. She would be dazzling in a bride's dress. She would be the most beautiful bride in the neighbourhood — why, the most beautiful in Delhi. The neighbours would all be so jealous. And then, after they got married, they would move to their own apartment, someplace overlooking the Ridge Forest, and together watch the first monsoon showers drench the thick foliage, washing off a yearful of dust, as if decking the trees out in the colours of the new life they were sharing ...

'And, checkmate!' Karl grandly declared.

'Huh?'

Neel Pandey had lost his game to Karl Dostovsky in just three moves. It was one of the worst defeats ever in the history of chess in the United States!

❡

'Hey, a guy here has won in three moves! Let's go to that table!' a reporter next to Angela said to his photographer. She looked at the table to which the reporter was pointing. A white youth and the Asian man she had earlier seen in the restaurant were getting up from their table and shaking hands with each other.

Angela decided to join the other reporters. The organizers, surprised to see the press suddenly descend in a pack on the two players in the middle of the room, requested Neel and Karl to be interviewed near the entrance. Neel decided to have fun with the moment – not only had he just booked his name in U.S. chess history, he was also going to be interviewed by journalists ... how cool was that? What if he was the loser? The U.P. trick solution would be to make the best of it.

'So how do you feel about your defeat? It's one of the worst ever for this tournament,' a reporter asked, smiling condescendingly.

'Worst in U.S. chess history,' added the one who had done more research.

Angela listened in.

'Well, I congratulate Karl on his stunning win. He played well, and he played better than me. He is a worthy opponent. It is true that if Karl had not checkmated me in that third move, I had an interesting surprise planned for him in the next move. But he played better. It is an honour to lose to such an opponent,' Neel said.

It was all great soundbyte. The TV cameras and the notebooks lapped it up. Karl looked puzzled. He never seemed in threat. He answered a few questions, and then the reporters turned to Neel again.

'So tell us about your opening, and what was it you had planned that would checkmate your opponent in the 4th move?'

'It was the Ranthambore opening. As for the second part of the question, I never discuss strategy in media interviews,' he said confidently.

'Ranthambore? Never heard of that opening,' said the occasional chess reporter of the *New York Times*.

'Well, it's a new one. We are working on it at the National Chess Academy in India.'

India? Angela looked up. Hmmm. Then she went back to her notes. Maybe she could write about this goofy loser and the Ranthambore opening.

'Wow. I must do a separate story on that. The Indians working on a new opening. You mind sitting down for an interview sometime?' the *New York Times* reporter said.

'Sure. I don't yet know where I will be staying, so why don't you give me your card, and I shall call you,' Neel said.

The NYT guy handed Neel his card. As if on cue, everyone else took out their cards and handed them to Karl and Neel. In the hall, a coffee break was announced and dozens of chess masters began to stream out. The passageway was getting choked. In the minor commotion, Angela realized she hadn't asked the players their names. Damn.

'Excuse me, can I have your names, please?' she shouted across half a dozen bobbing heads as the two men walked out.

Neel and Karl turned around and shouted out their names to her from where they stood.

'Karl Dostovsky! That's D-O-S-T-O-V-S-K-Y!'

'Neel Pandey ... That's P-A-N-D-E-Y ... Ciao!'

Angela stood there, in the middle of the humming, buzzing crowd, and felt the world cave in about her.

❦

Angela did not wait for the rest of the games to finish. The hall suddenly felt so small, so claustrophobic. God, why did these things happen only to her? There was no way this man could be the Neel Pandey she knew. After all, he had just called her the previous day from India! Besides, why would he come all the way after what had happened? Hadn't she seen him in a restaurant falling all over his new girlfriend? Maybe it wasn't him at all … just someone with the same name … maybe Neel Pandey is a very common name in India … he never said anything about playing chess … but then he never mentioned so many other things as well! O god … why did he have to show up now, just when she was coming to terms with everything? And even if it was him, she had nothing to do with him. It was over, remember?

As if.

She took the subway, rushed to her office and wrote out a quick story, about four hundred words, which the page editor cleared in no time. It was really a miracle that she had been able to finish it at all. But the actual reason was that she wanted to go home as quickly as she could and open the image with the picture that Neel had sent of himself — which she had so far refused to see, yet somehow never deleted from her computer.

Poof. In a second, the attachment opened. Oh my god. Oh my god. It *was* him. The same goofy loser. Neel Pandey's benevolent face smiled at her off the monitor. The same guy.

Angela took a deep breath and leaned back in her chair. He was right here, in New York. They had actually met, as themselves, and yet lost each other. Should she believe in destiny, like he did? But then why had he come with his girlfriend?

If they love you, they will find you, isn't that what they say, Angela thought as she began throwing her clothes into a suitcase. The bus is in forty-five minutes and it is my destiny to get on it, she thought bitterly. Let him be happy with his stupid Indian mistress. What an asshole he's turned out to be. What a smooth-talking, double-crossing asshole.

◉

The phone rang. It was Nyasa Okri. And she was breathless. Angela was not exactly in the mood to be upbeat and encouraging. She took the phone wearily. 'Hey, Nyasa. How are you?' she said dully.

'Angela! I have been trying to call you all day!'

'I'm sorry, honey. I was at a chess tournament, and then on the subway. The phone was switched off most off the time.'

'You won't believe this, Angela.'

'Try me, honey!' she said slightly impatiently.

'I got a call from this man this morning about the band. I was kind of rude with him in the beginning 'cos I was so bummed... Anyway, first I thought he was a prankster ... but then he started telling me about how impressed he was with our story, and all ... He knows you too ... Then he began to talk about how he had saved up money over the years to be able to live and work in America one day, but he didn't want to do it now ...'

'Sweetheart, can I call you later? I have a bus to catch ...' Angela said impatiently.

'No, no, you have to listen to this. So he told me this entire story and I was like, "Why are you telling me this?" Anyway, he finally said that he wanted to donate all that money to us so that we could go to the Orange Bowl! But the money was in his country, and he said that he could arrange to have it all wired to the school's account in a few days. *Twenty-five thousand dollars!*'

'*What?* I don't believe this!' Angela shouted on the phone, now genuinely shocked and genuinely happy. 'Oh god, Nyasa, this is the best thing I have heard in such a long time! Have you told everyone yet?'

'Yes, I have. I wanted to tell you first, but I couldn't reach you earlier...'

'That's fine, sweetie. So who is this guy?'

'Some guy from India. One sec, I have his name here ... if you want to do a story when you return ...'

'Huh?'

'It's someone called Neel Pandey.'

℃

Neel had pledged away all the money his grandfather had gifted him – the one lakh rupees that had become sixteen lakh over twenty years in the post office saving scheme. The money that had been set aside for his higher education. Or for the two-bedroom flat when he got married. He had already consulted his mother; she had given her consent, as well as her blessings.

Not just that, Neel had also inspired Rocky Randhawa to throw in some money for the kids' entertainment in Miami before he left. Rocky, a true connoisseur of bhangra and other art forms, knew the pure joy that erupts from one's being when kids belt out a heartfelt number. He had gladly agreed. Neel remembered Rocky's parting words to him: 'Don't mind, but I've got some inspiration from you ... I have also made a small contribution to Angela's band. For you, and for love in general, and for my own love in Saratoga. Hope those kids get to the Orange Bowl.'

℃

Neel stood clutching a bunch of flowers at the door of Angela's apartment, after losing his way several times thanks to the ridiculously lousy directions Matthias Baldenburp had given him. His heart was galloping like a mad steed on top of a Japanese bullet train. Should he knock? Should he run away?

He finally raised his arm to ring the bell. He would never admit this, but his knees were feeling wobbly and he badly wanted to go. When the most courageous of men become nervous, they want to go.

He rang the bell. No answer. He rang again. He rang a third time. He was desperate and worried. The hell with manners, he thought, and banged the door with his fist like a doctor hammering a patient's wooden leg hoping to get a response.

That is when the lady next door, an old black woman of about Neel's mother's age, popped out her head and looked at Neel with a degree of irritation. 'I was trying to sleep ... Are you one of Angela's friends, son?'

'Yes, sort of, Ma'am. I have come from very far to meet her.'

'She just left, son. Two minutes ago. She came to say bye. You might have crossed each on the way in.'

'What? Um ... I am sorry to bother you, Ma'am, but where did she go?'

'She said something about catching a bus out of town for a week or ten days,'

'She's taking a flight?'

'A bus. Now if you'll excuse me —'

'Um ... it's kind of urgent, kind of life and death ... would you know where she is catching the bus from?'

'Metro bus-stop. Just walk straight for two hundred yards, then take the first left. But the bus will leave in a few minutes, so you better walk fast ...'

Neel thanked her and briskly walked out. Once on the road, he broke into a run. It could be a blind chase. There was very little time left and he was looking for a passenger whom he didn't even recognize.

If there was ever a lost battle, Neel thought in despair, this was it.

☾

Neel stood at the bus-stop looking desperately for Angela Cruz. Was she a redhead? a blonde? a brunette? Was it that woman standing in the corner with a cola? Was it that one fighting with the ticket clerk? Was it that one smoking by the tree? Was she here at all? Had the old woman played a prank too?

He was breaking into a sweat. The passengers began loading their bags onto the bus. Children scampered in and started to fight for the window seat. The driver kicked his tyres. The ticket clerk struggled to find change. Neel watched all of them silently, trying to find the one familiar face that he didn't recognize. Nobody. This was a stupid exercise, he thought. He had no clue what Angela looked like, and unless she was condescending enough to recognize him, they might as well have been trying to find each other on Halloween night.

Then someone spoke to him. It was the last passenger on the bus. 'So what shall I call you? Neel Pandey or Neil Patterson?'

He turned around, startled. There was only one person in America who knew his secret identity. Angela Cruz. 'Angela? O my god —' Neel exclaimed, and stepped forward to attempt a hug. A futile effort. She was not done yet.

'You disgusting, two-timing, double-faced, twisted, perverted, demented, backstabbing —' Angela stopped screaming only because she had run out of adjectives. Her voice was firm, but not bitter. She sounded so determined, so herself.

Neel drank her in. A 5-foot-7 inch beauty with shiny black hair and hazel brown eyes. So *this* was the women who had turned his life upside down. This was the woman for whom he had crossed the oceans and defied five thousand years of caste laws. And, here they were, face to face, just like that, in the blink of a moment. In a meeting craftily set up by destiny six months ago when a computer malfunctioned.

But she wasn't exactly rushing into his arms. No surge of love, no strains of music, no flowers in blossom. He stood there, as if attached to the ground with a glue-stick, gawking at her like an idiot. She looked at him, emotionless, waiting for something to happen. Neel just wanted to laugh off all that had happened, let her fight with him all she wanted, and then walk away with her into the sunset. Because the moment he looked into her eyes he knew that he loved her and that he wasn't going home without her.

But she was in no mood to indulge him. 'Is that why you came all the way from India? For me? Then how come you're here with another woman?' Angela asked.

'Yes, Angela,' he replied, looking her straight in the eye. 'Because I love you ...' The bus driver honked. He was ready to go.

She shouted back: 'That's bull! You are playing games with me again. Where's your girlfriend? I don't see her? Why isn't she clinging to your arm and cooing to you that she loves you and tousling your hair? I saw the two of you together this morning, pawing each other in the restaurant.'

The driver honked again and looked at his watch. The passengers looked at them, expectantly, and then at their own watches.

Neel was laughing as he spoke, 'Yes, Angela, the woman you're talking about was about to get married to me, it's true. Yes, it's true. And...'

'You bas —'

'... And her parents and my parents almost fixed up an arranged marriage between us back in India. But then something funny happened.'

'Really? Did you find out that you were gay and slept with her brother instead?'

'No, but you are on the right track. She is a lesbian and loves another woman.'

Angela found his explanation so cheeky and unbelievable that she turned around and started walking towards the bus. The passengers heaved a sigh of relief, although they were a little disappointed by the outcome.

'I know you love me too, Angela,' he said just as she turned around. 'And I have turned over a new leaf.'

'Oh, and what a leaf! A fullblown, six-foot cactus leaf! In case you are forgetting, the two people who were in love with each other were different people, Neel. I don't know them. They were phonies. An American beauty queen in love with a white American man. As far as I can judge, you are certainly not him, and I clearly am not an American beauty queen.'

'Oh, I would strongly disagree with you there,' Neel said.

'Excuse me?'

'I said...'

'Are you hitting on me in the middle of a fight, Mr Pandey?'

The bus driver forgot all about his time schedule. This was fun.

'I love you, Angela and I think you are very beautiful. So please stop being stubborn. We fell in love with reflections of each other, and now it's time to fall in love with the real us. That's why I left everything behind in India and put everything at stake, just to be here and be with you. But you don't want me in your life. So all I can do is wish you good luck ... I hope the man you marry likes you enough to travel around the world to be with you.'

'Great. What do you expect me to say? Thanks a lot for taking a plane to America and let's proceed on our honeymoon? After all that has happened, how can I pretend it hasn't?' Angela said.

'We both pretended to be people we were not. We were both imposters. But we have to move on.'

'Excuse me? I am an imposter?' Angela snapped.

'I hate to say it, Angela, but you are. Aren't we all?'

'I must say, you are a lot less polite than you led me to believe, Mr Pandey.'

'And perhaps you are a little less of many things that I had imagined, Miss Cruz.'

The bus driver groaned. It was turning nasty. This was going into Act Three. He revved the engine.

'You know what? You are getting on my nerves! What else are you hiding from me? Do you have a wife and kids?'

'Sure. One wife in Sultanpur, one in Sitapur and one in Kanpur. The children are all in boarding school. What else do you want to know? And what about you? How many boyfriends do you have? God, I imagined you so different and —'

'And what did you find? That I'm an ogre?'

'No, that you'll make a perfect wife. Sexy and snappy! You are one wild thing!'

Angela sighed. 'Look, Neel, I know you are a nice guy, and thanks for helping out the band children, they mean the world to me. But the fact is that I fell in love with a man who doesn't exist. Now you come up to me and say you are him. But you are wrong.'

'No, Angela, I fell in love with a woman who *does* exist. She was just wearing someone else's clothes, but her soul can't change. And a name? What's in a name? In India, we address god by nine million names all over the country and worship him — or her — in a million forms. God still listens.'

Angela sank down on the small street-side bench and stared at her bag, which was now plonked in the middle of the road. She let it lie where it fell.

Neel walked up to her and sat down beside her. 'I know ours is a bizarre story, Angela. But it has happened. We have to get a grip on it and move on. Matthias Baldenburp has his knives out for me ever since he heard you are the woman I came looking for. He's making sure I leave the United States as soon as the tournament is over. The thirty other chess players with me are also going home...You have to decide. Are you coming with me?'

The bus driver could not wait any longer. 'Hell, lady, make up your mind, are you coming or not?'

Angela searched Neel's face for a long time. Then she stood up resolutely and picked up her bag.

BE IT EVER SO HUMBLE

A dream. It had all been a dream.

Neel Pandey opened his favourite left eye like a squirrel ending a long winter hibernation, pretending he was in another world. He pulled the sheets from over his eyes and squinted at the window.

The October sunlight lazily filtered into the New Delhi apartment. Shafts of sun rays peeped through the glass wherever they could, warming up long rectangles of space on the concrete floor. A large wooden rack in one corner stood next to an ornate teak box (but the love letters from Neel's past girlfriends had all strangely disappeared). The book rack was crammed with thick books. The walls were clean, except for a stunning picture of the New York skyline, a Rajasthani painting, and a Ganesha painted by some obscure artist. In one corner of the room, a Kishore Kumar song suddenly began playing 'Paanch Rupaiya Baara Aaana' on a CD player. The perky Bollywood wake-up call was programmed to play at this time each day. On the study table was a small pile of books on different types of Indian cuisine, a notebook with hastily scribbled notes, and a pair of earrings.

Wait a minute, did I say earrings?

Abruptly, Neel prised open his right eye, making all sorts of faces as the sunlight assaulted his sleep deprived orbs and panned his vision to find the other occupant of the bed. The love of his life, his newly-wedded, jet-lagged wife, stretched out a hennaed hand and tousled his hair. Angela Cruz smiled at him invitingly, 'Hey, are you going to kiss me or do I still have to dial a toll-free number to get you to do that?'

(

Neel and Angela had come home to India to a host of new surprises. To begin with, a new hatchback car that Ravi had bought with a loan, courtesy the same bank manager whom he had bribed to get a loan for his house, years ago. No, there was no bribe paid this time. They were neighbours after all.

And the other surprise: an Evergreen Beauty Parlour located some distance from their home in a just-inaugurated shopping mall. Its owner was a certain Narmada Pandey, who had started it with a low interest loan from the beauty school, with her husband as guarantor. Grumpy workers had grumbled day and night to finish their work before the flight landed from New York. The furniture glistened, the walls still smelled of fresh paint, and marigold flowers and gerberas decked the modest beauty salon. Narmada knew who the first woman to sit on the customer's chair was going to be: her daughter-in-law.

Angela had been whisked into the private recesses of the parlour and was soon being thoroughly pampered, her hair was dressed with sweet smelling jasmine flowers and she was draped in a stunning gold brocade sari. Narmada had personally put the henna on Angela's hands, a beautiful and intricate floral pattern that hadn't dried up yet. 'Your henna isn't dry as yet ... do you like it? This is one of the things Indian brides love most in their weddings. I have added clove oil and tea leaves to make the colour even richer,' Narmada said.

'I love it and I want it to settle in so that the colours show up dark and strong,' Angela said. 'I know that in India, they say that if the colours of the henna are still dark after the bride washes off the paste, then her mother-in-law will love her a lot.'

That was a surefire way to get Narmada all choked up. 'I hope you know that Indian mothers-in-law are very deadly,' Narmada said beaming through her tears.

'I hope you know that American daughters-in-law are every bit as nice as traditional Indian ones,' Angela replied.

They hugged and laughed like old college friends.

❦

Neel had put his foot down; no loud garish Indian wedding, and please, I will *not* ride a horse, he had said. So, the day before, they were married in a simple wedding ceremony in the holy town of Rishikesh, six hours away from New Delhi, by the banks of the Ganga river, in Narmada's favourite ashram, the Parmarth Niketan, flanked by the lower Himalayas. Dozens of monks in saffron robes held aloft oil-wick lamps, swaying gently as songs worshipping the sacred river resonated across the valley. Even Gavin the King of Sceptics had agreed: A wedding like that, with a thousand lamps reflecting in the glittering water of the Ganga and music echoing into the mountains, could not have been ordered from any wedding planner.

In ten days, the entire group was to fly back to the U.S., where there would be a Christian wedding ceremony in a beautiful Gothic-style church in New York, near Central Park. Then a small informal lunch at Central Park, and later that night, a party in Greenwich Village.

Ravi Pandey had agreed to all these plans. He had also given up his earlier insistence on never setting foot in the United States. If he came face to face with Bill Gates or George Bush, he had promised himself he would not be mean to them.

Even so, as his daughter-in-law was being dressed up at the parlour, Ravi paced up and down the corridor, twiddling his fingers and biting his lips. The reception was in an hour. His eyebrows were furrowed and his forehead wrinkled in deep thought. Neel, the radiant groom, dressed in a cream-coloured kurta-pajama, walked worriedly after him. 'Is everything all right, Papa? I hope you are happy ...' he said. The last thing he wanted right now was one of his father's famous temper explosions.

'Oh no, no, no ... Don't get me wrong ... I like Angela... lovely girl and all that... I am very happy with the marriage, but beta...' Ravi cleared his throat nervously. 'She *is* from a high caste in America, right?'

SOME MORE RAMBLING, SO HELP ME GOD

NEEL PANDEY set up a company that develops software and outsources services in partnership with his father-in-law. He travels constantly between the United States and India, and also visits the mushroom farm in the village when he can find the time. He is working on a software that women homemakers can use to run their small businesses better. At the call centres, he doesn't mind if his employees to fall in love with customers — but not on company time.

ANGELA CRUZ is now South Asia correspondent of the *Upper Plymouth Journal* and also writes occasionally for other publications in the same publishing group. She is based in New Delhi but snatches enough frequent flyer points or free spouse tickets from her husband to be able to fly home once every four months. Her brilliant series on outsourcing won an award last year from the New York based South Asian Journalists Association.

NEEL'S PARENTS are planning to start a second beauty parlour. Their customers include the Prime Minister's granddaughter, who got to know of it after some clever PR by Ravi at the office. Narmada goes to work in the new car, and they are moving soon into a bigger apartment. Ravi still goes to work on his old sputtering Lambretta scooter, and refuses to sell it off. He has recovered from the shock of Neel's giving away the savings as donation to the band. (The beauty parlour makes more annually, you see).

ANGELA'S PARENTS also bought a new house. Gavin grumbles much less and loves Martha much more. Martha now works in a senior position in the Mississippi State Education Department. They have just returned from a vacation in India, which they spent floating on shikaras and lazing in the houseboats of Kashmir. Gavin has changed his opinion about coloured people, and Martha suspects he might even have a crush on his African American secretary.

ROCKY RANDHAWA has vanished without trace. Uptil this moment, as this book goes to press, I have no idea where he is.

MATTHIAS BALDENBURP has left the police force to start a security agency that provides private guards to customers. He was acquitted by the judge in Kashmir in that old drug case. Matt is about to get married to a woman at the DA's office. He doesn't hate babies now — in fact he has already planned names for them. If it's a daughter, she will be Angela. If it's a son, he will be Angelo.

MEENAL SHARMA and Sonia Shah are now India's first legally married lesbian couple. They've adopted a baby boy. Meenal's parents visited her recently and her mother offered prayers for her grandson at a local temple. Meenal's father speaks only a few sentences each year to Sonia.

THE KID'S BAND will soon have their story featured on the Oprah Winfrey show.

JUANITA is back with her mother. She has decided to pursue music as a career.

THE VOICE was disillusioned by Rocky's sensational disappearance and desertion but quickly propelled himself to a position of power as Rocky's number two man. He now runs his own illegal visa racket from a two-storey house in Pahargunj, opposite the New Delhi Railway Station. Contact me for his number if the visa officers at any of the embassies are giving you a hard time.

Not that I was forgetting:

Arre bhai a big thank you to my parents, Dr S.B. Misra and Mrs Nirmala Misra, and Nidhi's parents Mr M.K. Razdan and Mrs Sarla Razdan, for the patience and good humour with which they bear my impatience and good humour.

Aur ji oye thank you to all the thousands of hard-working men and women at India's call centres whose nocturnal adventures gave me the idea for this book.

Aur to aur, another big thank you to my editor Nandita Aggarwal for wading through 83,000 words of pure balderdash even when her family was down with viral fever and her son had decided to stop a cricket ball with his face.

Achha, thank you to P.M. Sukumar, the CEO of HarperCollins India, for publishing the novel in the first place. And thanks to my friend Deepak Das in faraway Boston for labouring over the cover page concept, even as he and his wife awaited the arrival of their son a few days later.

Ye to kuchh bhi nahin, thank you to Shailesh and Aditi, and Nitin and Raka — and to everyone from Jhumri Talaiyya to Timbuktu who has ever fallen in love (and hence should read my book).

Aur khote da puttar, last — and certainly the least — thank you to my four-year-old nephew Aditya, the biggest brat in Noida, who is showing signs of falling in love with his neighbour and hence might read this book some day.